FOOD FOR JACKALS

Food for Jackals
THREE SHORT NOVELS

by
JOHN ZEUGNER

RESOURCE *Publications* · Eugene, Oregon

FOOD FOR JACKALS
Three Short Novels

Resource Publications
An Imprint of Wipf and Stock Publishers
199 W. 8th Ave., Suite 3
Eugene, OR 97401

www.wipfandstock.com

ISBN 13: 978-1-62564-758-0

Manufactured in the U.S.A.   05/12/2014

Part I of "The Tennis Player," appeared in *Perspective*, Volume 15, Number 3, 1968, and subsequently in the anthology *Short Stories from the Literary Magazines*, Glenview, Illinois: Scott, Foresman and Company, 1970.

Contents

The Tennis Player

HIT MOVING INTO THE BALL, AND OFF THE FRONT FOOT

The pro shop was small and he had to share it with golf bags. Each morning he pulled the bags out and set them along the white stucco wall at the back of the club house. He resented them more for smell than for space; by morning the stacked bags had transformed the scent of his room. At some point during the night the fuzzy, rubbery scent of Wilson tennis balls (he kept his lesson basket full—though he seldom gave lessons) the crisp tissue smell of Moody shirts and shorts, yielded to the greasy leather odor of the bags. He often wondered just when the transition occurred. He thought once of sitting in the room through the night and smelling every five minutes or so, trying to pinpoint when the change came. He was amused by that vision of himself. Balding, fattening, (from Moody 33 to Moody 36 in the last two years) and now at thirty-nine, he was constantly watching himself, projecting himself into various absurd poses, laughing and yet resigning to the present as an alternative to the seal of the future. That had been his great weakness: an ability to project all situations—failure to success, weakness to power, poverty to wealth, and then having so projected, fully experience, fully reject as inadequate. Four years before, his wife had summed it up, "You're a waste."

He dragged the last two bags out, pulling them along the terrazzo, over the lip of the sprung, aluminum door, along the outside cement, scratching them.

So it had come to this, he thought—the quiet pro at Cape Revere Club, twenty miles south of Hane, Florida. Grand developers from the East Coast of Florida had come over to project Cape Revere on the discontented

1

Haneites. Purchasing a solid segment of bay front (one of the last available pieces) they had begun the quick process of killing every living thing (thwarting the conservationist by releasing to the Hane Tribune, every now and then, the number of rattlesnakes butchered.) Pumping in the new land, beating it flat, white, arid, unfrustrating, and then moving back in a few cabbage palms here, one royal palm there to landscape, beautify, renature, the surface. And, most importantly, building the Cape Revere Golf and Tennis Club for residents. But not enough lots sold, and the Hane Tribune continually ran the contractor's advertisements exhorting Haneites to come down, join, enjoy the salve.

They had given him two courts, two hard surface courts because they needed no maintenance, or none beyond the sweeping that was the next job in his morning routine. If he could build interest, they would provide more courts, but they must have known he was not going to build interest. He was not a young, money-hungry pro. He had been that, made that projection, seen through it, and Peg and the two children as a result had left him. They went back to Westchester and he elected not to return for the lucrative summer. Once taken the decision made everything fall into place.

He went back into the shop, checked his lesson book — one lesson with Brian when Brian got there after school. Brian the ambitious, prodded by his parents, one of whom always sat at the side of the courts and jotted down Brian's errors. He was free then till 3:30 — a typical day. In May the club was vacant anyway, and there were continual rumors of not being paid.

He got the heavy, stiff bristle broom out from behind his hydraulic stringer purchased in that moneyed interval when he had been the pro at the Hane Country Club. The stringer paid for itself there in six months, but he regretted the evening when hours passed as he fitted first one clamp then another, one awl then another, waxed one set for crossing, then another. But there were always people at the Hane Club. Even at 11:30 at night when he left his elaborate shop, someone sitting in the moonlight by the pool would offer to buy him a drink.

"Come on, Frank, you can't work all night."

And then he got home later which made Peg madder. But the bills were paid, the house purchased, the car repaired. However, he played less and less, taught more and more. It was disappointing, so in a volley of self-will he vowed to reverse the process. That was not what they paid him for. It was an interesting struggle. He went to the mat with them. He fought, argued, insinuated, he got a tremendous kick out of that, but in end they axed him — with surprisingly little severance pay.

He dragged the broom out along the walk by the pool. Mike, the lifeguard, climbed up to his chair, his plump tawny body glistening with oil. He nodded to Frank, who cranked the broom handle in acknowledgement.

His own body had been blessed once in that summit of his game at twenty-two. When to quit singles, twenty-five? Thirty? Certainly no later. At twenty-two his body, browned but not oily plump, had been as good a retrieving and attacking machine as he would possess. But the toughest muscles, the tightest sinews then were only strengthened for what? A local ranking that would go down, and down, and find a level below sea level (despite Cape Revere's filled land) — a level so nicely summed up by two courts in need of no maintenance, adjacent to a vacant golf course, near a vacant club house, in a vacant season that never ended, never began. With the end of the broom handle he flicked the gate latch up. He never missed it. He always forced the gate on the first try.

MEET THE BALL AT THE TOP OF ITS BOUNCE, OR ON THE RISE

In the morning, dew sparkled on the link fence surrounding his courts, dew shimmered on the green background wind-break, clamped four feet from the ground and ending two feet from the top of the fence. To enter his courts was to enter, in the morning, a glistening pen of greens and rhinestones. Yet by 11:00 the irritant glitter was gone, sun scattered, traceable only in the coruscation on the galvanized wire. He stood at the east corner and plotted the brooming. The sweeping prevented boredom, so he thought. But it was not a matter of dragging the broom as on clay. On the hard surface the broom had to be lifted and stroke pushed, lifted, stroke pushed, and for all the effort not much accumulated before the bristles. Whoever used the courts? Brian on the afternoons — meticulously clean. Three old men on the weekends. On clay, at the Hane Country Club, he had liked to watch the ridge of claydust which ran before the broom and the even leveling after. Here, his strokes could not disturb the concrete surface and yielded no evidence of his energy. It was difficult, but a routine. And that was how to pass the days.

The rasp stroke of the stiff bristles dominated his courts. He worked quickly brooming from the back court to the net. On this surface that was the way to play, the way to broom. Get the fissures behind you. Get to net. Put the ball, the trash, away. And if at the end of brooming, if you had, after the careful lift stroke pushing (the tedious overlapping of one lane of cleanliness on another) if then, as you eased the bristles toward the final edge of the grass, if then, the steady broom delivered to the lawn only one gum wrapper brought all that way, what did it matter? An hour had passed — and the reward was the same for the keenest volley on the most crucial match point.

Beyond the fence, on the west side of the courts there was a white metal table and two aluminum chairs. He righted the broom, carried it out, flung it down so that in settling the long handle nearly whacked his leg, and then sat in one of the chairs. Just south of the courts there was a series of condominium apartments, offering he understood from Mrs. Silvern (whose apartment overlooked his courts) a paid up initiation fee for the Cape Revere Club with each purchase. A widow and bored, lonely, well to do, she pestered him—waving, laughing, cajoling, on her way to lunch at 12:30 every day but Monday in the club dining room. He could sit for her arrival, but he did not want to. What else was there?

At noon the sky was a solid block of blue, in which the bell of sun clanged and clanged, cringing the greens of his courts paler. Across the road which led to the main entrance on the west, Mr. Sweeting, the grounds keeper, atop a rotary tractor, was mowing the heavy lawn. There, at least, were lanes of cleanliness clearly marked. Sweeting slumped on the foam rubber seat, rippling with each jostle. He was an old man, a genuine Floridian, born in Hane and never beyond it. Frank did not think it possible for Mr. Sweeting to be outside of Hane.

There was the scent of fresh cut grass. Frank got up. He liked Sweeting. He never thought of him as hired help. He saw himself that way. Sweeting seemed, rather, a permanent structure in Hane who merely bent this way and that to let the recent Haneites flow by. Sweeting's face had apparently swallowed sunlight, was puckered in a myriad of needle-thin wrinkles, crow's feet, furrows and freckles. His eyes, always squinting, always recessed in the sunlight, opened wider in the shade. They filed with surprise at how Hane had grown—what Hane had attracted.

"I can remember when there was nothing here but swamp." Sweeting stopped the tractor, but the rotary blade still clattered whirling.

"Turn it off, will ya!" Frank shouted.

Sweeting smiled. The motor sputtered dying. "I'm supposed to finish this strip before lunch."

"Siroka tell you that?"

Sweeting squinted, adjusted himself on the seat, "Yes, sure did. Can't say that he can do much about it. I was thinking about you could get more lessons."

Frank thought about turning away. He could feel himself dropping, dropping—landing on that solid green floor of pretense. "It's mainly the lack of members," he was appalled at the business like tone he spoke in. "But the club will grow. I'll probably try to get a youth group going over the summer. It'll build. I'm on the job." He felt hungry. "Besides, I could always have your job."

"I reckon you could. Almost anytime, you know." Sweeting leaned down from the rusted orange tractor. Frank anticipated a joke. He never quite knew what Sweeting's attitude was. "You know I'm not even supposed to to riding one of these. 'Course Siroka doesn't care. But my doc doesn't think it helps my stomach at all."

"You want me to finish the strip?"

Sweeting looked at him hesitating. Frank stepped up on the machine.

"All right, old man, get out of the seat. I'll finish your goddam work for you."

Mr. Sweeting got down. He arched his back bulging a stomach which looked as hard as the tumor it suggested. "I'll take your lessons," Sweeting said smiling.

So he knew. Frank answered, "No, you take the youth group." He laughed. Sweeting chuckled.

"How do you start it?" Frank asked, then pulled the correct knob. Sweeting stepped away. He waved his arm in a slow rectangle, indicating how to finish the strip.

WHEN OUT OF POSITION LOB TO THE BACKHAND CORNER, OR SLAM TO THE CENTER

He made the rough rectangle smaller and smaller, then double cut the cuttings. Fine particles, needles of grass, spewed out from underneath — at first pluming behind, then on the second cut, misting. Mr. Sweeting had settled by the white table. Now he rocked back and Frank saw him fall into his standard half slumber.

What was better than the scent of grass? Orange groves? Perhaps. The thick lawns of Westchester. How green they were! How brownish, flat, under-nourished was Hane! Yet there, as here, what were the options? To go round and round. At the Westchester club the trip from the back to the fore court, the fence to the net, retrieving balls, standing at the cord holding a pile of balls, locked to the elbow in fuzz, and blandly stating, "Take your racket back. See the ball hit the strings. Turn. Shift the weight to the front foot." — was that not the same as the continual mowing of rectangles of grass? Around and around. Surely Peg could see why he did not go back. Surely. But no. She had gone back because that is what they had always done.

That was the order of things—an order for things: cars and houses; clothes and dinners out—in short, the unwasted life. As if purchase or movement or something could avoid the freckling sun, the crows feet and furrows. A southern girl she never tanned. She was always ashen. Her skin stretched so softly in eggplant smoothness. Oh Peg, nothing of the needle thin wrinkles of Hane.

He cut the motor. Mr. Sweeting, disturbed by the silence, leaned forward.

"Lunch?" Frank shouted.

Mr. Sweeting unfolded his arms, shook his head.

"What's the matter, food not good enough?" Frank approached him, "Siroka give you indigestion?"

"Henph! I don't care about him. My wife's coming. She'll bring lunch."

"She drive all the way down from Hane?"

"It's her day off."

"Well, that strip's never been cut better. Try to do as well next time, eh?"

Sweeting smiled, stroked his stomach, closed his eyes.

Frank went back through his pro shop — the scent of rubber and starch, normalcy. He paused. He was not hungry, but it was time. He knew after he tasted food his hunger would build. He thought about re-arranging the shop, as if he would have traffic, congestion, sales. He laughed a little to himself, opened the inside door which led to the open courtyard before the dining room. The gravel was fresh washed. Willie stood in the corner, holding the hose, moving it back and forth limply from his hand, dangling it over the stones to give them the polish of moisture, the luster which dried out.

There were sliding glass doors to the dining room. Frank came through right at the center. In the season he would have had to come through the kitchen. Now only the three waitresses retained in May sat at the large round group table. There were, however, two drinks on the table near Frank's entrance. Women golfers he thought. He took a small table by himself, near the bar. He did not hold that kitchen was different from professional help. He did not see the gradation—Peg did. But he simply did not care for the three waitresses. Thelma he found sweet but aging and cloying. The others dirty, acid tongued, demanding, what have you. He could not imagine marriage to any of them. Now, least of all Peg.

Thelma got his order. It was standard, no choice, (Siroka's rules) today: Welsh Rarebit on toast with cole slaw and a swimming fruit salad. The plate was filled with white slosh soaking into the toast. He ordered a Budweiser. Thelma shook her head as she put it down. He smiled. In eating he did become hungrier. The two women golfers came back to their table. They wore slacks and metallic blue and red blouses, were tanned, frowzy, and slightly high. In the dining room black topped linoleum tables needed tablecloths, which, because it was May, would not appear.

He piled all his food together. Because it was May. Because it was May, all the pros went North, all the pros who made a living went North, took their wives, their kids, their ballboy machines, practice nets, and baskets of Wilsons, boxes of Moodies — all following the sun or avoiding it. He had not adhered. Just as he had applied, some days, a layer of white sun screen to his nose, so he shut Westchester out. Shut Peg, the kids, the Wilsons and Moodies out. There would be no blisters, only the moistness of a meal clumped together, and a beer.

The big room was quiet. Once in a while he heard a glass slip into the soap-thick water of the stainless steel sink in the kitchen behind him — or the phone rang in the front lobby, and the short woman in the black sweater who had come to the waitress table shrugged, got up and ran back to the front. He chewed the soggy Rarebit, smiled at the women golfers, felt himself grow bloated.

Then Siroka came in. The small chatter at the waitress table stopped. He was a tall, very stocky man with slicked black hair, a metallic brown suit, black shoes, and nervous eyes. He stopped at Frank's table.

"Look, you got lessons on this afternoon?" he said, slicking back his hair. The voice, gruff, urgent, utterly sincere, amused Frank. Could it be Siroka lived the myth that his club was successful? Would he stand now in the empty dining room and truthfully ask, "Do you have lessons on this afternoon?" Was success such a deception-prompted thing?

Frank wiped his mouth. Siroka leaned in, seemed about to pounce. "One at 3:30," Frank said.

"Oh good!" he straightened up. "You'll be free then. When you finish lunch?"

"In a while."

"When's that?"

"Ten, maybe fifteen minutes."

"That's great," he slicked his hair again. "Good. Good. Look, I'll meet you upstairs in ten minutes. O.K.?"

"What's wrong?"

"Wrong? Did I say anything was wrong? Wrong? Nothing's wrong. I just want you to help me, that's all. A little job."

"I charge thirty dollars a half hour," Frank said.

Siroka looked down at him, hard, quizzically, then smiled. "Oh good! How come you're messing up another table?" He laughed, shrugged and went on.

The Rarebit was terrible, but to live out his time Frank ate every bit of it. Siroka was waiting for him. "I need to spray some of the rooms up here."

"What?"

"The rooms. My wife saw a couple of roaches last night. She won't let the kids back in the rooms."

"Why didn't you have Willie or Sweeting spray them?"

Siroka looked at him incredulously. "Look, they're *our* rooms."

"But the club owns them. Certainly it's part of club business."

"Of course it's club business. Of course it is. But they're our rooms. You think I let just anybody in *our* rooms?"

"Oh, I didn't understand."

"Come in here. I'll get the spray."

They went into his office. He dragged a large tank shaped like a milk canister from behind his desk. "This is a heavy son of a bitch. Grab hold will ya?" They carried it outside, then down the maroon carpeted corridor. Siroka stopped twice: once to rest and the second time to get a can of Raid from the closet at the end of the hall. They dragged the tank through a screen door, across an open porch, which overlooked the golf course, and then into another corridor.

"My wife is so damn finicky about bugs. Here we are." He opened the door, "My little girl's room. These rooms are supposed to be picked up."

The room was a narrow cubicle holding one spongy bed, a chest, and a secretary with a flap down used as a desk. There were dolls on the bed and books and two broken toys. Shoes were just under the edge of the spread trailing on the floor.

"We'll shoot the baseboard first."

"How old's your daughter?" Frank said.

"Eight. How old's yours? Drag that closer."

"Nine, I guess. Yes. Nine."

"All right, pull up that handle. That's right, all the way up. Now when I give you the signal push it down real slow. I don't want to flood this place. Set?"

"O.K."

"Good. Oh, good! Go ahead—push!"

As gently as possible Frank eased the handle down, feeling the fluid give against him. Siroka grasped the tube from the tank firmly and directed the squirt neatly along the baseboard. There was the scent not of cut grass, nor orange blossom, rather, a thick flour-ammonia smell which expanded.

"Stop. We gotta move the bed," Siroka smiled, embarrassed at how much work it had turned out to be. That Siroka could be concerned at all surprised Frank. They pulled the bed out from the wall, then the secretary and chest—each time spraying the baseboard. Finally they dragged the tank back out into the hall.

"We might not be able to finish this before my lesson," Frank said.

"Really?"

Frank didn't answer.

"Well, look, we'll skip my son's room. He's got to learn how to live with bugs anyway. We'll do Rita's room, ours. She's the one bitching anyway. She's the only one who could have got me doing this."

"Yes, I guess we can get that one done."

"Oh good. I kept saying, why cut myself out over a few bugs? Know what I mean?"

"Yes."

"If getting rid of a few bugs is all it takes, then get rid of the bugs. Why cut myself off? This getting lighter, notice that?" Siroka seemed genuinely surprised.

The master bedroom was filled with religious statues. Several madonnas stood on several corner shelves. Three crucifixes hung from the walls. And there were pictures and scapulas.

"Rita's very religious. We're Polish you know. Not much stuff to move in here." Siroka threw himself into pushing chairs. "I want to set it up so we can go right around. We gotta put it on thick, else Rita won't believe we did it."

This time Frank aimed the tube. The white bug spray trickled down off the baseboard, puddled on the green linoleum. He went right around the light, then right around the walk-in closet.

"Help me move the stuff back," Siroka said. "I appreciate this. It's not what you're paid for. I know that, and I appreciate it. Look, while I drag the tank back, you seal up this place and spray with the Raid."

"Around the windows?"

"No. Everywhere. I mean everywhere. Fill the whole room up. She won't be able to sleep in here tonight. She'll know we got the bugs—eh?"

"Close the windows?"

"Right. Good! I'll take this back to the office."

"O.K."

"Seal it up good and really spray it on." Siroka slammed the door.

After he had shut the two casement windows, Frank sat down on the bed. Ammonia scent and heat. The room was nearly stifling. Why cut myself off? He had to laugh at that. Fondling the Raid can he turned, looked at all the corners of the room and decided where to start spreading his film. He filled the closet with the gasoline scented mist. Would it stain the clothes? He closed off the closet, sprayed the windows, then the hanging corner shelves, spreading an oily frosting on the blue statues of the Virgin. Then, stepping back, he aimed the can high, pressed down full, and weaving his arm back and forth, plumed out a fine mist which fell too directly. He moved more quickly spraying thicker and thicker plumes. Some of the mist hung in the air, finally obscuring the view of the windows. He kept back stepping, still sending out arcs of spray. He made his cloud a delicate retiary of mist and moisture, bulbous and stretched almost to eye level. Above it though, from three walls there was Jesus in iron, in plastic, in wood, watching as he eased out of the door. Why should I cut myself off?

IN SERVING TOSS THE BALL TO THE MAXIMUM OF YOUR REACH, AND FOR POWER, FORWARD INTO THE COURT

He had a ritual for preparing for a lesson. He bent down and slid the basket of balls out from under the shelf which held his hand stringer. He eased the basket around in front of the counter. He took his favorite Kramer racket from off the pegboard clamp. Brian could give him a game. The gut strung racket would be appropriate. At the Hane Country Club he had given most of his lessons with a lesser Kramer strung with perfected nylon. He brought the gut out, then, only for special games against excellent juniors, or prestigious members. The nylon stood up better. He had given lessons right after a rain—sometimes even in a mist that would have doomed the gut. Now, Brian alone was his special case.

Today there was no mist, no breeze — sun-hammered sky, hot, forcing sweat, his favorite tennis weather. He banged the heel of his left palm into the strings, listening for the correct twang. He could string a racket by tone. 3:15. He put the racket down, clacking on the glass counter top. He picked up the tube of sun screen and using the plate glass as a mirror applied a careful layer to his nose. The cream was itchy, sticky. He felt momentarily like a warrior. His legs, he thought, took up a certain spring with the application. His shoulders felt larger, shoving at the Moody knit shirt. In deference to the May sun, he should have worn a hat, but today he didn't feel like it. He picked up the basket, wedged it awkwardly against his side, picked up the racket and went outside.

His dark glasses were still on the white metal table. He put the basket down. Usually Brian was early but not today. He put the glasses on, nudged the basket into the court, thought about hitting a few serves, but rejected the idea and sat down.

Then he saw Brian's mother. A short plump woman in tight Bermuda shorts and a green blouse, she waved to him and indicated by arm motion that Brian was in the locker room. She carried, as always, a large yellow pad.

"How'd Brian do in Orlando?" he said, "I didn't see anything in the paper."

"He got to the finals. Frank, how are you? But lost to a boy four years older." She firmly put the pad down, snapping it on the white table. "Lord, what a tournament! Mismanaged? I've never seen anything like it. And the finals in the rain. You know how rain bothers Brian. I, mind you, *I* got reprimanded for pointing out to the umpire—what a jerk — that rain spotted Brian's glasses every time he looked up to serve. It seems to me that's pretty unfair to Brian. But the other boy was local. I told Brian he had to expect that. In the sanctioned tournaments things will be different. Mostly it was his low backhands. I've never seen him hit so many into the net. Of course the other boy was smart. He kept feeding them to Brian. But Brian couldn't seem to chip them up. He was picking up the tape all, I mean all of the time. After the first set I told him, 'Forget about the corners. Try cross court with some top—anything. Get the ball back' But that only rattled him more. I should have stayed quiet. His father's smarter that way."

"He probably wasn't getting down to the ball."

"Yes. That's it exactly. But he thinks he just had an off day. He could have beaten that boy. I guess too many things were stacked against him. You're right. I should have told him to get down, bend his knees. You know he's so lazy. Course all of 'em at that age are so lazy about anything, anything at all. He chokes up, stops stroking, then it's just a matter of time, but he'll learn."

"Listen," Frank said, "He's a fine tennis player right now."

"Oh, I know that, but it would please his father so if he could win one or two big tournaments."

"Like Wimbledon?" Frank laughed.

She looked at him quizzically. "What's he going to do today?"

"Well, I guess we better work on low backhands."

"I wouldn't do that. He'll think I put you up to it. Why don't you just play him some. Just games, or a pro set."

Penalty for the Wimbledon remark, Frank thought. She was skeptical of his playing ability, he knew that. And doubtless since she had not been able to join the Hane Country Club, she was hesitant about accepting its cast-offs. But ah, how she belonged at Hane. She drew a chair up to the table, brought out her ball point pen. It was all decided. Brian would humiliate him.

"Well, I suppose that would do. It's my kind of weather."

She nodded, apparently writing a box score up already.

Brian came out through the pro shop. Short and pudgy, though his fat portended elongation, he walked slowly toward the courts.

"Get us a can of balls," Frank called out. "No practice today. We'll play some."

He pulled the basket of balls back out through the gate. He knew Brian was steady but no threat. At a moderate pace the boy could hit all day from the back court, but once the speed picked up, once Frank began rushing net, Brian's errors would multiply. He would begin to look pleadingly toward his mother. Frank swallowed, shook his head slight slightly. Had it come to this concern: how to clobber a fourteen year old?

Brian came back, "Mom tell you about Orlando?"

"Yes, that was great, just getting to the finals."

"I could have beaten him. But the umpire made us finish in the rain. It smeared my glasses. How come we're playing?"

"Seemed like a good idea."

"Brian," she said, "take a good long warm up." She smiled at Frank.

There came the usual hiss as Brian opened the can of Wilson balls. They went into the court. He took the north court, facing into the sun. He did not like to begin serving. The serve was the weakest part of his game. It fell apart in the tension of a match first. He preferred to work into it. Get a sweat up and then start serving. Would they spin to see who would serve first? He didn't think so. Ironically as the older, as the pro, he could say to Brian, "You go ahead and serve." It would be taken as a gracious gesture, giving the boy the advantage. And changing on the odd game would get him out of the sun for the first serve. He knew he was plotting as if Wimbledon had come to Hane.

Brian began the rally. His balls were coming short, a foot or two beyond the service line. It was a poor way to practice. In a match having warmed up this way, he might never find the range. But the boy was hitting smoothly, turning, stroking, nothing to suggest he was upset at the prospect of playing.

"Lift your sights," Frank called. "Hit deeper, aim higher over the net. Send a few out even. Get the feel of the court." He felt magnanimous, powerful, for he knew all he had to do was say a few more words and he could rattle Brian irrevocably. But he had limited himself. He could have suggested dropping a shoulder or changing a grip and then watch amused as Brian clumsily extricated himself from a new style. Brian's mother would have seen through it. So he had made the proper instruction. A good student, properly instructed, should excel his teacher. Wasn't that so?

And then he fell silent, lapsing into that pre-game euphoria somewhere between concentration and instinct, loping effortlessly, delighting in each shock of delivery as the ball leapt to his directing. He knew he hit with a mild slap motion. It was not a perfect stroke, especially on his forehand. He met the ball too far forward, compensated by cocking his wrist, flicking it at impact. But on a fast surface court, such as this, a slap stroke had its advantages. Hard hit balls skidded off irretrievable. He could really put them away. The surface gave him percentages. The slap stroke wasn't steady, but on the concrete he would have to hit less of them. Besides, he had always delighted in the speed, the thrust of tennis. He never cared to retrieve. A well hit slammed fault was more enjoyable than a cautious, well-placed serve. He had tried as a serious tournament player to correct that flaw in himself. It had cost him victories. But he could not entirely suppress the conviction that joy springs from going down slugging. On grass he could win slugging. That was an almost overwhelming experience—enjoyment and victory in one match! Now as if to drive home his feeling, he waited for a high forehand and when Brian sent one, slashed it away into the backhand corner. The boy, awed by the speed, did not even turn to run.

Frank felt Brian was somewhat comical: bulging stomach of early adolescence. Brian couldn't move very well—that would be his flaw—just as a certain power-lust had been mine, Frank thought. But who could tell what the boy would grow into? Frank followed a short ball to net. His volley was always the strength of his game. He hung in on the top of the net almost by instinct and when his reflexes were sharp (as on days like this) his slap stroke rifled points away. At the net he never came out of a crouch. Even his low volley had a deceptive sharpness to it. But there was no rhythm in net play—at least not with Brian. The boy had too much difficulty returning his volleys.

"Try a few lobs, please," Frank said. Brian nodded; the first one came too short to be hit as an overhead.

"Sorry," Brian said.

"That's normal. Get the range."

The next lob arched high but not deep. At the last minute Frank had to bend to get his racket fully on it. The third was better—over his backhand, high, deep, unwobbling. He back stepped, remembered to turn, leapt up, watched white fuzz against the blue until the ball fused with the sun in a prickling, white blast of light, swung, felt the shock, landed blinking. He had pulled it into the alley, but there had been pace, terrific pace on the shot.

"One more," he called out, though he could not yet see Brian clearly, blinded by periodic sunspots in his eyes. Brian's shot was short and on the forehand. Frank closed on the net, swung hard without turning, met the ball full. He slammed it into the forecourt. The ball bounced high toward the second court. Brian made a snap decision and went after it. He sprinted well, far into the other court, reached out and, though off the wrong foot, stroked the ball back up into the air. It was an excellent lob.

"Nice get," Frank said, catching the ball. "You look ready. Are you?"

"Yes."

He threw him the ball. "Go ahead and serve."

IN DOUBLES CHIP, IN SINGLES STROKE

His practice serves were all long, but he hit them smoothly. Brian didn't seem to tighten up.

"Ready," he called out, holding two balls up to indicate play was about to begin. He rocked back, came into the serve too quickly and faulted it in the middle of the net. Frank crouched down. The second serve would drop short. He instinctively shuffled forward waiting for it. There was no pace on it at all. Frank had time to turn, cock and slap the ball away cleanly into the backhand corner. He followed his shot to net but Brian didn't make a move to retrieve.

"Get the first ball in," Frank said sharply, "and deeper. Serve like that will get crammed down your throat every time."

Brian nodded. Out of the corner of his eye Frank saw Brian's mother jotting down notes. On the next point Brian double faulted. Rattled already Frank thought, the victory cheapening with each error. He won the game at love. When they changed courts he said, "You should have served more practice balls. Don't ever be afraid to take dozens of them."

There was no question of the outcome now. Frank felt himself relaxing. Once on top, the pressure eased. He could take more chances and that would demoralize the opposition even more. He could be magnanimous. He served easily and elected to stay in the back court. Brian returned deeply, rushed into position and they sparred at long range. There was the rhythm again. He hit easily, with the depth and loft, not so much of a stroke as a push. It was dangerous, but he was confident. Even with experience such casual soft hitting could choke him up, force him into a pushing game which would favor Brian who could run all day. By prolonging the rally he knew he was building Brian's confidence. But if he built the boy's game up a little, wouldn't it be more enjoyable? Wasn't he paid for that?

Surprisingly Brian chipped back one of Frank's short shots and closed toward the net. It was arrogant, but there he was, pudgy and determined, hanging in right on top of the net. Frank ran deep to the backhand, tossed up a lob. Brian backed up, eyed the ball carefully, but only half swung at the overhead. Frank was set for a slam. It was disconcerting. He had to leap back again, deeper this time to the backhand. He elected to go down the line, figuring that Brian would be set for another lob, but the boy had moved to the alley, outguessing him. He met the ball sharply, but was not far enough in front of it to get good cross court angle. His volley was within reach. Frank wheeled, lunged, opening the face of his racket, spearing a short lob neatly down the backhand line. It would be a winner. Frank straightened up, elated, but Brian had sprinted after the ball, had reached it, and now, his back to Frank, actually managed a backhand high enough, deep enough, to keep Frank away from the net, keep the rally going. Frank, winded, disappointed, back pedaled and stroked, adding a little pace. However, Brian, alert, crouching, was in position. He seemed ready to close on the net again. Frank was breathing harder. No matter how the point turned out he knew he would have to give away a few more just to rest. But it would be bad psychology to lose the point. He felt he had to stay in with Brian. And for the first time he felt he could not count on an error. He would have to force the win. His stroking steadiness would only keep him even. It was not enough to win. He would have to make the extra effort, take the extra risk. When had he first learned it?

He moved toward center court. Brian's shot had not been that short. Frank knew he should have stayed back but he hoped that by crowding in he might panic Brian. He hit soft and deep to Brian's backhand, then sprinted to net. Brian lobbed, short. Frank cocked, met the ball perfectly, put it away. He relaxed, panted. His legs felt dead.

"Good rally," he said. Brian nodded, took his position quickly, waiting for the next point. He's learning, Frank thought. He's trying to pressure me. Was it pressure or just the natural impatience of a youth who wanted to get on with the game —someone so utterly confident now that he wanted to speed time and the inevitable up. Frank was thinking back as he slowed, walking toward the baseline of another match twelve years before. A match which seemed now his last effort in exhibition—against a 16 year old who stroked flawlessly, relentlessly, and who burned to win. That dedication—that was the upsetting part. Frank expected to triumph but lost. He had fallen then, as now, into the natural sway of shots, but they had all come back. The exhibition had drawn well at the Hane Public Courts. A crowd, linesmen, ball boys, an umpire who was Chinese (former Davis cupper) and who shouted the score incomprehensibly:

"Oddvontage Surva!" Against a lanky junior who hit all the balls back. The Chinaman perched aloft, hunched over his score card, like Brian's mother over her pad. A sky as pale as this one, as hard, unetchable as this. More sweat then—longer rallies—a clay court. But the same perception. Steadiness was not enough. He would have to force the win. But the boy was tireless.

Frank served and followed to net. He did not know where he found the energy. Brian, awed (he guessed) didn't turn for position, rather chipped to Frank's feet. The low volley worked, went deep and cross court. Brian was there, tried a slashing backhand which only bulged the middle of the net.

"Oddvontage Surva!"

Frank thought he would have to go to net each time, every time. The long run pulling out his legs. The long run working its cold fingers into flaccid thigh muscles, pinching off, for an instant, calf muscles. What if the boy lobbed? What if the run up was only the beginning of the run back? Frank served hard. Brian thrust his racket out, blocked the serve and surprisingly lobbed perfectly. At the service line Frank made a wrenching turnabout, watching the lob as it drifted almost eerily toward the forehand corner. For an instant he thought, hoped, it would go out. But no. He sprinted back, ran hard. He hit a half lob return—regained position. Brian hadn't moved to the net. That was stupid. Had the boy crowded in, the point would have ended there. Instead, Brian loped easily to Frank's shot, returned it deep to the backhand then followed to net. Frank tossed up a good lob, but Brian went up on giraffe legs, cocked, slammed, angling the ball short to the forecourt, out of play. Frank was exhausted. Brian hurried back to position, not even breathing hard. So it was finished Frank thought. After a few points which experience might salvage, endurance would prevail. The longer the rallies the less chance of victory.

Frank rubbed his leg, bounced the ball before serving — letting breath slow down a bit. Not to this kid, he thought. From a private, desperate pre-serve he summoned enough energy to hit two blazing serves. Brian erred on both of them.

"Your game," Brian said.

"Yes," he answered. "Concentrate. My serve wasn't that hard. You shouldn't have missed it."

"It was the hardest serve I've ever."

"Oh, come on," Frank laughed.

"Well, it was. Do you know how hard you hit?"

"I'm a pusher."

Brian's mother laughed.

Not hard enough, not sure enough, not long or steady enough. The brittle, blue light sky astounding even through the dark glasses, and now not enough energy to last another set, not enough detachment to be amused at his own racking. And then too much detachment. The loser climbed right out of his skin, completed the stroking, rushed to net and was passed, leapt high and lost overheads in the sun, raced to the backcourt to face down drop shots, was continually lurching in the wrong direction.

The end always began when he started watching this loser, this alien mired in his own skin. It had to be somebody else—somebody else with aching, half cramping legs and no desire to win. He drew further and further away, thinking: on that distant, green court there's a fellow in white shorts and tired legs who's going to lose. He thinks well enough, but he runs poorly and very probably he doesn't care enough about each point. In a way he is amusing, getting caught flatfooted and standing straight up all the time. But he is going to lose. Leave him to his own devices. It's not a team sport. Let him lose separately. Would that salvage pride?

Brian held two balls up—a summons to get ready to play within the lines and according to the surface. The loser apparently hated the boy but Frank did not. The boy's impatience, the loser's hatred were veneered with amusement. The little game going on below. The separate Frank, the observing Frank, two figures refusing to blend and hence causing disaster. But merge of course they did — delusions only of separation. He felt them hug, loser and observer, beneath the crisp scratchy towel, felt them lock together in the ripple wave of cramp as he slumped against the fence. As he watched Brian lower his racket, all matches became one. He heard the Chinaman of that prior exhibition, heard him try to say the right thing, the right consolation for Frank's loss. But he had trouble with the language. He wanted to say "good match" but it came out "goo motch." A thousand points gone by, a million balls hit. Legs pounding, knees rising, earth receding, and the perfect consolation for the wasted man — "Goo Motch, Frank, goo motch!"

ON CRUCIAL POINTS DISGUISE YOUR SHOTS EVEN IF IT MEANS CHANGING YOUR STROKE

"Are we going to finish the set?" Brian said. "I'm hitting much better now. I'm getting down to the ball."

"Time's up," Frank said. "Besides, you were hitting too many balls back."

Brian's mother stood up, angry, thwarted. He expected her to offer payment for another half-hour, and he did not know how to answer this.

He projected himself before her on his knees, saying, "I decided not to go back North this summer, not to try again, and lately I've been so tired, as if muscles holding, now released, have given up. I don't think I can play another game, another rally. Forgive. Put your sweet white fingers in my hair. Ah, hold me up, Brian's sweet mother." What would she say? The scene amused him, especially now as she burned with frustration.

"We can try again tomorrow," he said.

"What time?" she asked.

"Oh, in the morning. I'm fresher then."

"So's Brian."

"Good then, how about 11:00?"

"Too late. I play golf then. Try 10:00," she said.

"I guess that will be all right. I'll get the sleep out of my eyes."

"Come on, Brian."

"Thanks," Brian said.

Frank nodded, picked up the stiff towel and raked it across his fore-head, down his arms. All business, they walked away. He slumped beside the white metal table. The sky was darkening. The court greens grew richer, and for the first time the fence cast a shadow longer than itself. He heard splashing from the pool. For a good while the delicious exhaustion of the game held him—not that he had played that long or hard. Ten games or whatever would never have bothered him before. But now—no matter, physical tiredness was the purest joy he knew. If only such enervation could persist. Renewal was the enemy. Resumption the terror. His feet flat on the grass seemed to grow right out of the earth, his body diffused to the air. All of the coolness now of the sky seemed to wrap him up, trading him for its currency: beads of sweat. To be so permanently tired as to be beyond pretense, illusion, ultimately care itself—that was the gift of the game. That and a good night's sleep.

Mrs. Silvern came out from the pro shop, stood hanging on the open door, her short yellow dressed body framed by the darkening aluminum strips. Then she saw him and came wobbling quickly at him.

"Is lunch just getting over?" he said.

"No. Why no. It's bridge day. You know that!" her voice, as always, was high, rasping, somewhat phlegmy. "I looked for you when I came over. I thought we should have dinner tonight. I'm a damn good cook, you know. And I thought with Peg away you might be getting tired of the fare." She pointed to the dining room. "Besides, you've never seen the apartment. It's scrumptious and I keep it just as neat as a pin—not that I'm a finicky woman. Harry used to say, 'Louise, you think dust undisturbed is no dirt.' Harry, now there was a finicky man. He was hell to live with but how I miss him. You hear me, Harry, I miss you. That's why I dust. Oh Harry, I do miss you so."

Frank was thinking, "I could have tried harder. I can try harder. If you can just stay with a junior—stay with him long enough, he'll fold up. They can't yet take the pressure. They will fold up, but you have to stay with them, keep the pressure on."

"What would you like for dinner? Nothing too elaborate now. Are you listening to me? Come on now. That's not polite. Harry used to do that too. I used to say the most elaborate things to him, and suddenly I'd realize he was a million miles away. Now, come on. What do you want for dinner?"

"A martini."

"Oh, good! But you'll have to make it. I never mix the drinks. Harry always handled that, and well too. So well! You hear me, Harry?" She turned, addressed the fence, the segmented shadows of the court.

Frank wondered if he could stand dinner with her.

"When do you want to come over?" she asked.

"Let me shower first."

She smiled at him with infinitely knowledgeable coyness. It flabbergasted him, for an instant an actual message came from her. But she was hardly Southern—tanned not ashen, rasping, not soft spoken, and easily to top it off, 78 years old. He shuddered internally. It had come to this. Exhausted by juniors, he had been left to fill the fantasies of seniors.

A meal at the club was no prospect. "About an hour," he said.

"Good," she answered, "that'll give me time to get the smell of cards off my hands. See you the. Apartment 10, right by the pool, on the ground floor. Oh, this'll be such fun." She made the move of kicking up her right leg. He had to laugh.

The shower smelled of sulfur. The soap filmed rather than lathered. Siroka must have cut the softener back. A typical move in May to reduce overhead. He resented it. Then he stood in the locker room, watching the grey asbestos walls. But there was a nice contrast. The evening sun had stroked the upper ventilation jalousies a rose color. Rose and grey—starchy concrete underfoot—and an ache the length of his body. He sat down on the blue green bench, rested his right arm on a locker handle. He thought about calling Peg. She never dusted well.

He got dressed, closed the shop, leaving the golf bags out till later. Dew would form. Manny, the golf pro, would be irritated but no matter. His anger might liven the day. He paused at the courts, noticed the broom, sighed, brought it back, unlocked the shop and tucked the broom clumsily in the darkness away behind the stringer.

He had no trouble finding apartment 10. Reflected light from the pool, blue, shimmering, clearly lit the number. Would she meet him in a flimsy negligee? He shook his head, knocked, and went in. The air conditioning was on, rumbling.

"The bugs," she called out from the kitchen. She had not changed her dress, merely put a green apron on over it. "You know those no see 'ems—that's what Harry used to call 'em. Actually 'no see 'em' is a southern expression and Harry never really was in the South. I don't know where he picked it up. Where did you, Harry? Eh, where? Where did a nice Chicago boy like you learn that southern expression? You didn't have a nice southern belle, did you? Oh, but the martinis. The bar's in here." She pointed to the end of the kitchen. "I put the glasses in the freezer. Harry liked that. He liked that. Harry demanded that. Oh, he was hell to live with, but you go ahead."

"Do you want one too?"

"I certainly do. We're going to have a party, aren't we?" She stroked his arm. "And it's getting cool in here."

"What's for dinner?"

"Oh now, don't you ask that. Don't you! You let me take care of that. I want it to be a surprise. It's going to be wonderful."

He made the drinks. She took hers and said, "Now I want you to see the apartment. It's bigger you know than a lot of houses. Of course I spent a fortune furnishing it, but I kept thinking—you know I'm not such a spring chicken, am I?" She slipped her arm around his. They walked out of the kitchen into a den which opened directly on the living room. "So if I spent a little more now on some things, who could care? All his hard money for frills like these." She pointed to the valence boards. "And wall to wall carpeting. The bedrooms!" She dragged him. He had finished his martini.

"Harry liked yellow of course, but not this much." She set her drink down, sat on the edge of the bed. "There's no view in here. All the windows are up high, so people walking out front can't see in. You never met Harry did you?"

"No."

"Of course not. That was before I moved here—four years before in Chicago. And the bathroom." Abruptly she got up. "Small, just the right size. Do your business and get out. But cheery. So cheery. I like a bathroom to wake you up, start the day right."

"Yes, do you want another?" He held his glass up.

"Yes. Yes, of course. But take a look at the guest bedroom."

There was no view there either and they went back from the yellows and blues to the soft pale browns of the living room. He made a second martini.

"You ever hear the people upstairs?" They sat in green velvet chairs, drank, watched each other and noticed the silence thickening.

Finally she said, "Eh?"

"You know, drop shoes, or what have you, upstairs."

"Of course they do. That's what an apartment's all about. Now the Mellows are moving out because the people above them have kids and the kids are always tumbling around, thumping. But I don't have to tell you that. How many children do you have?"

"Two."

"Mr. Siroka says you're going to stay the summer?"

"Yes."

"Now you know there's no business here in the summer. It's hotter than blazes."

"Winter either," he said.

She smiled at him, held her glass up. He made two more martinis. Standing in front of the gleaming formica he felt himself relax, subside under the velour of the gin, as if the props inside the skin had slid, part into part, like a telescope closing up. He could have stirred the pitcher for an hour, fascinated by the slosh-clack of the ice.

She took the drink and leaned back. The fluid lapped over the glass, down the stem.

"It is nice," he said. "The apartment I mean." Why had he forgotten to tell her that before? It was very dark outside. No trace of the sunset. Across the way the stucco of the condominium glowed bluely from the light of the pool.

Pointing at the pool Frank asked, "There any hours on that?"

"I don't care about noise you know. I'm used to it. I've lived in apartments everywhere. Evanston, Lake Forest, Winnetka, Everywhere. Here you can get more for your money. Thicker pile. Bigger rooms." She began looking about the room, motioning vaguely toward the bedroom. "More tile. Heavier drapes. Just more of everything."

"I was wondering about the pool."

"Would you like to swim? A swim! Say, that is an idea. That is a cracker jack of an idea. But it's so cold in here. I wouldn't want to come back in here in the cold. Besides," she leaned forward, crouching, "I haven't been swimming in ten years." She finished her drink. "Oh, don't you say it. Don't call me a killjoy. Why in my time. Don't you call me a killjoy. I haven't even thought about swimming in so song. So long. I love a party. Harry had to drag me home. Why, getting him to stay out till 1:00 a.m. was a feat. A real feat. Of course, he enjoyed himself more than he let on. Men are that way. I bet you do the same thing to Peg." She paused. He wondered if she recognized an impropriety. "But just to show you I'm no killjoy. I, I, what do they say now?"

"About what?"

"You know when you enjoy yourself. A party, everything."

"Swing."

"Yes," she ate the olive and spoke across green particles which slurred her pronunciation. "Yes, I swing. One more and then I'll finish dinner."

He got up, thinking, well, at least dinner has begun. But he was not really hungry. The gin had spun the threads of his concern out and swirling like cotton candy. It was quite enough challenge to stir the pitcher, plunk the ice, pour the drinks. She was humming "The Lady is a Tramp."

Slumped back in the chair she said, "Remember when they had that party for the young people at the club?"

"Yes."

"Ah, the parties. Harry was the best dancer and he never wanted to go home. My legs would ache and ache and, and. You dance?"

"Not the new ones."

"Oh, I mean dance."

"Not now."

"Who said anything about now? To tell the truth I don't think I could get out of this chair. What d'ya think of that Harry Silvern? What d'ya think of them apples? Them apples. He always said that. Them apples. It was his favorite expression. He'd throw a bonus on the dining room table. 'What d'ya think of them apples?' Oh, Harry. Find that record. Put it on."

"Not now."

"Oh, you're worse than Harry. What a stick in the mud. How old are you? Come on, how old are you?"

"Thirty-nine."

"Thirty-nine and too old to dance? Of course, some men don't like to dance. Oh, this is good, so good. And fun." She took another swallow of the martini. Closed her eyes. The long stemmed glass in her hand tilted ominously. He would have said something, but he felt sadfully settled, swayed by the drinking. He stared at the pool, listened to the rumbling of the air conditioning. He was thinking of someone for her. Someone to marry her. But he could think of no one appropriate. There was seventy year old Dr. Spanos who came down to the club, shuffled out on to the court, dumped an Abercrombie and Fitch traveling bag filled with tennis balls and then began practicing his serve. He stood hunched over in the backcourt, balls streaming away from his feet. "I had a game," he always said defensively, "but I guess he couldn't make it. I had a game coming." Her expression the same as his—a game who couldn't make it, wouldn't arrive. In the late afternoon near light, the old doctor, rocking back, tossing the ball directly above him—no need of power forward—and miss-hitting the serve. Did he want to rally? No. Why had he come? To practice what? For what? Their expressions were the same.

"Should I go back north to Peg?" he asked, wondering if Mrs. Silvern was asleep.

"Hell no!" she said, rasping, her face still against the velvet. "We're having too much fun right now. Why didn't you go back with her in the first place?"

Perhaps by keeping her eyes closed, her head turned, she's trying to say she doesn't care, Frank thought. "We had our problems. Maybe she was too religious. I don't know." He felt cornered, clumsy, angry.

"That's a problem?"

"Yes, it can be."

"Sure. Sure," she sighed.

Suddenly he felt very, very hungry—realized that she would not cook him a meal. He watched her raise herself enough to finish her drink, eerie blue-lit, pale. She dropped back against the chair.

"Mrs. Silvern, I think I better put you to bed. I'll get something to eat over at the club." He got to his feet. The pool seemed to grow brighter, began to move. He shook his head. "Mrs. Silvern?"

There came a faint "Whaa?"

"I think I'd better put you to bed." He paused, moved toward her.

"You're the doctor," she said extending her arms.

He held her close to him, walk-wobbling with her to the bedroom. He hoisted her up on the bed. She left one hand about his neck.

"Frank, Frank. Thanks for coming over."

"Mrs. Silvern, I've got to go back to the club."

She dropped her hand, let it reach for the other side of the bed. She patted the opposite pillow, then turned over.

ON SOFT SURFACES RETRIEVE AND RETRIEVE, ON HARD ATTACK AND ATTACK (EXCEPTION: GRASS)

He pulled the spread down underneath her, then brought it back, double folding it across her shoulders. He opened a closet, brought down a green blanket, spread it on the bed so that she could reach it later. She was out all right. He went back into the living room. The pool lights were off. He lit a lamp. Then wondering about dinner he went into the kitchen. Sure enough there were two Stauffer dinners, chicken breasts, in their trays, sitting in the unlit stove. He thought about cooking them. It would take too long. Of course he could maintain the next day that she had cooked the meal. That might make her feel better. He was sure she wouldn't remember, but it would take too long. From a roller near the sink he got some foil, rewrapped the trays of chicken and put them back in the freezer. Had she just forgotten about dinner? Who would take care of her? How often did she forget? He didn't notice any pictures of children or grandchildren around the place. How did she get along? It occurred to him that he might have been the very first caller in the new apartment.

He thought about leaving a note. Instead, he left a full glass of ice water on the night stand by her bed, and put a can of V-8 in the refrigerator to chill.

It was not a clear night. In the late afternoon in summer clouds piled up from inland, cooled approaching the Gulf and sent quick torrents on Hane, on the whole west coast. But May, though hot, though buggy, was still not summer. Evenings, afternoons, passed without rain. The threat was there, obscuring the moon. He could see a few stars and also, strangely, some low mist. It was moist but cool out. He breathed deeply. There was a little difficulty walking. He tended to lurch, his shoulders led his legs. It amused him. Each time he was scared that his feet might not shuffle fast enough to catch up. He expected any moment to be staring face to face with the grass, but he kept on his feet.

He went through the pro shop, clattered through the darkened dining room, and made his way to the kitchen refrigerator. It was not locked. No one was around. Siroka had not made his final check. Frank eased the door open. Not much—two plates of chilled Rarebit and five squat bottles of Budweiser, beading up beautifully as he leaned on the open door. He took a plate of Rarebit out. Upstairs a door slammed. He listened. He was entitled to dinner, but he still felt thievish. Overhead Siroka was saying, barely audible:

"What d'ya mean? What d'ya mean, *deliberate*?"

"You know perfectly well I can't sleep in there. D.D.T. on everything."

"Oh, that."

"Yes. That. Yes, that exactly. *Deliberately.*"

"I can't win."

"Don't start that. Don't you dare start that."

Frank picked out three bottles, all he could hold in one hand, closed the refrigerator with his hip. He took up the plate and snuck back out through the dining hall. He put the plate down on top of the counter in his shop. There was an opener somewhere around the stringer. He stepped on the broom which snapped at him, and finally found the rusted opener. The Rarebit clung to the soggy toast and he ate it like a sandwich, tough custard almost. He opened two beers. He gulped the first down. Cool, thirst quenching. The Rarebit seemed much saltier in the gelatin form. Then he sprawled out on the floor in front of the case. He stretched his legs, reached up and brought down the second beer. After the first swallow it occurred to him his room was too large. "The golf bags," he thought. "They must be covered with dew." He took another sip, contemplated leaving them out all night, rejected it, got to his feet. He eased the door open. They were still there all right, like headless animals on the dark ground. Irons like silver legs speared out in the grass. He drew a five iron out from the nearest bag.

Golf was a less competitive game—an older game. No enduring juniors. Terms only with the wind and grass. He put the beer down, unzippered the ball pouch and spilled three balls out onto the grass, kicked them further from the building—arranged them for blasting. He clasped the iron's handle firmly, locked his fingers, and took a few practice swings. The pressure was off his legs. Tension became more naturally located in his torso. The swing was easy, swooping through the rough. He addressed the first ball. Yes! He whacked the ball, pulling off a little as he started into the down stroke, seeing how it would go, waiting for an unused muscle to twinge. But it was natural right through the shock of collision and follow up. Not lifting his head, he delighted in the metallic clack of club on ball. It must have sailed 100 yards and though he couldn't follow it, he knew it had gone straight.

He let himself go on the next ball, flailed through, straining all the way. Harder shock. He connected lower. A longer wait till the click as it dropped on the distant fairway. If only he could have seen it. On the third shot he jerked his head up determined to follow the whiteness all the way. He topped the ball—laughed as it sluffed, tick-bounced out of sight. Perhaps in the morning he'd hit a few more. There was something to the game, some quality removing it from time, making it less demeaning than a set. Nobility, maturity. That was it. The game had a maturity, a certain maturity to it.

He put the iron back and one by one dragged the bags inside. He stacked them in an L shape, leaving him space to sit on the floor. He finished the second beer, tossed it in the waste basket. He uncapped the last Budweiser. He closed the shop door, and using the stacked bags as handles eased himself down onto the cold terrazzo. There was a terrible darkness. The chrome buckles and zippers barely flickered. He took a deep sniff—still rubber and starch, still Wilson and Moody—not leather, wood and iron. Not yet. He smiled, took a long swallow of the warming beer. Still fuzz and rubber—not leather. But some time the change would come. He sat back hopeful, but not confident, head against the glass of his display case, that the exact moment of transformation would be revealed to him.

PART II

"If I want lectures, Mr. Sweeting, I'd at least go to somebody who could speak the language—and who knew something besides."

Sweeting harrumphed but there was a smile and Frank relaxed. Was Sweeting sensitive about his literacy?

The DeSoto rattled. A convertible purchased a month ago, it once had been the pride of some neighborhood; now Frank was only thankful that after an anxious length of low combustion coughing the engine would always turn over.

"You always get salty after you speak to your Daddy. You call him?"

Frank slowed down. Ah, Sweeting the perceptive.

"As a matter—"

"I knew it," Sweeting put his hand on the dash. "Your Daddy—"

"It's his birthday," Frank cut him off. Sweeting would see, wouldn't he, that it was nothing special—only a dutiful birthday call and if in the conversation other than birthday exchanges had come out—Peg had stopped by (how shrewd, isolating the enemy) if other things had been talked about, didn't that go to show only that "dutiful" was, after all, an expansive word, expansive concept. Family extended up and down, forward and back—from baseline to net. Had his father reminded him of that? Not in so many words. Would Mr. Sweeting? Not in so many words. Illiterate words! "Yes, she and the children — they looked tired—stopped by on her way to Westchester. It was good to see her."

The phone had suddenly felt slimy. Frank had not figured on it. The well composed letter explaining so tightly how things were, what they had become—so that the old man, widower, alone in his large Philadelphia apartment which cruelly reminded him everywhere of Frank's mother—so that this man would see how things were, what they had become—the letter, scrapped by Peg's resourcefulness. Concern on her part for the old man? Surely his father accepted that. And doubtless Peg accepted the old man's grudging coming over to her side. Frazzled woman, lonely children—not a male in sight—who would not be moved?

And was the girl (Delores?) in the tight black sweater listening in from the club switchboard? Was Siroka over her shoulder beaming?

"You have to take care of this problem, do what's best. The most constructive." The old man came back again and again to that word *constructive*.

What the hell was *constructive* anywhere? Anyhow?

"Where you going tonight?" Mr. Sweeting said. They passed the massive green stretch of the Hane memorial park—perhaps ten more miles to the city proper.

"You are a nosy bastard," Frank said.

"Eh?" Mr. Sweeting pushed back in the seat, folded his hands like a child on the bulbous tumor of his stomach, crossed his ankles in the space below the dash, a perfect freckled Buddha—implacable. Sweeting apparently knew things that non-real Haneites might only discover after a lifetime of scurrying. Watching such scurrying only made Sweeting cross his ankles. Frank did feel pressed by his own desire to do something, by Sweeting's tanned censure. He regretted coming to Hane.

"Have dinner at a Chinese restaurant and drive back," he said.

But Mr. Sweeting didn't answer.

All the way to the shopping center where Mrs. Sweeting worked they did not say another word. Frank felt embarrassed. Sweeting shook his head getting out. Frank looked, leaned over toward him.

"Look, you know we just kid around. You know that."

Sweeting shook his head, blinked. "I must have been asleep," he said. "Soft car puts me right out."

"See you tomorrow."

"Catting around, eh?" Mr. Sweeting smiled, turned toward the Winn-Dixie where Mrs. Sweeting was taking off her white apron. Frank saw her through the endless plate glass which now began the reflected blinking of the dusk-controlled Center's lights.

He liked Chinese food, eminently digestible. He liked the martinis Mr. Wong made. He did not like dining alone. Taking a corner seat he tried by proximity to become part of the conversation of three women across from him. It was not dark yet, and the restaurant, made from solid Ocala blocks, needed darkness to complete its décor. The overhead lights seem extraneous. He felt he was in a bowling alley or a well-lit cellar. The gin he hoped would change that. It did. His nose tightened; face gradually stretched back more taut, his forearms tingled, legs felt as dead as after four sets. It was a good feeling. What a pleasant place it was! What a pleasant fellow Mr. Wong was! How warm, smilingly friendly, the three women were. He had another drink. He wanted to keep the feeling going. He thought of winning tournaments. In the interval of the walk to the back court before the game began he never failed to imagine he was at Wimbledon –certainly not the courts of Hane. If that had never happened, if clay never yielded to grass (but it did in time, or were they only weeds?) then such unfulfillment was only cause to clarify the situation with another drink.

He had egg rolls, wonton soup, shrimp with lobster sauce and a fortune cookie that read, "The night is full of charm." When had he seen that dentist's wife last? She had come to watch the slaughter—his last exhibition at the Hane Public Courts—watched bemused as that sixteen year old pounded him relentlessly into senility. He had not seen her since. He could not see her now. It would be humiliating. Had there been enchantment? Perhaps? But more likely not. She must have sought a stable of twenty-two year olds, sun darkened, athletically fit. When they lost matches so they lost her. Was that the way it was? Apparently. There were others. He would find them. Others prettier than Peg, less individual, more accessible.

When he left Mr. Wong, he took the main four lanes through Hane proper, passed the Exxon, BP, and Sunoco Stations, the drive-in movies, the airport, the Hane museum—donated by the original Sam Hane who had made a fortune and a half in first the carnival and later the bakery business— then row upon row of motels, most closed, all with advertised vacancies. In May the tourists never came. He stopped at a bowling alley. He was all alone there. The silence was oppressive. He heard his rented bowling shoes creak like tissue on the carpet. He selected his ball, turned back around. He thought, it's so quiet they must all be waiting for me to serve. But no one was waiting. There was a bar counter at the back, illuminated as if it were a drugstore, and the bartender was not watching him, not waiting for his serve or his hook at all. He was reading a paperback. Frank turned around, slumped down, dangling the bowling ball, gauging the distance to the foul light, squinting, blinking, refocusing on the pins down the alley. He planned to hook in on the one-three. He propped his arm back, began the quick steps, arched the arm way back, slid forward, released the ball. There was some loft. The ball bounced, settling in about six feet beyond the foul line. The place came alive like an echo chamber, the terrifying crunching relentless rolling sound of his lone ball down the alley. It seemed the roaring rolling got louder and louder. Everyone would be watching his ball hook all the way across and into the opposite gutter. He waited and waited—hearing the roar of the rolling. He turned back. The bartender was still reading his paperback. No crackle of spilled pins—only the quieter sound, miniature of the first, his returning ball.

He bowled finally a 138. He had two draft beers with the bartender who seemed irritated to have his reading interrupted and who suggested another bar with authentic go-go girls. Driving there Frank realized suddenly that the bartender only wanted to get rid of him.

He took the first causeway to the key. Surprisingly the Sham-Rock Club was crowded, poorly designed but crowded. It was evident the architect wanted to be covered for all contingencies. The club was designed that should it fail, three stores could immediately be made from the building. A U-shaped bar ran the length of the three distinct rooms. Mounted above the bottle racks in the center of the bar was a caged platform. A saucer-eyed girl of perhaps nineteen sat shivering in a bikini on the edge of the platform, waiting evidently for the music to start. Her hair was extremely long; her breasts did not seem more than representational, but her legs, at least in the pose she sat, appeared huge, arresting, constricting? He took the stool opposite her, but their eyes did not meet. She peered beyond anyone, a practiced non-seeing. He ordered a gin and tonic. The music started. A roaring ta-thumping of the drum and bass guitar overrode any finesse on the part of the other instruments. For an instant he was back in the bowling alley, every ball in every lane lofting in syncopation.

The girl got up walked to the end of the cage and turned on an improvised spot light. She began to undulate. Her legs looked less impressive now glowing and dark in the red illumination. He ordered another drink, but he would not get high. He sensed it. The food would strangle relaxation drunkenness. Drink would, throughout the evening, make him logy not happy. Perhaps the music. But it was not music *per se*—only rhythm. His mind came back to the girl. Snapping her pelvis she saw nothing, merely pranced forward and back in a supreme daze, eyes glossed unblinking, a mechanical marvel. Still, there was that always arresting softly taut stretch of skin out in circles from her navel. Those two little bulges of such soft flesh extending down to the top of the bikini bottom. So soft, soft. He took a deep sad breath.

An hour passed, perhaps two. He felt his heartbeat fall in rhythm with the music. The girl moved onto another cage further away. Another took her place, this one dumpy, overly fleshed, colossally ignorant looking. There were more drinks, more people entering all the time. When the music stopped the air thick with smoke seemed charged with distant ice clinking and giggles. The air it seemed was a squirming thing.

"Frank! Frank, come over here."

Someone was shouting but there must have been a myriad Franks in the Sham-Rock, in the world. Oh, melancholy starting—perhaps, he thought, the drink would work after all. After several hours, several drinks he could lurch unevenly to his Desoto, struggle into the front seat, anneal these tears in his eyes—a figure of responsibility abandoned. The stars behind clouds and God's soft hand via the Negro station in Memphis which played Bo Diddley and hawked hair straightener.

"Frank! Over here."

Someone calling him? Not likely but he turned, peered into the darkness beyond the white flashing teeth of the bar-stooled happy souls. There was someone standing motioning, but he did not know him. Gathering up his drink, yes the legs were wonderfully unstable, Frank yielded his seat to tall man who had been breathing on him for some while. Frank eased around the edge of the U but it was tough going. Patrons were bunched in tight.

"Frank—are you deaf or something?" It was Siroka, Siroka standing, conducting the smoky air, carving it up with fat, beckoning arm motions. "Good, Good. Have a seat. How long have you been here?"

"A good while," he looked down at Siroka's table. Of course no Mrs. Siroka, but a strange woman about his age, thin, yet with a puffy bulbous face and an eye which seemed to move a fraction of a second after the other one. She wore a knit tennis blouse and apparent short tennis shorts perhaps a skirt (he figured shorts) for her bare legs came around (as if in quest of his eyes) the solid black legs of the table.

"This is Suzy."

"Sooci. Soo-cee," she corrected, smiling at Frank.

"Sooci," Siroka delightedly corrected himself. "Sooci Kling and Mr. T. Hall Cullenoon."

T. Hall stood up pulling across his stomach an expensive cardigan tennis sweater. A sweater in May, Frank thought, something awry here. "And of course Paula." Frank sort of backhanded a motion toward the tall, dark-skinned woman in tennis clothes. She stood up. Frank shook hands with T. Hall.

"I remember you. Oh, do I," Paula said. "You used to be the pro at the courts.

"I played there a lot."

"Of course."

"Sit down everybody," Siroka commanded, then laughed to take the tyranny out of the line.

Beside Paula there were two young men, college boys? Her sons? Or part perhaps of another table, he couldn't tell. She swiveled away toward the collegians making room for Frank, next to Siroka. She made no effort to introduce them. Frank felt strangely good about that.

"Been playing?" Frank asked.

"Not me," Siroka interrupted, "not by a long shot. That's a young man's game." He nodded at the collegians.

"You're just a lover," Paula said laughing.

"Good, good," Siroka answered taking a drink.

"Where do you pro now?" T. Hall asked Frank. Frank mulled it over—pro now. Does one pro? Hustle? He was amused by the idea of *pro-ing*, especially at the Cape Revere club. T. Hall fidgeted and Sooci looked around at him. She had heard the question and now seemed interested that Frank had declined to answer. Even Paula leaned in some. The noise from tables grew more audible.

"Did I ask the wrong thing?" T. Hall said.

"No," Frank answered slowly, delighting strangely in the little tension of his decline.

"He works for me," Siroka said loudly. "Down at my club now. Does a damn good job. All the members are pleased. Very, very pleased. Good, good. Good job. Let's get another round. I'm buying."

"Of course," Paula said. Siroka stood up, started waving at the waitress near the bar.

"I'm sorry if I seemed to pry," T. Hall said. "It's such a natural thing to ask what a man does and knowing that, where he does it."

"What do you do?" Frank said.

"I work for a bank here."

"In loans?"

"No, in directorial capacity—I'm actually semi-retired. Newspaper business in Kansas."

"And now banks in Florida."

"It keeps me active. Tennis keeps me fit. You ought to know that."

"Yes."

"Yes sir, it's a great game. When I see some of those old duffers on the courts I feel pretty good about the game. It keeps a man fit." He patted his fist on the table. Sooci reached over and patted the top of his hand. T. Hall nuzzled into her hair. Frank heard him say, "Let's get out of here."

Sooci shook her head. Why? I'm in this game, Frank thought. And the flesh of the dancing girls is made to be pressed and covered, kissed and licked. Yes.

Siroka brought the drinks. Seven glasses. So the collegians were a part of the group. Siroka ceremoniously handed out drinks leaving the last two on the tray. The collegians reached across Paula and snatched them up.

Sooci's slow eye fixed on Frank. She watched him, even as she drank. The liquid actually flowed over the lip of the glass, graying the front of her terry cloth blouse. Was she really drunk? He couldn't tell. She laughed, wiping her mouth with the back of her wrist. The music started again. T. Hall looked unhappy. He leaned down into Sooci's hair again.

"Who won?" Frank said.

Sooci smiled, leaned away from T. Hall. "Won what?" she asked slowly.

"The set."

"Oh, oh well, I only play night tennis about once a month with T. Hall, and a few of the lights were out."

"You lost?"

"Oh no. I won. But I wanted to make myself look good."

Couples were shoving toward the tiny elevated dance floor. Abruptly Paula got up. She pulled on the shoulder of one of the collegians. Shrugging, he got up, feigning drunkenness, the last stilt of dignity. Old men pretended to be sober, young men pretended to be drunk, which left Frank dangling and for the first time wondering.

"I think you look very good," he said nodding toward feigned intoxication.

"Oh, I meant concerning tennis," she fairly fluttered.

T. Hall put both hands on the tall, frosted glass of his Gin and tonic, let his lower lip fold over his upper.

"My competition," Siroka motioned toward the collegian Paula led to the floor. "Good, good."

"It's not a foot race, pal." T. Hall said to Siroka, who smiled lamely. "Cash wins," T. Hall went on, this time turning a stare into Frank. "Come on, Miss Sooci, let's go away from here. I know a spot."

"Oh, there you go," she answered. "Well, I'm not ready." There was an awkward pause. Siroka started to laugh. "To be rude to this nice young pro who's come over to sit with us."

T. Hall sat back, looking the magnate. He rubbed his throat. "I can wait," he said.

"Oh, T. Hall, I know you can. You're so sweet."

"I'll get us another round," Siroka stood up.

"No. This one's on me," T. Hall bolted up, catching the edge of the table with his thigh. For a moment he went ashen, grimacing. Frank thought he was going to fall. The table juggled, settled. T. Hall limped toward the bar.

"Lots of energy," Frank said leaning over to Sooci.

"Oh yes, and so sweet."

"Not too much coordination though."

"Co-ordination?"

"Yes. You know ability to—"

""Oh yes," she smiled, "are you going to spend the summer?"

"I think so," he said watching her. So she did not want to knock T. Hall. Cash wins. "I used to go up to Westchester, but not this year."

"My husband lives in Larchmont." She watched his surprise. "I'm divorced. I'm going to send the children up in June three whole glorious weeks."

"You're planning to spend the summer then?"

"I don't know. T. Hall doesn't think I ought to."

Siroka leaned into their conversation. He ran the fingers of his right hand over his left fist. He whistled and watched the dance floor. Sooci looked annoyed; his whistling didn't harmonize with the music.

"Do these dances?" Siroka said to Frank.

"No."

"Neither do I. Not dances, not like we did, eh? Not dances nowadays at all." He began whistling again.

T. Hall brought seven more drinks. He tucked a new Gin and tonic down in front of Sooci and said quietly, "Now this will be the last here." She didn't acknowledge his statement. Paula and the collegian came back, sweat on both foreheads.

"Lover, you ought to try that. Ha, ha," she said to Siroka who continued to whistle. "Boy that'll take the starch out of you."

"He wouldn't want that," T. Hall said.

"Neither would I, I guess. Ha, ha." She picked up her new drink, "Who do I thank?"

Siroka pointed at T. Hall. "It's him."

The collegians snatched up their drinks.

T. Hall said, "Miss Sooci and I are going to drink up and then we're going to have to be leaving." The tone was flat, menacing, directorial.

"Oh, T. Hall, I have a better idea: why not have everybody out to my place?"

"The kids a—"

"The kids are asleep, like stones."

A collegian laughed. "Like stoned!" he shouted and finished his drink in two swallows. Siroka whistled louder.

"Like stoned. Get it, Pal?" T. Hall laughed, finished his drink. "Come on," he stood up pulling at Sooci's shoulder.

"No. Wait a minute, T. Hall. You shouldn't just go tugging on me like that. Now wait a minute." T. Hall pinched his nose. "Now how's about everybody coming out to my place for, for a swim. I'm right on the water. How's about it?"

"Great idea! Great idea," Paula stood. "You come too," she motioned toward Frank, but clearly the sweep of enjoinder encompassed the collegians. They in turn got up.

"Yes," Sooci said smiling. "You be sure to come, you be sure now."

"Done!" Siroka said. "Let's go." He took Paula's arm. The collegians closed ranks behind her. Siroka stood at the door. T. Hall and Sooci had already left. "Come on, Frank, you follow me out," he shouted.

"A party! A party!" Paula said and took the arm of the nearest collegian.

IF NECESSARY, PLAY A WAITING GAME

Beyond the rectilinear, freight-car lines of Sooci's house the Gulf of Mexico's froth slapped the sand tirelessly. It was a clear night and through scrub palm cabbage, palmetto and sea grape Frank saw the familiar phosphorescence of the water. T. Hall's Lincoln was pulled in right next to the wooden stepway that led to the kitchen. The house, brown-tired, obviously weathered, sat on four-foot stilts—not the sort of place, Frank thought, to get drunk in. He felt logy, vaguely unhappy. Paula bounded out of Siroka's Caliber, the collegians piling out after. How tireless she appeared doing a mock pelvic dance with the boys as she swiveled her way to the living room. Siroka got out, joined Frank on the steps.

"I'm not going home," Siroka said to the parked cars. "I'm not going home."

There was a moon, full-disked, and as light-giving as any streetlight on the causeway. The worn paths to the house, the tire tracks, the dead places of previously parked cars, the whole, unpaved trail-like driveway from the road, were all stamped with an aluminum glowing patina. Even Siroka's sweating face looked silver in the moonlight.

"Who said anything about going home?" Frank said.

Siroka turned around hotly. "She did, of course." He went in the kitchen.

The floor sloped, the linoleum was turned up, cracked in places, and moldy. Salt air scents mingled with the odor of grease and stale garbage. She was a pig, Frank thought. It made sense. Perhaps with bad eyes she didn't actually see the stacked, egg-caked dishes, the half-filled glasses, the rusting SOS pads. With her eyes she didn't care.

From the living room the sound track from the Beatles movie *Help* jolted him out of his mesmerism over the shards of a week's eating. There were gnats and, strangely, two flies over the sink.

Help! I need somebody.

Help! I want somebody. Paula's voice made the lyrics clear. She stood in the center of the wood paneled living room and gyrated against one of the collegians. There were three lights in the room in the corners. The wood paneling—old, darkened, seemed to pour from the ceiling down the walls to the floor underneath like a coating of oil. T. Hall and Sooci sat like an etching on the narrow short rattan couch. Siroka leaned up against the table holding a boombox. The second collegian was prone on his back on the floor and watched as Paula flounced and sputtered. Frank stood in the kitchen doorway leaning against the greasy jamb.

When I was younger, So much younger than before.

Sulking, Siroka finished his beer. T. Hall put his arm around Sooci who rather obviously dropped her right hand onto his thigh. He stormed into her neck. Would it be an exhibition then? Paula and the collegian, T. Hall and Sooci. A foul foursome in the oil slick grease smelling room before the metal sheathed windows, and then a flying exit to the sea? The sexuality in the room began a rotation arresting and absorbing.

I never needed anybody's Help in any way.

Now I'm not so sure

Was T. Hall despite himself calling for help? Frank got a can of Budweiser from the refrigerator. Thirteen more cans right below a half eaten bowl of jello — Sooci's concession to haute cuisine?

The collegian had both arms around Paula now. He was trying to trip her but she was agile, kept pressure on the small of his back. T. Hall looked up amazed.

"Why don't you knock it off, kid. You're gonna fail. You're gonna fail." He turned to Sooci. "How about getting rid of the Boy Scouts?" She rubbed his thigh. Siroka shrugged. The song ended. Paula stepped back apart.

"Oh boy," she said. "Oh boy!" grabbing breath, "You're too much!"

"You're gonna fail," T. Hall shouted again, but it came out mumbled by Sooci's neck, hair.

"Oh boy! How about a swim to cool things off a bit," Paula said. "How about it? Come on. You got no life." She latched onto Siroka, who ostentatiously crushed his beer can.

The standing collegian turned, shoved his way past Frank into the kitchen.

"Easy," Frank said.

"What?" The boy looked up from the open refrigerator.

"I said take it easy."

He laughed. "Yeah, I'm gonna fail." He took two beer cans out, "Excuse me," he leaned away from Frank in the doorway sarcastically harrumphing. He dropped one can to his buddy on the floor, opened the other.

"Well thanks a lot," Paula said, feigning insult at her neglect.

The collegian turned to go back to the kitchen for another beer, but Siroka bounding across the room cut him off. "I'll get." He hurried past Frank. Paula and the collegian practically rushed to the front screen door, bolted down the steps toward the Gulf. Siroka came back to the doorway.

"I guess I'll drink this myself," he said.

"You're gonna fail," the collegian on the floor said and faked passing out. Sooci got off the couch. She stretched. "Why don't we all go for a swim?"

"Sharks," T. Hall said.

"Well, stay inside the sand bar."

"Sting rays."

"Well, walk slowly through the water."

"It's cold."

"I'll warm you up."

"Ah, for Chrissake, why don't you just get rid of the Boy Scouts. Get rid of everybody."

"Stop shouting. You'll wake the kids."

"Ha! That's a laugh. Goddam music would wake the dead. The kids for Chrissake."

"You're gonna fail," the phony corpse muttered.

"You'll go swimming, won't you Frank?"

"Why not?" he said.

"Oh good! Then let's go, all of us."

T. Hall got up from the couch. Siroka sat down.

"Can you swim, Pal?"

A little immediate communication of despair, "I don't swim," Siroka answered.

"You can hold the towels," Sooci said, using an organizer and vote-gathering tone, dispenser of something for everyone. The collegian on the floor laughed—echoed, "You hold the towels."

"Shut up," Frank said stepping out of the doorway. The collegian's right eye opened. Frank watched him. The eye closed again.

"Come on, come on. We'll change on the beach." She held the door and an armful of towels. Frank stepped out down the wide steps, wooden and faintly moist. Was Paula frolicking in the surf with her boy, a pair of pelicans devouring smelts or what have you?

"Oh, come on, T. Hall. Come on."

T. Hall came through. "It's too damn cold. For Chrissake why don't you just send the Boy Scouts home? Why play games all the time? For Chrissakes!"

"You're gonna fail," came the steady slurp of the collegian now alone, prone, nearly passed out, genuinely passing out.

The beach was a long way away. The path studded with sand spurs stretched a trickle of white lamination separating growth low and ominously dark. They had to step over a log. T. Hall stubbed his toe.

"Oh, for Chrissake," he howled. "You just go on. Play your goddam games. But not with me. Jesus Christ! I banged the hell out of my foot. Jesus Christ! You just go on. But not with me." He turned back toward the house.

"T. Hall, oh, come on! Don't be that way," she turned to lurch after him, but Frank, his shirt already off, grabbed the tops of her shoulders.

"Come on yourself. He's gonna fail," he said.

She swiveled toward him. "Oh my, you're ahead of me."

"Jesus Christ!" T. Hall cursed again but nearer the house—vanquished, doubtless curling up now on the couch or wheeling the big Lincoln out the drive.

Sooci licked Frank's chest. He nuzzled her hair, his arms clamping at various intervals down her arms, her sides, the top of her buttocks. She propped back offering her lips and he clamped in on those feeling simultaneously the thrust of her tongue and her pelvis. He yanked her up close to him, hoisted her beyond the log, wobble-walked with her entirely off the ground toward the beach.

"Ow, that hurt," she whispered in his ear. He eased her down, knelt himself, sharply bringing the palms of his hands into the back of her knees. Delighted, holding his head, she crumbled backwards toward the sand. He lunged in on top of her.

"Oh my, we certainly are aggressive, aren't we?"

"Oh, yes," he faked a moan but already he had begun to draw away from himself, began to watch as his arms fumbled with the back of her tennis shirt, his legs clambered in and out, over and under, hers. The clasping rasp of clutching bodies amused him, the awkward way his fingers sought out the side zipper of her tennis shorts. Her own tones growing toward involvement but as yet distracted, conscious, all voluntary and hence sterile. It was such an endearing performance, such a performance indeed. In a flutter of sand, a hail of crunching particles trickling from her hair, his forehead, he managed to get her blouse over her head. The bra fell away of itself. He swished his body across her letting her breasts trickle the chest hair, but he was still detached, all too conscious of the sand in his mouth, too aware of her sand-snarled hair and the slow eye that watched him an eerie appraisal of its own.

He kissed her again. Again let his tongue trace an abrasive path down her neck across the nubbin of soft white collar bone toward her breast. She pinched, stroked, the back of his neck, guiding prodding, controlling. He arched his body up on elbows. Her hands went to his belt, unbuckled. He kissed her again. There was gin on her breath, that mild smelling scent, faintly etherous. Would she taste the hot mustard, the stale shrimp?

Her thumbs hooking over the top of his belt she inched her hands down, riveting the sides of his buttocks, thighs. He mouthed her breasts, unzipped the shorts. She ran a closed fist up his spin column, a practiced stimulator. Was she reading a technique manual over his shoulder? And was the lapping of the surf that gentle slap on his thigh, or perhaps a slurping tongue slithering anointment of his ear?

Sand was everywhere, screeching across their naked parts, in hair—a honey layer of abrasion on her back. A gritty earful of distraction. Her slow eye ever open, ever watching, ever evaluating, and he himself again aside somewhere watching the gyrations, the flouncing of trouser, underpants, socks and shoes. Mindful of the long tugging on the white basting of her underpants, a tugging that sent them topsy turvy, rolling on the beach. But she must have sensed, as he did, that there was no involvement yet, no commitment. Perhaps the abrasive distractions were too overwhelming, the grit too enervating, or perhaps there were psychic incapacities suddenly freed by a little tumbling on a less than silk façade. Could she see all that? She must have, he thought, for before things reached an embarrassing crescendo she shook events, particles and panties off, stood up and ran into the water. No teasing attempt at heightening, he thought, sitting in the filthy mounds of his moist shoes. No indeed. A device for saving face — his. She was practiced, indeed compassionate, had no stomach for imitation, no damnation for what might have been his failure. T. Hall trained and used to this? It was an interesting thought.

He got up, leaned down on one leg and took off his socks, tossing them by the shoe hummocks. Was she gesturing from the sea? Phosphorescence streaming around her, a trail of blazing fireflies that lived magically underwater. Ah, a sylph in a fragrant lacquered night.

If the sand had been inhibiting, the cold sealed the issue. When the water reached his navel he began rippling the phosphorescence by an entirely involuntary shudder. She was lolloping further out and he was afraid suddenly of getting wet above the chin. He shrank down in the eerie waters and watched her slip along the sand bar. Eyes following her little hopping jumps, eyes etching out the solid lines of her prancing form in the moonlight, he leaned back dipping his head momentarily, and as if in summation of his prior excitement, his present possibility, passed a warm urination.

Later, mutually wrapped in towels, he carried her all the way back to the house, a token for her understanding, he thought, but an effort beyond her deserving. Nothing was, he figured, worth a hernia. She was docile, moist, affectionate, renewing. He kicked the screen door open, gratefully slipped her off onto the floor.

"T. Hall's gone? Siroka?" he asked.

"Oh yes," she turned to him, making only a half attempt to keep the towel up.

"And the collegians?"

"Gone too," she answered. "They'll be gone all night."

She gave him a fumey passionate kiss, pulling at him toward the couch. "You have a bedroom?"

"Oh no," she answered. "The kids, the children, are in there. Here is just fine. Turn off the lights."

"And T. Hall?"

"He's gone, all gone." Another kiss, the towel slumped at his feet. She folded back on the couch. He moved around the room pulling the fine chrome chains, flicking brown switches, dousing illumination.

"Oh, hurry up." The first harsh tone from her. It interested him. Thwarted at the beach she would not be compassionate here, could it be? He climbed in under the couch cover.

"You're cold," she said.

"Wait a minute things will change."

"Do you have a wife?"

"Yes."

"Oh."

"She's in Westchester."

"And that makes it all right?"

"Absence makes the heart grow fonder."

She laughed, put a hand across his back. "Do you do this often?"

He didn't answer.

"Do you?" she persisted.

"If you say so."

"Oh, but I didn't say so. I just asked."

"What difference does it make?"

"Oh, I'm very interested in those kind of things, that's all."

He kissed her, slipped a hand onto the top cream smooth part of her buttocks. She entwined a leg. He felt himself begin to shudder, squeezed her tighter. She scratched his neck, his back, his hips, his stomach. What difference does it make?

Under the crowded cover, salty-moist, warming, as he reached and embraced, hardened, shed distraction, feeling almost the vaguely hissing tenderness of her, he suddenly was aware that someone else was in the room, someone close by. On his side and facing the wall he pretended not to have such sensation, but it was no good. Someone was there. Siroka? A vision of his wife? He crimped up his arms, yanking Sooci in tighter, biting at her hair. But still, though diminished, there was a presence in the room, watching. He reached outside of the coverlet, extended his arm up and back into the darkness. He was afraid to turn over and look. Moonlight from the windows might have provided enough light. He slumped to his arm a wider arc and then his hand reached across a face, a small smooth face standing by the bed.

If there had been a drop of terror, he washed it down with a glass of shame. Sooci stood up tugging at the cover.

"Jonathan! What are you doing out of bed. Go back to bed this instant. Really Jonathan!"

The boy didn't answer, turned silently, headed back. Clutching the cover Sooci bounded off following him. Naked, suddenly chill Frank got up, stub-stumbled through the kitchen, went back down into his car.

T. Hall's Lincoln was indeed gone. Frank slumped on the train-like upholstery of the Desoto. He would leave, but how could he naked? His clothes were on the beach. He thought about getting them, thought about Peg, Tracy and Matt. Was there a strange hand on Matt's face at 3:00 in the morning? He leaned down, ticked his teeth on the steering wheel. Fear and shame, anxiety all mingling, he heard a voice above his mindless ticking— someone near or far, inside or out, T. Hall or collegian. "You're gonna fail."

PART III

"What do you want?" she said in such a tone that if there was menace after the amenities, he did not gather it.

"I want you to talk to Ray and see if I can still get the job."

"They have a new pro already. And talk louder I can barely hear you."

"Oh."

"Well, you didn't expect to have everybody standing around holding up everything for you, did you Frank?"

Should he hang up?

"But I think. . . It's so wonderful to hear you like this. How I've missed you! At night I've been so scared. The house is so big and it creaks and creaks."

"What did you think?"

"I think there's another job. Ray mentioned it to me. A new club, not much money."

"I'm used to that."

"Oh, good. Good. Please. Come up. I've missed you so terribly. It's awful without you."

"I think it's what I want." The desire to gloat, to shut off her loving need, seal it in a tub and then step in for a long wallow. Was there anything on earth worth more than that?

I've gone too far, she thought. "What do you want?" she asked.

"I told you. If Ray can handle it, tell him I want it."

There was a pause in which he heard his father clucking out the word *constructive*. It sounded only partly enunciated—*tructive* came through clearly enough.

Humor him, she thought. "What do you really want?"

He didn't answer. A flattering thought, understanding, compassion. Preparing what? A trap?

"What d'ya mean?"

"Oh, Frank please come up. We miss you so."

"I said I'm coming up. I'm going to tell Siroka this morning."

"When?"

"Right after we get through talking."

"But you haven't told him anything yet."

"No."

"You won't change your mind?"

"Look, I don't make up my mind easily about anything."

"I know that, brother." Too much joy, too far? She couldn't tell.

Taking liberties already, he thought. So I've become something to cuff around, taken for granted already. Change that. Get back into the tub. "Hell."

"Please, Frank." Too far indeed. What a child he was, so petty. Endearing? Perhaps. "Frank, please. Matt misses you so."

"Tell him I miss him too."

Perfunctory, unemotional, mechanical, dry. Maybe he shouldn't come. Maybe more time. She thought, I'm riding the current; perhaps I shouldn't open the gate. Let it build up pressure. Let it learn to shove. Heartless? Practical! But how?

He cut in on her plans. "I said, how's Matt?"

"Fine, of course." Good inflection, distance, a trace of reserve. Things were not what they seemed.

A pathetic attempt he felt to mash her emotions, a new game. She wanted to dangle the plum. Plum of what? Body? At thirty-eight no Sooci; heavy in thighs and waist, flopping in breast and face. Plum of family? Ah, family. No information then, nothing on Matt and Tracy mysteriously run over. A bitch. If she should care. Then nothing but retreat, smoke screen confusion. Frustration. Her flesh needed kneading. He needed to knead. Indeed! Or kneaded to need. Sooci again. Bugs in the bedroom.

"Frank?" she summoned. "You're not saying anything."

"How cold is it up there?"

"Not cold."

"What's that?"

"Warm."

"Oh, funny. Very good. Like what? Ninety?"

"Heavens, no. Just nice. You can walk outside. You know how it is up here." Unalterable fact: he made the call; he initiated the action. Everything else—hesitancies, little games, long sighs and threatening silences—only that: games. And in a way delightful because the outcome was known. He made the call and now apparently a little dance of pride, gavotte of masculine kowtowing before the capitulation. She could tolerate that. "I dream of you."

Loving need again and on track She will learn, he thought. Dreams. Yes, dreams. "Nightmares," he answered.

"Certainly not, though you gave me cause enough." Oh, too far again.

Again the little cheap acceptance. He thought of hanging up. Thought of egg-rolls and being twenty-two, of plastic rain globes on Jalousie windows, and a slow eye of time and for the first time frightened again. Frightened again. *Constructive*, the old man repeated. Alone in his Philadelphia apartment—too big for one person, but refusing to leave because every inch of space reminded him of what could not now be anywhere *constructive* of her. Peculiar idea of *constructive*. Living it out with the ashtrays she once used and the hat rack and card table and tiled kitchen and dreadful vanity, and bourbon undrunk and newspapers uncollected and the same late radio show. That awful happiness exchange and refusing every shred of change, every tidbit of possibility. *Constructive*. Hell! What was *constructive*? There, was she speaking?

"And of course you know how much greener it is up here." Fill the silence somehow, cover with talk until a thought comes. "It's a shock, Frank." Frank, my darling, my dear inevitable darling. Inevitable? Apparently, yes apparently now. No. Kids and weather. Fall back on Ray's stipulation, but Ray was such a fool. "You know you get used to Hane and you brainwash yourself into thinking it's a tropical paradise, but up here you suddenly realize how barren, how void, how sterile it is." Taking that all ways, including the wrong way. Fear. She put the phone to the other ear. God! The wrong way. "No flowers to speak of there. The foliage is so thick and Matt has a real woods to explore. The kind you walk around in, and no snakes. No snakes."

Except one, he thought, and was amused. Little torrent of geographic details. Ah, she was off balance. Deliberately? It was impossible to say. "I know it's nice there."

"Nice? Eh? You have no idea."

"What does that mean?" No sarcasm in her voice. Blind censure then?

Ah, piqued interest, a little splash of jealousy. How manipulate that? Think! Think! But nothing came. Lurid suggestion with Ray. How ridiculous! How uninviting. Nothing. He leaves me as always unimaginative, she thought. "I miss you."

"Look, will you talk to Ray?"

"I said I would."

"Good."

"It won't be much money," and you'll have to come right away, she thought—mustn't say that. No, indeed. The little boy can only be led to the toilet. It was degrading, this cajolery. Degrading. But what else was there? That was life, then, cajoling what you could, ignoring what you couldn't.

"It can't be worse than here. I give a couple of lessons a week. Even Brian's cutting back."

"We can manage I'm sure."

How assertive! How predictable. He might have hoped for the allure of something new, a relationship somehow not written down before, but no—no, indeed. It would be the same. Absence, time, only made things more stale. He looked out the door of his shop at the green rolling lumps of golf course. The Hane-manufactured hills glistening unspoiled, unmarred by golfers. In the air-conditioned shop he had to imagine how muggy and distasteful that outside was. For a moment, in comparison to her predictability, it looked almost satisfactory, adequate, inviting.

"Yes, we can manage, I'm sure," he said.

"Look, Frank, you made this call. I'm here. I'm getting along all right." His damnable lelthargy, his arrogance, sarcastic, ironic, was overwhelming. Perhaps it would not be heaven to put up with him again. She resented his casual slurs more than anything else. Oh, but be careful. Without him what else was there? What could there be? Spewing children across the country and hurtling toward more and higher degrees? Her legs began to itch. Oh God, the little slurs against her very sexual identity.

"Don't get hot," he said.

"Look, I didn't make this call. Don't tell me not to get hot. Frank, please. Are you mad I kept the books?"

"Books?"

"The records, you know, finances."

"Yes, I know. Finances."

"Are you mad?"

"Mad?"

He was toying with her. That was good. So it was she felt, inevitable— why not saw off the embellishments?

"You want me to talk to Ray and call you back?"

There was a golfer now. Far away and old, pulling bag on wheels behind him. He evidently took out an iron, for there came a chrome flickering, an instant mirror wheel, as he stroked against the green.

"Frank?"

How she intruded on his dreams. Her kitten voice squealing through his possibility.

"What?"

Couldn't he listen to anything? Even the simplest statements. Oh, Frank. "Should I call you after talking to Ray?" Or didn't he want the inevitability brought home that quickly. Of course not. Back off. "I've found a good morning camp for Tracy and Matt, run by Christian Scientists, but very nice and they seem to like it."

Reminders of responsibility. How clever she was. At the crucial moments she'd shift to emphasize his cares. The golfer seemed so free, though sweating no doubt and anguished by his stroke, obviously awkward, filled with hitches, even to Frank's appraisal from his cool room 300 yards away. She was buried in *constructive* things.

"That's good. Takes them off your hands."

"What do you mean by that?"

"Just what I said." The golfer started up the hill.

"Oh brother! You're a fine one to talk about taking something off your hands. You're a fine one."

"Would you give me Ray's number?"

"I'll have to look it up. I can take care of it for you and call you back."

"I wouldn't want to burden you."

"Very funny."

"Just get me the number so I can call Ray."

"Oh, right away, master."

The old golfer was pulling, lugging at the wheeled bag, but at the slope of the hill the tiny black wheels turned harder in the soggy rough. We are all golfers pulling our loads, waiting for our wives to hunt up the phone numbers of our employment. Pull, old man. Frank thought about putting the phone down, rapping a key, an opened beer can, a can of tennis balls, on the thick window, signaling the old golfer.

"977–2211," she said, "and of course the area code."

"Of course."

How his lethargy slipped into sarcasm. How allied they were. She understood that. He never would. For of all the possibilities open, one remained closed. She could never teach him anything. Damnably lazy and unteachable. Now, nothing on the phone. She tried a tentative, "So?"

"So?" he parroted.

"Frank?"

"Yes."

"Why did you call?"

I shall not crawl, he thought. She wants that or perhaps only wants reassurance. "Because—because I called. Because I'm unhappy, I suppose, pulling things around here. Because I missed the kids, because I missed you."

"Please come up. Please." Suddenly she felt very near tears.

Don't cry on me, he thought. I would not take that. Such emotion is alien to us both. All right. The, reassurance. Reassurance. "I said I was coming. Why don't you believe me? I have the number and I'll call Ray and tell Siroka and then I'll come up. Why don't you see that?"

"You're there. Please come up, come up now. Why can't you call him after you're here. Please Frank. If you had only to explain to Tracy and Matt."

"You haven't said anything to them?"

"Not directly, but they know. They were the first to know. You couldn't avoid that. Believe me you couldn't."

"You tried though didn't you?"

"Why? So you could be confident that I'd play out your charade. So you'd know that when you wanted to stop playing, stop toying, that everything would be as before and nobody would get hurt. At least nobody of consequence. Nobody you cared for, just me. Well, that's not the way things go in this world."

"This world," he sighed into the phone. The utter relaxation of his comment untying her completely.

"Well, it's not. I know that. You can't play and toy and fool without someone, everyone, getting hurt. I know that, Frank, better, stronger than you. That's the way things are in this world. What do you want? I'll give you everything I have, everything—go on giving. Is that what you want? Oh, Frank, please."

"Get a hold of yourself." It was fantastic the little stops women could pull out—going from phone number to hysterical shrieking, sobbing in less than it took the old man to chip to the green. "Calm down."

"Calm down? Is that what you called up here for? To have me calm down by prodding me into—"

"All right. Just shut up and listen." He heard sobbing at the other end. Phony. All her tears seemed phony. Her best crying had a certain artificiality to it. "Are you listening?"

"Yes."

He paused. What was it he was going to say? The old man had apparently about a 15 foot putt. A challenge. What was he going to say? She seemed firmer, in control. He didn't like that suddenly. "Why did you stop and see Dad?"

"Because I thought he'd help to get you back."

The truth? Or flattery or both, he couldn't tell. Had the ring of truth, he thought. We all have 15 foot putts to sink above the sobs of our wives he thought. The old man hunched, struck, then walked over to the flag. He didn't pull it out. Was the putt good then, wedged against the post or was he merely giving himself the benefit. We all have to walk to the next tee. What more was there to say? Ever? The sobbing stopped entirely. "You have a hold of yourself now?" He liked the clinical exactness, the detachment of his tones.

Having no comprehension, no control, over major issues he delighted in absolute capacity for smaller ones. The voice was firm, the man not at all. She could not go on with this. "I don't think we're getting anywhere," she said.

Getting anywhere? That was the key to her philosophy, getting somewhere. Off to the next tee, for example. Ah, the long, the long, long *constructive* fairway, getting to the next flag, which unaccountably was stuck in a new semi-solvent, open-for-suggestion-and-tuition club in Westchester. Getting nowhere. Getting up there. Better to bake in the Hane silt, than mold in the leaves there. But it was too hot in Hane. Twice on the courts with Brian he had gotten short of breath. Salt tablets and sunglasses. Getting somewhere in Hane. Getting somewhere in Hane.

"Maybe we aren't," he said, "but I'm still coming up, I guess."

I guess. Ah, the deliberate tenuousness of it. Deliberate? Yes. Of course. How sadistic of him. "Is that what I'm supposed to say to Tracy and Matt: "He's coming up, I guess."

"You don't want to accept anything else apparently."

"Don't want to? How can I? Frank, you better get a hold of yourself. You're getting yourself into a position where you won't be able to come up."

"What difference does it make?" What difference indeed? What difference? There or here? With them or without. In family or out. *Con—or de—structive.* Didn't she see that it didn't make any difference?

"It does. It does."

I wonder, he thought. "Don't you see?" Thinking—we all are born, we all live, we all die. We all walk to the next tee and some of us develop a strong forehand or a weak one or none at all. Some are rich and famous, powerful or loved, defiled or indifferent, but ultimately we all share the same emotions: embarrassment and distance before our fathers, anxiety, wonder, closeness before children. At death we all lisp the same and shit the same, gag, rot, sear the same and the levels we sought prior to death make no difference at all. Saying, "What does make a difference Peg? Please tell me what does make a difference. What, for God's sake, what? The people we cared for? Those we felt responsible for? The recognition of the game. Is life over in an instant then?"

Her answer though cool, though arresting, absolving, nonetheless had tucked in a furthest fold a certain note of jollity. "Have you had lunch?"

"No."

"All right, have something to eat. Then call Ray. I'll talk to him too. Then tell Siroka and pack. Get a plane. I'll meet you at the airport."

"Should I tie my laces?"

She thought: "Yes, and go wee wee before you get on board."

PART IV

On the Saw Mill River Parkway road crews were burning leaves, the residue of a previous autumn. And for a moment driving away from the center guard (newly erected for safety reasons) he was carried over to October. He was returning to, not leaving Hane. So they burned leaves in the spring as well as fall. And the brown faience of dead leaves spun up from the little hummocks of blackening cinders as if to reclasp the branches that nine months ago had cast them off. Whatever else was here, there was indeed energy, if only the energy of endless cycles. In Hane, all circles broken, the net shards were bits of indolence and precious few clips of energy.

She sat beside him and seemed mesmerized by the greens of the Westchester parkway, by the careening brownish white of the road, the flashing pines. She was doubtless reveling in the solidity of the earth here. The permanence till subdivision. So it was better than Hane, more beautiful. Was she happy? She seemed to be—fairly jumping up and down in the sunstruck, smokey corridor at La Guardia airport. Her kiss was sweetly receptive, mildly inviting as if there were time before the baggage check, and she looked better than he had remembered. She had only a surface commitment to her appearance—as if nakedness were her more accustomed state. He liked that. Was she basically academic—an intellectual nymph who grew radiant in the chase? Ah, yes. He put his hand out onto her thigh. She covered his fingers.

"A beautiful couple," he said, snorting faintly.

But she looked out the side window, a brief view of a golf course.

He wanted to say something better than that.

"Siroka wanted to come along."

"What?"

"When I told him, he didn't say anything for a while. Then he said, 'I wonder if they need a first class manager up there someplace.'"

"First class?"

He laughed. "He wanted to come along, all right. His wife is giving him a lot trouble."

They let the tire drone, the click of concrete segments churn around his statement, though both had prepared rebuttals. There was a merciful distraction, a sudden traffic light.

"Ray's coming by this afternoon," she said.

"I know. We're going out to look at the club."

"It's brand new. Not even finished."

"I know."

"And Ray says the manager is a real go-getter."

"Is that the phrase he used?" Frank emphasized the "he."

"Yes," she answered lazily, seeing through the challenge. Whatever else Frank was, he was not a go-getter.

"They've dropped the limit."

"Yes. There were some accidents, Ray said. So they slowed everything down."

He reached for the radio knob. There seemed a stale compression suddenly in the car, as if subtly windows had been closed and they had begun a sightless soundless coughing. What was wrong? Was it not spring? Full-bodied, fat leafed spring, the honest resilience of earth and oak-stifled sky? Maple, birch, hickory, and dogwood's clovers of pink white against the starched scrub of lilac, laurel, fern. The air—was it not moistly chill out of the sun, and overwhelmingly soft. She was better than he remembered.

"Don't," she said, taking his hand from the radio. "Let's just ride."

"Okay. Let's just ride," over slopes of green and knolls of brown, down the glens toward senility. Let's just ride and ride and ride.

"Kids at day camp?"

"Yes. They'll go to the Bixler's until we get back."

We have time then, he thought. Time for what? A little tussle behind the orange sand barrels the highway department set out for winter hazards. It was a long way till January. Time to discover that nothing had changed, nothing could. Time rather to resume. The same old stretch marks on her belly. The over floating flapping of the backs of her thighs. The same scent of avocado tinged with lemon. Ride and ride and ride.

At Exit 72 they took Highland Avenue and began looking, not riding.

CROWD A HOPPING SERVE

Ray's tan Lincoln was parked before their house. The driver's door was open and they saw Ray reading a newspaper. A studied casualness, Frank thought, so typical of Ray. Most likely he had begun arranging himself the minute the engine stopped. When the driveway stones crunched Ray thrust the newspaper open onto the seat. Stock market returns, Frank thought. Ray bounded out, all bachelor frenzy which he would pass for energy.

"Well, how do you like it? I told you I got you one helluva house. How about it, eh?"

Frank got out of the car. "Impressive," he said, shook hands with his uncle, countered a certain raucous jerking motion by clamping down hard enough to see Ray wince.

"Still in shape, I see," Ray answered the handshake by bouncing back. "Come on I'll show you around." But Frank had turned. Tracy and Matt came bounding across the wide oval of grass separating the drive from the Bixler's house. Tracy, a little calculatedly, was running with her arms out. Matt kicking the grass as he went.

"Daddy, Daddy," she called out and jumped up onto him (rehearsed by Peg? He couldn't tell). He snatched her up, twirled her around. She planted her lips, slathered his neck. Then it was Matt's turn. When he set Matt down, Tracy, a few steps away, said, "Are you going to stay or what?"

Ray laughed. "Stay? Of course he's going to stay."

"Good," Tracy said, turned, almost afraid to pursue the question, and headed for the door.

"You like the house, Matt?" Ray asked.

"Yes."

"Yes? Is that all you can say?"

"Yes," he answered with dumb politeness.

Ray laughed again. "Well, one thing, your kids sure have minds of their own."

Peg, who stood near the front door, nodded. They carried the bags in. There was a rather sullen interval in which, under Ray's guidance, he explored every aspect of the house. Matt and Tracy went outside again. It was a perfect day, warm in the sun yet derived from winter in the shade. Peg inexplicably went upstairs to the bedroom, left him to Ray's counsel.

"We're supposed to see Abbott at 3:30. If he okays it, you've got the job."

"You mean I might not have the job?"

"No. I don't mean that. Old Ray's better than that. I just mean Abbott has to okay it. He will. This is May, for Chrissakes. How many pros are floating around in May?"

"Thanks."

Ray laughed loudly. "Let's get going." They walked back to the front hall. Peg came to the banister overhead.

"We're going now," Ray shouted.

She smiled. A little triumphant moment, Frank thought.

"Good luck," she said. Mentally Frank arched up, leaped and smashed an overhead neatly to the opposite corner.

Abbott was a tall man who had the nervous habit of running three fingers back behind his left ear, then down along the side of his cheek bone.

"We're just getting started. You'll find things a little shambled up, heh, heh. But we're growing so fast that I think we can promise you a real income here. A lot of our members have never played tennis before. Naturally they're very anxious for their children to learn. We have one good junior, ranked, I think. Lloyd." He pointed beyond the unfilled pool, chalking the slant sunshine, toward the two courts beyond a brownish putting green. "His parents are extremely concerned for him. They'll want to meet you."

"Now?"

"At your convenience," Abbott stroked his ear. "At your convenience, of course. I believe he's on the court now."

"I don't see any backdrops, windbreaks, on the fences."

"Pardon?"

"Canvas. Something on the fences to break the wind, provide a contrasting background."

"We should have those, I take it?"

"Yes." Frank was watching Lloyd serve. He looked about sixteen but tall, a southpaw. It was a good motion, although like all sixteen year olds, he tried to hit the ball too hard. Then suddenly, as if he sensed he was being watched, Lloyd switched to a twist service. How the ball hopped! The reverse spin a left-hander so naturally got. Frank thought once of learning to serve left-handed in order to get that murderous spin.

From a white table at the side of the courts a man got up. He began hobbling toward them. Abbott led Frank and Ray around the pool to meet him. "That's Dr. Wilson, Lloyd's father."

The doctor made an increased effort to reach them sooner, but his leg only seemed to drag further behind.

Abbott said, "He'll be your best customer."

For an embarrassing moment they all simply stopped and watched as Dr. Wilson hobbled up to them.

"Doctor, I want you to meet our new tennis pro, Frank—"

"You're the pro, eh?"

"Yes."

"Well, you work him." He pointed back toward the courts. "You work him. Really work him! The lazy shithead would rather watch T.V. than do anything else. I'd work him myself but this damn knee keeps me down. I swear to God I wish the game of football had never been invented. He's talking about playing football, as if he couldn't see what it does." He slapped his knee. "Look, you work him. I don't care how long or how much, you just get him working. Where you from?"

"Hane, Florida."

"That on the east coast?"

"No, the west."

"The west? There's no action there, is there?"

"Not much."

"Well, what he basically needs is somebody to hit with, somebody who can get the ball back. There's nobody here who's ever even picked up a racket, much less discovered what it's for. If Abbott would get off his tail and round up some members he might save us all a little money. But I don't care about that. I want him to hit a million balls before goes to college. You've got to hit a million balls to get into the big leagues in this game. And he's too damn lazy to do it on his own."

"He's a good boy," Abbott said.

"He's the laziest son of a bitch I ever knew. What a fuck-up!" The doctor swiveled awkwardly around. Lloyd was watching him from the courts. The doctor shouted, "What are you waiting for? What the hell are you waiting for? You got half a basket yet. See what I mean? He's so goddam dumb. I told him to hit the basket out. The minute I leave he stands around with his thumb in his mouth. Look, I want to sign him for a morning and an afternoon. One lesson and a session."

"Session?" Frank said.

"Yeah, session We had a pro in Greenwich who gave sessions. He'd just hit with you. Cheaper than a lesson. One lesson and a session later in the day. You know, to see if the lesson sank in. Fat chance with that shithead. He'd play in traffic, if you didn't watch him. How about it?"

"I'll have to think about that."

"All right. All right. You win. Two lessons, then. Anyway you like it. But you just work him. You understand? Make him sweat. He's as strong as a damn bull, but don't you tell him that. Just work him. Hane? I never heard of it. How's tomorrow at 10?"

"All right."

"You work him, the little shithead." He turned around, "Go on, go on! Pick up the balls. Walk around and pick up the balls. Hurry up. Tomorrow we start for real."

While his father shuffled across the putting green Lloyd sulkily collected the balls.

"I told you he'd be your best customer."

"Yes."

"Do you want to take a look at the courts?"

"Not now."

Ray walked back over to the pool. "This one looks bigger than the Westchester's."

"Bigger and better when we get it finished," Abbott said.

Ray laughed.

There was seepage of mud about the edges of the pool. Ray jumped back. "When you gonna sod?"

"Next week. Come on in. I'll show you the clubhouse proper. It's finished. Bill Reynard did the decorating. I think you'll like it. We're considerable more modern than the *Club*." They walked toward the long glass partitions. "Quite uncolonial," Abbott explained, "more effective I think, don't you? Why block up the view with panes and dividers?" He slid one of the partitions. "This area here before the sliding doors is going to be polished white stone." They were standing now on brown soggy boards, alternately squishing, as they shifted weight—secretions of mud between the planks. Abbott scuffed his feet on the edge of the runner for the glass panel and stepped into the emerald cavern. "Our grill room," he said. "Nice. Functional, but a touch exotic too. The sloping ceiling is papered with a fabric. It shimmers in the right light." There was a long yellow tiled bar, black topped tables and a tough thick green carpet. "there's nothing quite like this room anywhere in any other club." Each table held a yellow vase of yellow plastic flowers. No one was sitting in the grill. The bartender in response to Abbott's entrance had turned a faucet on and pretended to be cleaning a shaker. Frank thought the rushing water completed his image of the place. Abbott turned and walked toward what looked to be a coat room, but turned out to be a light-trap passageway into the main dining room.

"The light trap is very effective. Also deadens sound."

"I'd hate to come through it drunk," Ray said.

Abbott laughed. "We've had a few mishaps but it gives the entrance both ways a little, a little drama."

"Yes," Frank said. The dining room was huge, high ceiling, done in maroon with beige drapes and a light blue wallpaper. Slit windows rimmed the room. But there was no view out. White table cloths and maroon napkins.

Two waitresses in black stood by a revolving dessert stand. And one lone woman sat in a far corner. She looked at least seventy. With utmost care she spooned her cup of vichyssoise. There was a faint humming in the room. Frank looked for a discreet ceiling fan but saw none.

The next room was vacant, furnitureless, smelling of new plaster. "This may be a poker room, or maybe an extension of the lady's locker room. We don't know."

He took them through the men's locker room, which was carpeted in soft-sheet linoleum.

"There's even a tunnel entrance direct to the grill. Our members think that's very convenient." They came out into another corridor. Abbott led them down to a door, the upper half of which was made of translucent glass. "My office," he said. Unpainted, uncarpeted, on the bare concrete Abbott motioned to the two straight back chairs and took a seat himself behind his gleaming metal desk. The room reminded Frank of a large white confessional. Plaster mist seemed to tread the air.

"What we want," Abbott began, clasping his hands on the desk top and staring directly into Frank's face. "What we want is somebody who can run with the ball. Somebody young enough to take the long hours our members will demand, and incidentally reap the profits they're willing to pay out. Nothing here is halfway. I'm not interested in that. I'm interested in building a first class club, with a large select membership, and teams—tennis, swimming, bowling—that win."

"Frank here—" Ray interrupted, but Abbott cut him off.

"I have a theory about teaching sports. It's a separate art, if you will. I don't think it's important that a pro play well. In fact, the best pros don't play at all, or only discreetly. Nothing's worse for a club than a pro who'd rather play than teach. I don't mean an occasional game at the request of a member. That's different, but here we've got a lot of ground to cover, not a lot of time, and I need somebody who is all business. I don't have to tell you that there's plenty of gravy in this kind of a set-up. We need somebody to pick this operation up and run with it?" Abbott sat back, pulled his hands to the lip of the desk.

"You only have two courts," Frank said.

"I like that answer," Abbott said. "You're thinking along the right lines. With the right. No. Let me put it this way. The right pro will get up four indoor courts by November."

"Then you're thinking in terms of year round."

"Not this year. Not next. I don't pretend to be cutting you off from the Florida largess. You fellows have it pretty shrewd."

"You can't get the lessons out of commuters you can from vacationers," Frank said with a delighted coldness. Ray turned to look at him.

Abbott went on, 'I said not this year, not next, not until the pro thinks it's right. There's lots more money here, lot's more. The main thing is we want a pro who isn't happy just getting along. We want, we'll get, somebody to run with the ball."

He kept coming back to that football analogy. It almost amused Frank. Behind a grey desk before a sparkling white wall, in tones earnest, imploring, yet firm. Of course! He was in the locker room again and the coach was set to persuade. The scent of leather, sweat, liniment, damp towels filled the sterile air of Abbott's office. Of course the coach was speaking. Frank strained to listen, leaning in off his polished bench in line with the other fellas, the horses, in high sneakers and low T shirts, panting the air with bravery. What was the score? Who was ahead? Listen to the coach:

"Your background frankly seems a little erratic."

What a slob the coach was, heavy gut bulging against the stained sweat shirt. The braid-held whistle almost lost in a fold of stomach. And Frank, though leaning in as hard as the others, as transfixed as they, still couldn't quite follow what the coach was saying.

"However, I understand there has been some marital trouble."

Distracted? Perhaps. The way the coach stepped around the brown wet paper towels at his feet was perhaps more interesting than his message. But surely there were others who had been gathered up. He felt the tense union of the bench around, felt the leap of soul as the bench followed, almost forced the coach's harsh harangue. The coach had gathered them up, made them his. Frank could feel it. The team would follow the slob anywhere. But what was the coach saying? How Frank wanted to feel the tense exhilaration of coach-prompted care! The team would follow the slob anywhere. But what was the coach saying? Why was the steady drip from the gleaming chrome nozzles louder than the coach's talk? Why were the water marks on the mirrors of the locker room more commanding?

"So that about sums it up."

The coach was saying nothing. Mouthing. Frank knew it. Mouthing the phrases by which everyone found the energy to get up off the bench and head back into the game. The torn, riveleted, sneaker-splattered paper towels knew more than the coach.

"Frank's your boy all right." Ray stood up shouting. "Why he took that Hane Country club and put it on the tennis map. Ranked players right and left, and more interest than you can imagine. How many new courts they build that first year, eh Frank?"

"Six."

"Six courts. How about that, eh?"

"That's what we want."

"Then, let's sign," Ray said.

Abbott stood up. "Well, there are terms. Things that should be discussed at greater length. Frank, why don't you bring your wife by for dinner tonight, right here in the grill."

How would Peg like eating in the grill, Frank thought.

"What time?"

"Say, 7:00."

"Okay. Fine. We'll be here."

"Thanks so much. I'll be looking forward to it." It seemed Abbott wanted to reach for an intercom, to summon someone to direct them out.

NEVER COME OUT OF A CROUCH

On the planks across the mud Frank turned to Ray. "Marital trouble?"

"I had to explain something about your leaving the Hane club. I couldn't just leave it up in the air. Abbott's smart. He would have found out."

"So now he wants to meet my wife."

"That's standard."

"In the grill."

"Look, you know how things are up here, anywhere. What did you expect? He's got to cover himself."

Frank laugh-sighed— precisely the reaction he knew Ray could never accept. The hard asphalt of the parking lot seemed to solidify Ray's unhappiness. "Look, I don't give sermons. I just don't. We all want our little flings. But we're not kids anymore. This is a good beginning, something you need. You better grow up to it." Ray seemed almost embarrassed by his words, as if he had caught them somewhere else and recited them more perfectly than he believed. Frank looked at him for a long moment.

"You go on back and tell Peg to come here about seven for dinner. Tell her to bring a coat for me. Maybe a tie. What do you think?"

"Out of place in the grill."

"You tell her that?"

"You're not coming?"

"No. I'm going to take a look at the courts and the golf course."

"You mad at me?"

"Yes." Frank smiled.

"No. Look, all I wanted was to help you out. This hasn't been so damn easy for me to set you up you know."

"What else would you do with your time? Play father to somebody else's kids?"

"Now wait a minute," Ray backed up against his Lincoln. "Now wait a minute."

"Just tell Peg to be here before 7:00"

"Now wait a minute."

"You just tell her, Ray." Frank turned away, started off toward the courts.

Although he watched the fence surrounding the courts he listened for the start of Ray's Lincoln. Ray's anger was always ineffectual, but Frank still expected to hear the peel of mad tires. Nothing. He walked across board bridges to the courts. Lloyd was gone. The sun was just topping the tall thick pines beyond the second court, casting tents of shadows on the green Har-Tru surface. Where Lloyd had been serving the scuff marks looked a lighter green. Like a lot of power servers he dragged a toe leaving a series of curved ruts behind the baseline. Lefthanders had the advantage—perhaps worth a set among equal players. And the southpaw serve, the twist, always hopping more or less than was expected. What an advantage the southpaw serve was! Even if you could gauge where the ball would be, its spinning force would deflect it off your strings unpredictably. It could be handled two ways: you could crowd it, move in on it, half-volley it, cut off its spin, or you could back way off, let it take its full bounce and hit it from the backcourt on the drop. Either way was difficult. Half-volleying required perfect timing, and falling back just gave net control to the other player. Frank preferred to crowd a hopping serve. Be constantly available for Lloyd's father. It came to that. One could crowd in, make the time go faster, accumulate and accumulate, or one could drop way back. One could grow up to accumulation, regress to welfare, move forward to responsibility or lope away—listen to the coach or watch the nozzle drip. What was the coach saying?

He heard the absent thunking of a rally never begun, never ended. The Har-Tru surface needed watering. It would bake out in the sun without moisture twice a day. But there were no sprinklers visible. A typical construction. Abbott wanted the best, but did not understand it. In a month without sprinklers the courts would be as solid as bricks, as dangerous as ice, as useless as a parking lot. The idea pleased him. What was left? Crowd in and run with the ball, run up and back at the direction of legions of Lloyds, battalions of Brians, who in turn were running up and back from the epithets of "shithead" or "lazy." A lazy day? Not at all. The sun behind the pines now, chill air moved about him. He wished for a training jacket. Was it autumn or spring? The chill air swilled into him like a draught of ice water. Ice water to be spit out doubtless on the flaking hard-tru surface, the hard, true surface. Run up and back. For the reward of what? Solvency? Accumulation? The choosing of running up and back. He liked that better. The reward was the choosing. Could he live the summer on the thought?

And the diversions? The little aspects, episodes of fun, that made the choosing all right, made the choosing good, what were they? Flashes of anger at ineffectual bachelors; rages against unworthies. Tirades in another language at another people. Run up and back. Joy of niches in social conscience. Pleasant children, loving. The flab of Peg's thighs. The rewards of choosing? How the hard, true surface needed watering. He scuffed at it. Dust rising. Already thin fissures in the green topping. He stood at the service line, crouched, feeling the tightening at the tops of his legs. Crouched deeper, watched an absent southpaw serve, though only the tapes were visible in the darkening shades of green—court and pine—across the net. Crowd that hopping serve. A perfect half-volley, cross court, that caught the kid flat footed. Your best serve and neatly chipped away. One reward—one—once a set.

Once a day, a year, a decade, until Peg should join that old woman who ate alone in the dining room and talked shly of her husband's ex-whims. At her white table in her maroon room, viewless, attended by black-suited waitresses, did she still nurture thoughts of "swinging"? Still swallow martinis until all that could be managed was a hand pat on a plump, beside pillow? He would have liked to have understood the pat as a consequence, but of course it was not. Not a consequence; for any choosing led to it. That, he thought, straightening up, made the choosing reward enough. He kicked at the dust. The serve fell short. He chipped it away, down the line, catching the kid flat-footed again.

Icebreaker
John Spradlin's Journal

Just packing the seabag starts the constipation. Wedging in boondockers, pea jacket, work jacket, turtleneck, watch cap, ten, or is it twenty, soft T-shirts (extra skivvies, Spradlin, for the long arctic night) is like wedging soft plaster of Paris in my own intestine. With the snap of the lock on the seabag, I know my bowels have been sealed.

Everything stops—frozen—cemented for forty-five days. "It is, Mr. Spradlin, a simple case of anxiety. The roll of the ship may be part of it," a mythic perfect specialist in disorders of the lower intestinal tract explains, as I slowly gather into a fetal position before him. I see him as a youngish, starting-out kind of doctor, with watery rabbit eyes and already the lilting recitation which fascinates him so much more than his solidifying patient. "But more than the physical changes, the rolling and pitching, I would think the psychological changes, the fear of the wrong step, the anxiety over being accepted, the fear that as a reserve and assigned only for part of the voyage you may be tried in some special way—all these conspire to prevent normal excretion."

"But I love to shit."

"Pardon?" In the strain of hoisting the seabag, he vanishes.

How heavy, how logy I feel. Coming down the dock was like walking on a trampoline. But even as I felt the legs wobble, I could feel my innards lock. Oh, he cannot void. He cannot void. What, precisely, is the threat?

Begin with the chief—his whitening knuckle locked around a solid, white china cup handle, he efficiently blows across the top of the coffee cup.

Eyes watching my arrival. He is, I sense at once, the antagonist. My age, too, twenty-eight and already a chief petty officer—a ferocious go-getter who shrouds himself in low key, stony competence: the quiet command, the firmly glinting eyes. He looks, in his green foul-weather jacket, in his sharply planed face, like something off a billboard. I had thrown my seabag into the berthing area and come topside and forward (which is to say back up the stairs—ladder, fool!) and through the hallway (passageway) to the dining area (mess deck). I don't much like the coffee or the Coast Guard, but I've learned to pretend. There are compromises to camaraderie and we all have to get along, don't we? I mean it would be unpleasant if we did not get along, wouldn't it?

"Your gear stowed? Rack squared away?" the chief says slowly, using his syllables to cool the coffee, eyes just meeting mine.

"There's no linen for the bed."

Do his eyes flash at this little irreverence for jargon? Not that I can see—though I sense a few of the seamen sitting to my left are aware of drama. The chief, in a motion which does not move the top surface of his coffee, merely reaches into the pocket of his jacket and then rifles a huge packet of keys onto the linoleum tabletop where the seamen sit.

"Stephan," he says quietly, the clack of keys having stilled the entire mess deck, "break open the linen locker so he can get his rack squared away. Give him a foot locker too. Then bring me the keys on the 01 deck." Having made some point of power, he turns away.

In the berthing area Stephan volunteers, "The chief can be a prick, but he knows his stuff."

"That's nice," I answer, constructing sloppy hospital corners on the rack.

"You here for two weeks' active?" Stephan continues. He is bull-necked, affecting a kind of thug accent, but apparently intelligent.

"No. For forty-five days."

"Forty-five? How come?"

"I'm a fuck-up."

He smiles, silenced, then points to the rack opposite mine on the other side of twin poles which hold the chains for the upper racks. "There's a re-serve there, too. He's in for two years."

"A real fuck-up."

"Nah. It was in his contract."

"Imagine two years here." I lift my rack up and open the footlocker.

"How you gonna get off?"

"What?"

"We pull out in a coupla days for a six month's tour. How are ya gonna get off?"

"That's their problem."

"Man, they'll keep you here. I never heard of a reserve assigned to an icebreaker."

I let the rack drop. The hardest part of beginning a tour is the nasty adjustment to the omniscience so handily thrust at you from all sides. "I bet you've never heard of a whole lot of things."

Stephan eyes me like the chief. I think about apologizing, but remake a hospital corner instead. Stephan turns. I resign myself to another antagonist, but he merely goes over to the other rack and sits down. "How'd you fuck up?"

Can I be hearing respect in his tone? "What difference does it make?" I carry forward the truculence, since, apparently, it has engendered awe.

"I never met a reserve who drew forty-five days."

"You'll get over it, grow out of it."

"Yeah, sure. You and the chief should have a lot of fun," Stephan says, fondling the keys and going out of the berthing area. Who is the other reserve?

Day 2: The first day is not the hardest. It's usually half a day spent handling those details of a "new life." Making a rack up can take several hours if you know how to manage it. The second day begins a muster routine, and there is, ostensibly, work. The seamen soogee and soogee and soogee, an exotic name for washing the decks and bulwarks (walls) down with soap and water, an endless, trivial task as easily and pointlessly stopped as started— the perfect bureaucratic employment.

The first morning muster on the second day I meet my comrades: Stephan and five others making up one of the deck force groups under the charge of George Malae, a Samoan about five feet four, with powerful shoulders and inexplicable black protrusions (like warts, but not warts) on his face.

"Where's Watley baby?" Malae says as we stand at a slumped parade rest, minutes before the raising of the ensign (flag).

"He's due back tomorra," someone answers.

"He's due back today!" Malae counters.

"Fuck you, George. He's due back tomorra."

Loose discipline here. Will the Samoan, eyes flashing, cudgel this insubordination? Hardly. The reaction is extraordinary. George rises up on his toes, puts his index fingers into his ears and shouts, "Woo whee!" He backpedals toward the boat davits (we are on the 01 deck) turns completely around, then faces his crew again. He takes his hands out of his ears and, laughing insanely, slaps the third class petty officer patch on his work jacket. This brings laughter from everyone. The ensign is raised and we come to attention. George turns, but the triangle of his salute rustles with his laughter. I do not understand.

Afterwards, George says, "Canino, you, me and you," he points at me.

"Spradlin, John Spradlin," I answer.

"And you go down to the storage locker. Rest of you, soogee down the fantail nice and clean." He smiles, "Stephan, you in charge, right?"

"Right, George."

I follow Canino, a black giant who explains as we come off the 01 deck that he is Puerto Rican. Behind me, George is blowing his nose into his hands, which he then wipes on his work jacket.

"Undog that hatch," Canino says pointing to the stained gray deck.

I begin the process of turning those five, or six, or a hundred worn handles on the lid.

"For Chrissake hurry. The old man's watching."

I turn to look back up at the bridge. The chief has clasped the railing below the flying bridge. He stands, legs braced, arms locked, a peerless stone chieftain surveying the prairie of New York Harbor. I cannot turn one handle. From over my shoulder, with a thumb and two fingers Canino sets the handle spinning. "What did you say your name was?"

"Spradlin."

"Your first name?"

"John."

"Well, John, your hands are going to have to get stronger for the work around here. Lotta reserves never get so they can—"

"Woo whee! Canino! Get your ass down there. Here comes the chief."

Canino pushes me aside, flips the hatch open and lowers himself, filling the opening. I follow, then George.

It is dark below. I am aware of ropes hanging and stacks of rain gear, but Canino's voice comes from a distance—there must be space, an open area. "Where's the light, George? Where the hell's the light?"

George is laughing, poking at my shoulder from above me, shoving at me. I can't decide whether it is playful scrapping or a shove to speed up. Then, moving away from the ladder, I suddenly think: it's is a ritual, an initiation. They mean to beat me up, throttle me in rubbery rain gear or wrap me in thick hawsers.

"Woo whee," George is saying, softer now, with perfect sinister intonation.

"The lights, George."

"We can see," George says. He is down now. Suddenly he puts a shoulder into my side, shoves me across a narrow walkway into a stack of rain gear, which gives with the impact.

"What's going on?"

"Reserve," George says with a soft laugh. He hawks, then spits back into the hawsers. His nose is still running, so he blows it into the palm of his right hand. "Come on, reserve," he says, holding his hand out. Light from the hatch shines off the top of his greasy hair. Canino, I can now see, is on a lower level some twenty feet away.

"George, goddamn it, where's the fucking light?"

"We can see, we can see. Reserve, where you from?" He comes toward me, wiping his hand on his work jacket.

"How long you had the cold?" I ask, bracing my right leg against the stack of gear and raising up. It is very confusing. I've heard of little reception parties given to reserves as they report for duty, but Canino seems as ignorant as I am of George's intentions.

"Bad cold," George answers, "bad, bad cold. One bad cold! Everyday now, may be two weeks."

Suddenly a packet of keys drops clanking on the walkway. The chief's head appears in the hatch opening. "Put the lights on, George, then toss 'em back up here."

George smiles at me, winks or twitches, I can't tell. "Right, chief," he answers, then fits a key into a switch for the light.

The first toss is short of the chief's flailing arm. There is mutual embarrassment which the chief covers by shouting, "For Chrissakes, George." The second toss is high enough, but off to the left. The chief wedges himself into the hatch and swirls outward, just catching the keys. For a moment it seems the opening has grown a shoulder, an arm and part of a neck. In that instant, when the chief's head is turned back toward the bridge (a thrust to get more reach below) George winks at me, then brings his fists together as if snapping an invisible pencil. He rolls his eyes upward. I can't decide who the threat—if indeed it is a threat—is directed to: the chief overhead or the weak reserve below. But with George's snapping motion, I hear bones crack. The past slides away, a little initiation of sorts.

"See you at chow," the chief says, pulling the keys out. In the circle of sky I see him fit his cap on, tug at the sleeves of the foul-weather jacket, recommend a cigarette to the world.

The rest of the day is spent lounging on the rain gear—listening to Canino recount his one year of college football. Before evening chow, I give George my bottle of Coricidin. He takes three pills, then sits down to his meal, which he eats—all slopped together—from a Bakelite bowl.

There are five rows of tables, the last two given over to snipes, pale sweating engine room workers. Food is off of metal, compartmentalized trays. Strangely, dill pickles have been offered with each meal. George chews impassively across from me when a voice overshoots the din of conversation, the torrent of casual obscenity.

"Hey! Reserve!"

New quiet.

"Hey reserve! How come you're on for forty-five days?"

I do not recognize the voice. Stephan and Canino stare at me with, I suspect, faint smiles. I continue eating a pickle. But the mess deck has become silent. Even the Filipino cooks have stopped ladling.

"Hey, Reserve! How'd you fuck up?"

"You always talk so loud?" I say, loud enough, then chew furiously on the pickle stub. George looks up from his bowl, smile widening.

"How'd you fuck up?"

I cannot think of a reply. Respect and camaraderie—how to call them simultaneously into existence? There could be no explaining that the weekly meetings were boring, intolerable, and therefore I simply stopped going.

"Whadya do?"

I am listening to the voice, catching its tones, trying to imagine who owns it—a gangling snipe? It sounds young, hostile. The whole mess deck is waiting.

Then a role hits me. I shout, "I was tripping at meetings."

The ladles fall, the line moves, the conversation grows again. George returns to his bowl, and I cease to be a reserve. Ah, perish that designation. In the whir of acceptances, between chews on a pickle I have become respectable. No reserve now—a full-fledged drug freak. Awe swells.

With luck, before the meal is out my footlocker will have been searched. George takes out the Coricidin bottle, shakes it, then stares at the little red pills. I start to laugh, and laugh harder as his eyes flicker around in hesitant but growing upset.

Day 3: The morning begins with two Four-Way cold tables. I pass up the eggs, eat mounds of cereal, drink four glasses of the weak canned orange juice. The toast is kept in what had been the pickle tray—garlic and orange marmalade.

But before morning chow, a peculiar thing: at about 4:30 a.m. the engines turn on. I pull my pillow up over my head. There comes a pawing at my shoulder.

"What's that?" A voice from the parallel rack (bed).

"What's what?" I answer. So, the other reserve is back.

"That noise. It's unreal!"

"That's the engines."

"We don't leave till noon."

Ah, someone more ignorant than Spradlin. "On the big white ones, fella, they warm the engines for at least six hours before shoving off."

"No shit," he says without a trace of sarcasm.

In an instant he is asleep again. But the engines keep me awake. In a half hour Toonay, the Filipino cook, gets up to start work in the enlisted galley. As he goes out, the berthing area under the fantail is illuminated, a spiderweb of chains, draped blankets, white cotton shoulders and flung-out pale arms. Shoes on the deck, in the momentary shadowing, march around by themselves. I hear them stomping on the bulkheads across the overhead two racks above and away. The other reserve's breath wheezes in the now darkness. The little assertion of my superior knowledge makes me feel unreasonably happy. Ah, dangerous thing, this elation from a reverential "no shit."

At morning chow George says, "You meet baby?"

"We spoke this morning."

"We did?" Watley turns from the other side of the table, "When?"

"When the engines turned over."

"Oh," he chews on a soggy piece of toast. "I'm Andy ," he shoves his hand across the table "Sorry I woke you up."

"You didn't. John Spradlin, another reserve."

"A reserve? Unreal! Another reserve! Soon we're gonna outnumber you."

In the head, after chow, as I contemplate in pain another crapless day, Andy monologues from the adjacent stall: "the important thing is to be inconspicuous. Keep your head down, know what I mean? There isn't too much of an anti-reserve thing, but there's enough, and never volunteer, know what I mean?"

He doesn't know it is my last tour of duty—the things I could tell him. But my concentration is elsewhere.

"And never tell 'em you can type or you'll go right to the bilge. And don't fuck with the Exec. He's a real prick. Everybody hates the Exec."

Watley, it is clear, immensely enjoys this pontification. I expect him to come clambering over the metal partition. I say, "Right," a few times to keep him happy—sure of his captivated audience.

"I mean, I came on board here. I was pretty green. They gave me tangled heaving lines, stuff like that. I wasn't too hot, but I'll tell you something. George can be a lot of help. He doesn't hate reserves. I guess he kinda figures he's getting screwed himself, so why fuck anybody else up? Know what I mean? I mean he knows more than any first class—especially the pricks who walk around here with their coffee cups. You see 'em up at the mess deck during break, standing around with their cups, fucking the dog. So big! Don't let them know you're a reserve. Christ, they'll badger the shit out of you. But George never will make first and he knows it."

"Why?"

"Cause he's a Samoan, for Chrissakes. Can you see some of these pricks taking orders from a Samoan? Or letting him stand around the fucking coffee pot. Unreal! Never happen. Never! Where you from?"

"New Jersey."

"Where?"

"Somewhere."

"What does that mean?"

"That means I used to live in New Jersey, but now I live here. Here in this palace of steel, and stain-filled with these sweet people whom one would never talk to on the outside."

"That's got it exactly! It's the pricks you'd never see, much less live with, on the outside. That's what makes the Guard suck. The Coast Guard sucks!" Watley shouts.

The Filipinos at the mirrors shaving turn around and snicker.

I get off the commode. He cannot void. Will a headache form? Standing at the doorway, watching the Statue of Liberty in a cloud of greyness frozen at her feet, I wait for Watley to finish. Will he become my buddy? Ah, the buddy system. Little exigency of shipboard life—the soulmate of despair, necessity of cramped quarters, someone to reveal all hatred, all fear to. Not this fool, I think. But then, who?

Washing up, Watley says, "You seen the watch list yet?"

I had forgotten the watch routine. Once we're underway, every four hours there is a watch change, round the clock—five watch-standers required at all times. I stood a flying bridge watch once aboard a training cutter in November. Like a rain-suited panda, I rocked on the highest point of the ship, during the darkest part of the night, and in the howlingest storm imaginable. They tied me to the stanchions and said, "Whatever happens, don't open that voice tube (the only way to communicate with the bridge) or we'll get swamped down here."

"You draw a watch?" I say to Watley, looking down now at the gum-wrappered sea scumily floating this icebreaker.

A storm to remember. Machine-gun rain and waves like sick bears heaving on themselves. When I passed through the NCO berthing area, even the jaded first classes were wearing life jackets in their racks.

Watley says, "Yeah, four to eight. You spell me for chow?"

Chow, I remembered, flashed immediately over and beyond that brass voice tube, out directly into the sea, which for a moment curled its paws to accept my puke, not ten feet from my aching throat. Then the bow lifted, and before another wave I was eleven stories above the grey water bears that ground up whatever it was I had tossed out to them.

"Will you?" Watley insists.

"Sure. Where?"

"I'm the telephone talker at six."

"Eighteen hundred," I correct him.

"Yeah, man, you're a good reserve." He shoves me into the passageway out of the cold.

New York harbor is oil smooth and chill, and I am fighting down yet savoring (they are, after all, only mine) memories of swells. Swell swells— once upon a swell time.

Noon chow. Then cast off.

"Take in four!" the chief bellows from the catwalk.

Ah, the exhilaration of the voyage. The going out is all. I stand behind George, pulling in the fat hawser which is line four. It snakes behind us. I attempt to coil it down, but it's awry against the grain of spirals, twisting up in the passageway.

"Take in three!" the chief shouts, ridiculous in earphones on the catwalk. No one would emulate this fool's smoking now.

George turns to spring toward the bow, for line three is mid-ship. He stumbles in the raised hawser, sticking up like giant yellow wet pipe cleaners. "Woo whee! Where you learn to coil that line! Woo whee!" His laughter verges on fear.

"Take in three!" the chief shouts again.

Three has been tossed from its cleat, dead on the dock. George squats at the opening to begin the heave in. The passageway is narrow. This line must be flaked out (laid down) else there will be no room to take it in.

"Take in three. Goddamn it!" The chief has walked to the portside, leaned over from the catwalk, restrained apparently only by his telephone line. I expect to see him leap the stanchion, knock us both into the sea.

George stands up. "You pull. I put her down."

"George, goddamn it! The line's still on the dock!" the chief bellows. His deck crew makes him look bad to the old man. I crouch and begin a methodical hand-over-hand. The hawser is far heavier than I remember.

"Woo whee! Faster than that, John. She's dropping in the water."

Indeed, she does drop, nearly pulling me out. I let her slip away. The neatly flaked-out line plays out. George steps on it.

"Grab! Grab hold," he shouts.

"Release the cable!" the chief shouts.

From the stern, Canino looks back at George, who brings his hand sharply down. Then he nudges me aside, snares the dropping hawser and holds it.

I think, *what the hell is the cable?*

Canino takes three turns off a cleat and lets a stern line run free. The stern is swung away from the dock. A black cable comes into view off the portside. Then, in a loud click it releases, whipping toward the dock, then flailing straight down into the enamel-black water. For a moment the hook at the end of the cable, which had apparently been connected to Canino's line stands upright in the air then plunges straight down, amid line three's hawser floating on the water. Any fool can see they are going to snag. George moans, grabs the line and hauls. He actually takes up the slack but the loop on the water doesn't move until the descending hook plummets into it, like a marlin spike.

"Woo whee! Now we see some shit!"

George groans at the chock, hauling and hauling. I lend a hand. We take up the slack again, but it is as if the loop of the line has found an invisible cleat at the water line. We actually haul a bit of the cable with its four hundred pound set block, up out of the water. George takes a turn on the cleat to preserve what we have.

"Canino! Stephan! Notari. Here!" George hollers, leaning back in the passageway.

Instead of swinging away from the dock, the stern of the ship actually starts back toward it, obedient to the cable's dictate.

"Take in one!" the chief shouts, unaware that the ship is still attached to a mooring.

"What'll happen, George?"

"Woo whee! We drag out that block. Maybe run the screws into a camel. Woo whee! Canino!"

From opposite ends of the passageway, the deck force descends upon us. Canino plunges in, nearest the chock, grabs hold, and begins to haul in.

"John, get the pole," George shouts, motioning overhead.

I reach up, unclamp a ten-foot stick with hook and spear at the end. Canino, George, Stephan, and Notari are pulling, pulling, pulling, Has the old man yet figured out what has happened to his strangely sliding stern? Watley joins in.

"We get her up. You knock her off," George shouts to me.

I moved toward the fantail, still holding the pole above my head. The hawser-cable coupling is perhaps now fifteen feet off the portside and down. I lunge at it with the hook. Out of reach. George and Canino yank again, actually make the huge hawser flex, shaking out frost drops of water. The snag comes closer, but is still fifteen feet away. I make another lunge, scraping the hawser but not getting to the hook at the cable end.

"God, George, what's going on?" the chief calls from above.

The stern still swings in toward the dock. I climb up on the railing, lock my legs, lean out.

"Heave!" George calls to his crew, hauling.

I lean out, jab at the frosty space, lean further. Thirty feet below, the green-black buffer logs (camels) turn slowly like confident creatures. Oil swirls over their turning backs, spilling out in purple-red ellipses. I jab again, find the hawser. The cable's hook is now only a foot beyond the pole.

"Heave!" George hollers.

I hear the chief bounding down the only metal stairs aboard ship. Has he tossed his telephone into the sea? And what is the skipper thinking on the bridge? I can see him, a slender, mustached, ice-cold skipper, the perfect idol for our chief. There he stares at the burgeoning harbor. A formation of applauding seagulls. "Nice launch, skipper," says a fawning Ensign (a man I could have been), but the stern slams into the dock. It does not, of course. Not yet. I lean out further. The pole locks onto the hook. I spear. George shouts. The crew hauls. The chief arrives.

"Gimme that thing," he snarls, still low-key but furious. Below, the camels turn beckoningly.

I spear again, but the chief already has his hand on the pole. He yanks down. My leg-locked balance goes awry. I pitch forward. The green-black sea comes swirling beneath my arm. The side of the ships comes at my head. I let the pole go, make a splendid grab for the hawser, now almost parallel with the chock. The engines suddenly lessen..

My left hand catches the hawser. My legs come loose from the stanchions. For a moment I imagine I will have to hang from the taut hawser. I actually think about scrambling down the line, unhooking the cable barehanded, and then swinging in toward the ship, as George and the crew pull me up. A spectacular vision: the triumphant reserve. He has saved us from the dock. But of course, the dream is absurd. I reject it; too risky, too heroic. Besides, George has got the snag within reach and my legs have locked again on the railing. I make two karate chops toward the hook but its point is buried in the hawser. The dock looms only eight feet away. The camels below are bunching up and back again. The pole slams into the hook breaking it free, just as my left hand hatchets down on the hawser.

There is a blur of release. My hand, the descending hook, the spear of the chief-driven pole, tangle in a hot second, then part. I am yanked upwards, back aboard. The cable plummets again. The hawser swirls through the chock. But the back of my left hand is shredded—a mealy, red-spewing, lettuce-looking sight. I stare at it dumbly.

"Woo whee," George says, rubbing his lips. For some reason I imagine him sucking on the wound. The crew watches. Do they feel admiration for my courage? Envy of my daring? Satisfaction at my ignorance? Justice for my status? The chief terminates reverie.

"Lay below to sickbay and get that put together."

George offers his crumpled handkerchief which I fold over the gash. At last we are pushing out to sea.

Day 4. Before the TN gets up for morning chow, before the watch-standers change at four o'clock, I am awake. My hand throbs. After his watch, Watley had said, "Man, wasn't that unreal? I thought the chief would shit! We thought you were gonna shimmy down that line and unhook it by yourself."

"No chance." We had watched *One Hundred and One Dalmations,* my head on a boondocker. A mass of sprawled seamen and snipes on the cleared deck, cartoon dogs running on a strung sheet, and beneath: the drone of motors. A sound to get used to. For a moment I imagined that the vibration would be beneficial, an intestinal rearrangement to foster smoothness and ease.

At 3:30 a.m. I get up to use the head. The fantail berthing area is warm enough, but the passageway to the head goes outside, and so I get dressed. Clean skivvies, black turtleneck and fresh bells, a kind of ritual to prompt excretion. None of it will work, I know, but for a moment I forget the throbbing paw. I can still work the fingers. The fingers are not mine, however, mere stumps attached to a maroon and mounded bandage. I put on boondockers, work jacket and black watch cap. All this dressing is no good. Nothing spontaneous, and hence, lethal, and stifling.

I start toward but never reach the head. In the outside passageway I turn toward the fantail. Braced by the sight of the white water and air colder than new steel, I edge along the railing toward the ensign flapping on the stern. A rumbling peace—motor, ensign, wind. I wedge my left thumb into my armpit, clamp a gentle pressure to support the wounded hand, watch the froth dissolve out into the way. Far back is Coney Island, the lights along walkways between apartments there, no more than doll flares. At the very tip of the stern there is no railing, open space to let anchor chains run free. I move along the railing to the ending nub. I begin to count the throbs and I hear distinctly the swelling of each interval of pain.

It is cold, wind-whipping cold, but I feel myself sweating. Forty feet below, perhaps twenty, I can't tell, the screws are working beautifully, turning over froth like unwounded fingers through sand. I draw closer to the empty space, contemplate putting the toe of the boondockers over the edge. "Throw yourself in, Spradlin," comes a funny plea. "Go on, throw yourself in." A pert emanation from the salve-smelling bandage. I listen again. Why not? I imagine the little movement it would take, the littlest rocking movement to launch off the *Northwind's* stern. Out billowing into the shell-black night, arching against the doll lights of the distant island, floating for an instant above the white froth and then, like the cable hook, plummeting into the dark and solid sand below.

Leap, Spradlin. Go on. I take hold firmly of the rail, pull it toward me, arch my toes, edge forward, lean out, peer down the white, stained sides of the *Northwind's* stern.

Go on, Spradlin, leap! I feel a terrific rush of conviction. Yes. Yes. Into the dark night, out into the doll flares, out into the rolled-flat sea. Yes, perfect, perfect unconstipated fate. I reach out with my left hand to take a firm launching pull on the railing. And the moment I hook stub fingers over the stanchion, the moment those fingers, nestled in elastic, start to tug, searing swallows the jump. I actually drop to my knees and haul like a thin hawser my flaming arm back into my armpit. I am rammed back through the chock doorway of the berthing area and settle fully-clothed on the rack. For a moment there is the warmth of twenty contemporaries sleeping.

Day 5, or 6: After morning chow George explains, "We big buoy tender today. Woo whee! We get to paint a lighthouse."

"Are you shitting me?"

George's eyes flash delight. "We get into rain gear and lay to the 01 deck, break out the davits. We going over the side."

"Christ, George," Stephan says. "It's too damn rough to go over the side. A small boat'll swamp in a second."

"The chief," George says, smiling. "We look bad launching. Make up for it. Woo whee!"

"What lighthouse?"

"You see her—dead ahead. Nobody live there now. Put a new light in her. Make her white again. Right down the sides in bosun chairs." George's eyes glisten. "Make her white again in bosun chairs."

"It's gonna rain."

"Chief says, 'Do it.' We do it."

"Christ!"

"Stephan, you and Watley break out the davits. Notari, you, Canino and you—"

"Spradlin."

"Yes, you get the paint, chippers, brushes, all the good gear. Just like a buoy tender. We make the chief look good today."

"Yeah, by drowning."

"Nah," George says, "we drop that boat perfect in the trough. Up and down, drop her perfect. Make the chief look good."

"Fuck the chief."

"Woo whee! You fuck the chief, you get stuck for sure."

In the paint locker, Canino is not pleased. "What a prick. What a prick! Over the side in a small boat with four-foot swells."

"Yeah," Notari says, "he'll wave to us from the 01 deck."

I think, *not so.* I'm sure the chief intends to go along. I feel that, know that for sure. For him it is the only action—a leader goes with his men, leads them. In tailored rain gear, he will plunge us all into the sea. Canino hands me a paint can. Unthinkingly I grab hold of it. The finger tips yank, the arm catches fire. The can drops, rolls on the metal corrugated floor.

"Sorry," says Canino, apparently contrite enough.

I put my left hand between my knees, squat for a second, enjoying the sympathy, when a familiar packet of keys resonates on the deck behind us.

"Canino, break out the generator."

"What?"

"Pardon?" the nifty, soft retaliation, as the chief holds a coffee cup, rocking it in perfect unison with the mild pitch of the *Northwind.*

"Where you want it?" Canino answers, humbled.

"On the main deck, below the davits. We'll put her in the boat on the way down."

Canino gathers up the keys. I shift to one side. He opens the interior lock, tosses the keys back up. Catching them with one hand, the chief simultaneously draws a long swallow of coffee, then says quietly. "Getta move on. I want to beat the rain." He turns, pockets the keys and moves up the ladder.

In a very quiet, very real rage, Canino actually hauls the three hundred pound generator out from its cage. "We're gonna chip up the side of the light. Chip away fucking hydraulically, electrically." Canino says. "I hope this fucker sinks the small boat." He kicks at it, slumps against the cage and says, looking back at the ladder, "Prick!" He looks down at his boondockers, scuffs them. "I'd like to bump that prick. Fucking generator."

Notari leaves, opens the cargo hatch. We use the steam wench to lift the generator onto the main deck, then drag it back along the railing, leaving it in the passageway outside and a deck below the boat davits.

I lean out to watch them swinging the small boat out. A wind gusting to perhaps thirty miles an hour comes flat at the *Northwind's* superstructure. In one gust, the small boat's painter (its lead line) actually flies up in the air, strung out like pennant. Hatless the chief leans out over the edge of the 01 deck, pushes on the bow of the boat, then moves to the other end of the davits and pulls on the bowline trying to swivel the boat's stern out over the edge, ready to be lowered into the water. But the wind pushes the boat at him, flapping the collar of the foul-weather jacket against the back of his neck. He looks down, notices me staring. For an instant I expect a barked order. I see myself flailing up the metal steps, grabbing the painter, hauling the small boat out into the grey air, leaping beyond the *Northwind*, painter in my teeth, and settling the boat, the generator, the lighthouse, the sky and the chief's smile into the envelope of the sea. It feels wet, cold, sweaty.

The chief stops smiling. George has come to the other end of the davits. They are both yanking, learning further out from the rail-less 01 deck, slanted against the wind, soles of feet wedged against the curl of the deck's edge, supported by the painter, arms wrapped around it close to their chest pulling. Suddenly, the *Northwind* rocks toward them, to port. The small boat now rushes out past them overhead. The tension holding them fast is reversed. They now have to pull the painter back, not out, to keep from dropping off the deck.

Bodies almost parallel to the sea, the chief's feet slip. The wind is strong, but I hear him howl. George adroitly braces him with one leg, hurls his shoulder into the chief's back and actually drives him back onto the 01 deck. That recoil disengages George's feet, but he merely clings to the painter, swings naturally out from the ship and then on the return of the rocking drops neatly into the passageway of the main deck. He misses the generator at my feet by six inches. Smilingly, then giggling like a clown, he kicks his left foot in front of his right, as if to indicate a kind of judo trip, puts a shoulder into my side, then, fists held together, snaps another invisible pencil. I am up against the bulkhead. He says, at the conclusion of the mythic pencil snap, "Pop!" and bounds away toward the stairs to the 01 deck.

Notari arrives dragging a box of paint cans; Canino behind him armed with chippers, brushes, rags and two cans of gasoline. Overhead the davit winch starts and the small boat, rocking back and forth as the *Northwind* pitches, begins a slow descent. For a moment it seems the boat will slam into the edge of the 01 deck but George halts it here before then.

The chief appears in the passageway.

"It would have been a wet one, chief," Notari says, tentatively laughing.

"You would have liked that," the chief answers in a sure monotone.

"Yeah, that woulda been some sight. Rough water!" Notari says, going nervously further.

"Yes. Some sight. Stack the cans and we'll need two cylinder batteries. We'll leave the generator here."

Canino reacts without thinking, "What?"

The chief reaches his left hand into his jacket pocket. I think he has a Luger, a black Luger with a silencer; and in a few little puffs, we'll be nothing but maroon splotches on the sea. A Luger or a pipe.

"Seems like," the chief says, hand still in pocket," this reserve is the only one not full of lip today. Lay below and get the batteries. You—"

"Spradlin," I correct, advise him.

He removes his hand, "All right, Spradlin, lash that generator down, using, clove, timber hitches and a bowline." He smiles, leans out, looks up and shouts, "George, lower her level to the main deck."

I remember a clove, execute it sloppily, but by then the chief is preoccupied with the small boat. My granny bowline, granny timber hitches go unnoticed.

"Load on," the chief shouts.

George has brought the boat parallel to the edge of the main deck, but we have to load across the railing or through the one small opening. The small boat is flat against the fenders, for the ship seems permanently listing to starboard. We have drifted just past the lighthouse. The tide has lowered some; moist, glowing rocks have appeared, strangely sharp-edged, glistening even in the overcast day. For the first time I can see the peeling, old white paint, the streaks of guano and the peculiar grey shutters to the narrow windows on each of the five stories. The light itself looks like a weak flashlight beam, dull faint orange. Someone in a shawl should live there. Or the place should be crammed with hay.

Canino, now in the center of the boat, hugs each battery, wrestling them to the bow. I cannot even get one of them off the passageway. When the last paint can is loaded, the chief orders everyone out of the boat. He gets in and signals to George to lower away.

The winch starts again. The chief recedes. I expect to see him scatter bits of bread to a collection of seagulls mewing in the air. But he merely waves for George to stop the winch. The boat remains some five feet above the rolling water.

"When I signal down, George, let her run free," the chief shouts, then buckles on a life jacket.

"You drop her in a trough?" George calls out.

"Right. When I signal, let her go."

The chief turns, hatless harpooner surveying the swells. Close to the ship it seems they are not severe—perhaps three footers—but further out they break on the rocks of the lighthouse with viciousness. "Canino, lower the fenders," the chief calls up. We drop the tires and rope bumpers so that if the small boat comes into the hull of the *Northwind,* no real damage will be done.

"You ready, George?"

"Ready, chief."

Notari says, somewhat awestruck I feel, "If George drops him wrong, she'll swamp."

"Goodbye, prick," Canino mutters.

Below us, the chief looks like a very little man. I expect him to proffer a cleaning agent, or to remark on the long-lasting polish of the sea. He raises his arms, spread-eagled against the orange of the small boat and the dark, muddy grey of the water. Then like some hyperbolic conductor, he plunges his hands down. The boat drops perfectly into the trough, squarely onto the back of the octopus sea, which sends out hundreds of white curling tentacles, bordering the boat for an instant like an orange and white gilded flower. The chief almost loses his balance, but he straight arms the engine cover, scrambles to the stern, unhooks the pulley there.

From above us, knotted climbing ropes reel downward to the boat. Grabbing the first line, Watley from the 01 deck starts the descent, an eager kid swinging back and forth. He drops onto the engine cover. The small boat rises to meet him. George comes down next, using the knots as foothold, lowering himself easily.

"I can't grip the damn line," I shout to Canino who is already up on the railing. George drops near the batteries in the bow.

"Come on, reserve," Canino says, holding George's line for me. "Lock on using your elbow."

"I can't."

"Fuck you, you can't. Come on. If that prick can do it, you can." Canino yanks on my good arm. I take hold of the rope. "It's only ten feet, anyway," he assures me.

With my right hand I reach as high as I can on the line. Canino steadies me on the railing. The boat looks miniscule, swaying back and forth on the sea like a dog tugging at a towel.

"Grab on. Put your feet on a knot. Lock your elbow around the line."

I lock my left around the line, hug it to me.

"Come on, come on!" Watley yells.

Suddenly—it is miraculous—I feel the need to excrete. Yes. It is extraordinary. I feel that the days of stultification are lumbering toward relief. "I need to crap, lemme down."

"What?" Canino shouts.

Has the wind increased? Gulls seem so thick as to darken the already grey sky. The welkin has been smeared with their easily spewed guano.

"I need to crap. I need to crap."

Canino merely knocks my feet off the railing. I swing out, legs locked on the line. I find a toe-hold, drop down a knot, then another. Watley has hold of my belt, then my crooked left arm. The sloshing deck of the boat rushes up.

"Let go of the line," Watley says. "You're in. Let go of the line. You're in."

Indeed. In. In. In. Bound, knotted. Cemented again. Secure in head-ached safety.

"I missed my chance, " I say to Watley, who is standing up as Canino, like a dark zeppelin descends.

"What?"

"I had a chance to crap and I missed it."

"That's too bad."

"You have no idea."

"Yeah."

"No idea."

"Yeah, watch your head."

Stephan brings down the last paint. Watley unhooks the forward pulley. We slam once, twice, into the fenders of the *Northwind*, then pull away. The chief from the stern now aims the small boat expertly athwart the rolling swells. We spear, lift, thud through the waves. Unthinkingly I put my bad hand out to brace against the engine cover. The shock of pain actually brings tears to my eyes. There is a hot moment when I contemplate crying out.

Watley turns back from dragging his hand in the water steaming from the bow. "You have a lot of trouble crapping, don't you," he says too loudly.

I nod, putting the bandaged hand up in my armpit.

"That's a shame. Must be what you eat. Lot of starch. You need more ruffage." He momentarily slumps against the gunwale. "You know, cabbage, lettuce, celery. Raisins are very good too. Even carrots." He turns toward the lighthouse which has grown larger, then turns back. "Also corn."

"Thank you."

"I know what you're up against," he says, facing the lighthouse again.

"You have no idea."

"I know that it's not the same—"

"Yes, Watley, yes. Every individual is different. Every individual is a sacred, unique entity, with identity and configurations of existence given by God. No one can transpose himself. Only ignorant insolence can make such a transposition. Insolence or indifference, or incapacity. Or indolence, or innuendo."

Watley turns fully around. "Fuck you. I know all that," he says waving me down like a dumb relative.

"What you say?" Canino shouts.

"Nothing."

"Lotta words for nothing."

"Woo whee!" George says. "Chief says we gonna land her. How we gonna land her?"

While I have been contemplating ruffage, the small boat has circled the tiny island holding the lighthouse. There is only one landing place—a long flat rock. But immediately beyond and above it are sharp piled boulders catching the spray from the rolling sea. Ominously tucked between the boulders are fragments of cement which toss out rusted spears of rebar. It is as if a foe had deliberately blocked the way. We circle once more. There is no other place. Then, too, the long rock is on the leeward side, and it seems the waves are lessened there. We come back to it. I can't decide if the chief means to pull the boat right on top of the rock which slants out of the water, or if he only plans to use it as a graduated bumper.

The approach is tricky enough. Though the waves are smaller, about three-foot swells, they are still enough to toss the boat forward jerkily or swerve it suddenly to one side. The chief works the forward and reverse handles in syncopation. The boat steadies, holding true with each passing swell, now about twenty feet from the rock. Seagulls call, fluttering up from the dry cement chunks near the lighthouse entrance. Rain apparently starts, though, for a while, I am convinced it is only sea spray.

"Notari, you want to leap off first?" the chief calls out.

Notari doesn't answer. The rock landing approaches quickly.

"Okay. Okay," the chief shouts. "Stephan out first. That's an order."

"Jesus," Stephan mutters and clambers to the bow, shoves Watley aside.

"You wet this time, Stephan," George says.

"Fuck you," Stephan answers, leaning over the bow, motioning the chief to the left, then right to bring the boat in.

"You're going to have to jump early," the chief shouts.

Stephan nods, kneels on the gunwale, then sits on the very point of the bow, his legs outside the boat. Above him, the lighthouse looks like a huge rain-streaked and soggy roll of paper toweling. On its far side, sea spray plumes up, spreading against the overcast horizon like light through a dirty curtain. The seagulls have moved to the railing of the second storey.

"This is as close as I'm bringing her. Jump, Stephan."

There is a moment when the motors seem silent, the sea almost calm. Stephan moves toward shoving himself off the bow, then delays. The boat moves back some. He leaps out. But it is deeper than he thought. Doubtless far colder too. He sinks past his waist, slips, hurtles backward, submerges.

"Back off! Back off!" George cries. He grabs hold of a life ring, prepares to toss it. But Stephan rights himself, bursts through the water, rises on the rock, shouts "Motherfucker!" and claps his hands over his head.

"Throw him the line."

George tosses the nylon line out. Stephan begins to haul us in. But the chief cannot cut the motors. The sea is too rough, too rolling.

"All right, Notari. Now it's safe." An utterly new mockery enters the chief's monotone. "You and Canino take that line up to the light. Run it through the chock on the second storey, right by those gulls. Then bring it back down here. Don't get your feet wet."

Notari moves to the point of the bow. We are as close in as before. Like Stephan, he hesitates.

"Go, goddamn it!" the chief shouts.

Notari and Canino scramble off the boat, struggle through semi-submergence, thread their way across and over the cement obstacles, climb the steps, pass the lines through the chock and splash their way back to the boat. Canino wades out, gleaming like a dark seal, and passes the line up to George, who secures it to the towing cleat in the middle of the craft.

"George!" the chief calls out, "Take over. Keep her in reverse. Keep a lot of tension on the lines. I'm taking the high road, high and dry."

George scrambles over the engine cover, as the chief comes toward the bow. The lines slack. Then George slams the reverse hard, pulling them taught again.

"Out of the way, Spradlin," the chief says, taking off his lifejacket. "You can follow me up, if you don't want to get wet. Just hold her in reverse, George!"

The chief swivels, his back on the bow, takes hold of the lines, pulls himself further out from the boat, locks one leg, then the other, over the lines. The boat lurches forward some with a swell. The chief now some eight or ten feet away from me, dips toward the water.

"Goddamnit, George," he laughs, "don't get my ass wet." He shimmies faster on the lines. George accelerates in reverse. The chief is gathered higher, goes higher as he climbs along the rope. "You can start anytime, Spradlin. You like to hang from hawsers," he calls, shimmying quickly. He says something else, but the spray off the rocks muffles it. Sky over his wrists, above his knees, must look like a rippling gray curtain. Two seagulls fly over to investigate this cork bobbing on a line.

The chief is suspended now over the sharp rocks; in another minute of shimmying he'll pass the cement-held spears of rusted steel. The line is taut, but occasionally reverberating as swells rock the boat.

A classic stunt, but out of character, I think. Demonstration of vigor for whom? Canino, the ex-football hero? George, the champion Samoan? Notari or Stephan? They might be impressed. For Spradlin, who already knew where all the power lay? Out of character. Is the chief, beneath the sure monotone, beneath the calculated impression, restless? Insecure? Could the chief be a frustrated frat boy, throwing himself from the fifth storey into a snow bank because last night the brothers out-drank him? Or was it that the new initiate, by hanging from a hawser, out-vigored them all? Too absurd for thought. Simply staying in shape then? The good chief never gets his ass wet, especially if in avoiding it he can demonstrate feats which awed reserves will not duplicate. Is the whole stunt an affirmation that he has seen me? Ah, the arrogance of the interpretation.

I watch the circling gulls, perhaps a hundred feet above him. Will their guano drop on his defenseless face? Do they contemplate excretion, or are they stoppered too? All right. All right, Goddamnit, I think, there will be no humiliation here. He can do it, I can do it. The slop of the sea against the boat gets louder as I start to swivel, reaching for the lines. Then a new sound. The reverse stops. Has George thrust the boat forward? The bow dips. I watch stunned as the chief, as on a trapeze, swings toward the steel spears. Like Tarzan backwards on the vine, he makes a parabola flush into the rust blunt poles which actually pop into his back and through him. The popping noise comes through the gull screech and sea splash, through the engine rev and heart-stoppered ears.

"My God, George!"

But we are in reverse again at full throttle. The lines come up. The chief is still clinging. Cement slabs actually lift, then tear loose, haul out scarlet gobs of the chief's back. He hangs, dripping, suspended above the rocks. I turn back to George, who merely pushes harder and harder on the reverse level. He swallows and swallows, looks bug-eyed at the dangling mess.

Canino and Notari and Stephan leap down from the lighthouse porch, bob across the rocks and come below the chief. Watley plunges out of the boat to help.

"Lower it, George. Lower it."

"Woo whee!" George says, still pushing on the reverse lever.

"Lower. Go forward, George. Go forward! They can't reach him."

"Woo whee! Woo whee!"

I jump over the engine cover, lift George's hand. The bow eases forward. They unwrap the chief, start toward the boat with him.

The boat starts to slide off. I push down on George's hand. The line straightens, holds. The boat is in a fixed position, bobbing but holding fast. George slumps down beside the handles. I step across him.

"Bring it in, bring it in!" Canino cries out. "You're too far out. Bring it in."

Watley, Stephan and Notari are holding the chief by his chest, stomach and legs. His back bubbles redness. No one can survive that, I am sure.

I ease up on the reverse handle; the bow comes down, slips to one side. Canino grabs the painter, wrestles the bow in. "Christ, ease off. Ease off, you're fighting me. Ease off."

"I can't hold her steady."

"Just ease off!"

"We'll bust up on the rocks. I've got to hold her, I've got—"

"Woo whee," George sighs, puts his head down between his legs.

Holding the bow with one hand, Canino reaches back to take hold of the collar of the chief's foul weather jacket with the other. Like some giant, he actually yanks the boat and the chief's body together. Watley has come around to the side, climbed aboard. He takes the chief by his belt and head, drags him in, and hauls him onto the engine cover, splaying him out chest down, arms and legs over the edges. The gashes on his back bubble more blood. He looks like a mutilated starfish. Canino vaults in, hauls up Notari and Stephan, one on each arm. Watley casts the line free. I push down on reverse.

"I can't drive this," I shout.

Canino pushes aside the chief's arm, takes the levers, steps over George who is crying.

"John, take that ensign out and wave it upside down. Wave the shit out of it."

Working both levers, Canino turns the boat and we head back.

Notari fashions a pressure pack on the chief's wounds, using a thin rubber seat cushion and two life jackets. He presses down to stop the oozing, but the chief's face is grey, white, grey-blue. His eyes have rolled up. I think: this is the first dead man I've ever seen, touched, smelled. Like a wildly enthusiastic drum majorette, I wave the inverted ensign back and forth, back and forth, listening, as the snapping of the cloth coincides with George's gurgling.

Day 7: The Executive Officer seated across from me appears immaculate, as brushed, smoothed, lint-less as the green felt of the tablecloth on which my hands rest, palms down. No aces up my sleeves.

"We understand that the moment of the accident, you and Boatswain Mate Third Malae were in the boat, is that correct?"

"I think so."

"You don't know?"

"I'm not sure."

"I see. Perhaps you could say who was outside of the boat. Who was in the water or at the lighthouse."

"Canino, Stephan and Notari were up near the lighthouse. I guess Watley was in the water. Yes, he was getting into the water." I think, Watley was always in the bow. He must have been going into the water.

"So you and the third class were in the boat?"

"I guess so."

The Executive Officer takes a long sniff of air, not exactly a sigh, but hardly an asthmatic reaction either. He brushes, using three finger tips, the hair back of his right temple, looks at the captain.

"Mr. Spradlin, where you from?" The captain's voice, appropriately enough, is richly paternal, reverberating.

"New Jersey, sir," I remember to add at the last moment.

"North Jersey?"

"Actually central New Jersey, sir. Near the water."

"Can't you be more definite?" The Executive Officer says interrupting.

I understand he's not talking about my Jersey location. "Yes, sir. Watley was in the water. Canino, Stephan and Notari were on the rocks of the lighthouse."

"You and the third class were in the boat."

"Yes, sir." I'm adding "sirs" everywhere now. One need only get the hang of it.

"Thank you."

The Captain takes up again, "Which way, Mr. Spradlin, were you facing when the accident occurred?"

"I was watching the chief, sir."

"And what happened?"

"Well, it seemed like the engine cut or the bow dipped or something, because the chief's back just swung into the, in the pipes."

"Then what happened?"

"The boat backed off and the lines came up, ripping the chief free, sir. Then, Canino and Stephan and Notari came down under the chief. He was still hanging there."

A pause. I hear notes being taken behind to my left. I think, I should talk more slowly, distinctly, though there is a recorder going at the end of the table.

"Then what?"

"George still had her in reverse. He was sort of frozen to the levers. I went back and eased the boat forward so the lines could come down a little and they could get the chief off."

"Then they brought him into the boat?"

"Yes, sir. And Canino brought us back. I waved the ensign." Should I be rewarded, commended for this?

"How long had you been aboard before the accident?" The Captain asks.

"Several days, sir."

"And what do you do when you're not on active duty?" The Executive Officer follows up.

"I'm out of work. Forty-five days active make it—"

"I see."

"I've held a number of varying jobs, sir, in New Jersey and Florida."

"I see. Well, sir," the Executive Officer turns to the Captain, who has been watching the slowly turning reels of the Sony recorder. "Is there anything else?"

"No. No. Thank you, Mr. Spradlin."

"Sir," my mind is racing, but the Captain seems amiable enough. "Could I ask a question?"

"Sure," he replies, turning off the recorder.

"I was wondering, since this is an icebreaker, how I was going to get off at the end of my active duty time. Forty-five days, sir."

"Spoken like a true reserve," the Executive Officer says, with strangely pursed lips.

The Captain laughs—a sanction, I sense, for insolence, if, indeed, insolent I have been. "The mail copter will take you off. But, but," he coughs, pats the recorder, "this will delay us for a day or two extra. The copter flies a fixed schedule, dropping mail on the forty-second day of the voyage. I don't know how long it will take to get you back from Nova Scotia. I assume you'll come down by military hop. But," he stands up. "I gather you have no pressing problems with your employer, and the chow is pretty good here."

"Very good," says the Executive Officer.

I stand, salute, exit.

After evening chow, Watley occupies the stall next to mine in the head. "What a prick the Exec is," he says, in what I sense is a preliminary probe. My concentration is elsewhere and my hand has begun to throb. "But the CO's okay. Really nice, don't you think?"

I ignore the question, but Watley leans around the doorless partition. "Don't ya?"

"Sure. It's the old high school game. The Principal's a great guy. The Assistant Principal's a prick. Somebody has to be the hatchet man. It's inbuilt."

"Yeah, I see what you mean. Somebody has to be responsible for discipline. So the XO has to be a prick."

"Sure, and when he becomes the CO, you'll discover right away what a swell fellow he is. He'll radiate niceness and the new XO will be a prick."

"That's the way it's gotta be," Watley decides.

"Those are the rules."

Watley finishes, steps down onto the tiles, comes into my doorway. We have docked at a military base in Rhode Island. The air coming into the head is soft and cold.

Since he's still in front of me, I ask Watley, "Where were you when it happened?"

"In the damn water," he answers.

"You sure?"

"Of course I'm sure. I got my ass soaked, didn't I?"

I nod. "You sure did." But Watley has walked off.

Later, while *One Hundred and One Dalmatians* runs across the rippling sheet on the mess deck, I sit with George in the forward recreation area. We have a booth to ourselves. Over his shoulder I can see the small stores cage. Once outside of port, it will be opened to sell cheap cigarettes, contraceptives, deodorant and soap.

"How long will we be here?" I ask.

"District gotta say everything okay," George answers.

"That shouldn't be any problem, should it?"

"I dunno. Chief pretty big."

"Accidents happen. How's your cold?"

"You got more pills?"

"In my footlocker. I'll get 'em later."

"Thanks. It was an accident," George says, staring down at the faded, blue, thatchwork-patterned formica.

"That's what they concluded, I'm sure."

"You sure?"

"About as sure as I can be. They want to get on with the tour. The idea is not to delay, isn't it?"

"We gotta lotta ice to break," George says, smiling. "Woo whee! You never broke ice before?"

"No. I don't think so."

"Woo whee! She bobs up and back, slide her up on the ice nice and light, then fill her up with water. Crash her through. Pump her out, slide her up again. Crack her through. All day. All night."

"What does the deck force do?"

George looks up, smiles. "Chip and paint. Chip and paint."

"Outside?"

"No! Woo whee! Too cold. No outside work. Your nose break off. Chip and paint inside. Lay around, get fat. Pull on yourself. Watch the movie." He points toward the mess deck, then looks back down at the formica. The orange overhead lights are such that no reflection comes off the table top. Still George stares at it, as if trying to see himself in the faded blue. For some reason I imagine the chief splayed across the table. I see George and perhaps myself pulling steel out of his back. Then, longer silence. George picks at the dirt in the crevice where the chrome edging meets the formica. I listen for the yapping of cartoon dogs and then say without thinking about it.

"You like him?"

George shakes his head.

"Don't worry about it." I get up, go topside to the head. This paternal pose is a new experience for me, and while unsuccessfully attempting excretion, I see myself straining to lead Samoan natives to the light. What light? Self-knowledge? Humane inclination? It seems they've figured it out better than I ever might.

Before the metal mirror Artiga, the Filipino steward mate in charge of Officer's Country croons loudly watching his flashing teeth. Outside I hear a football being passed around on a wooden deck. I think, this is an old munitions loading dock. With the right dropkick, we all go up in fragments. There is comfort but not relief in the thought.

Another Day: At 4:30 a.m. or so the engines kick over, jangling the chains of the empty racks. So District has accepted the official version, I think. Watley, arched in a fetal position, sleeps with his back to me, the grey blanket half off his shoulders. I doze off again. Then at 6:00 a.m. the bosun mate of the watch comes through.

"Get up. Everybody outta the rack. Outta the rack! Get up! Get up. It's another right day in your Coast Guard. Get up! Get up! Outta the rack! Everybody up!"

From the blanket-draped depths of the back fantail comes a furtive, "Fuck you."

The greeting goes on, undeterred. "Outta the rack. Everybody up. Outta the rack."

Watley sits up, hits head, swears, twists the edge of his fists into his eyes. "You drew a midwatch," he says.

"Where's that posted?"

"I saw it, I saw it. On the rec. deck."

"That's great."

"What the hell, you get to sleep in. Besides, George is bosun mate of the watch. He won't bust your ass."

"Great."

"I relieve you."

"Great."

I rummage in the footlocker, contemplate a suppository, then opt for milk of magnesia.

Watley in his skivvies comes around the rack, sits on my mattress, puts a foot on the top of my locker.

"We get our new chief this morning."

"You're a regular little fountain of information."

"Yeah, I had the eight to twelve last night. District gave us the go-ahead."

"Us?"

"The *Northwind*."

"An identification of interests. Very significant."

"What does that mean?" He gets off the mattress. I am jostled by passing seamen on their way to the mess deck. Watley sits, then pulls on his bellbottoms. "The new chief's an E.T."

"That's nice."

"Nice? Hell, what does an E.T. know about being a bosun mate?"

"Some of the best electronic technicians started out as bosun mates. Besides, they're smart."

"Yeah!"

I push by Watley, go to the head, sit stonily awaiting some kind of reaction. The head smells of Right Guard. Giving up, I shave, and go to chow.

At our table Notari and Stephan are curiously quiet. Canino eats five fried eggs. Watley informs everyone of the new chief. And at the end of the table, five snipes do not seem interested. Then George comes in, followed by the new chief who looks immaculate in pressed blues. For a moment I get the impression George has an invisible tether on the E.T. An impression which is not dispelled.

"At ease, men," the new chief says. He wears steel-rim glasses, is about twenty-two years old, and looks every inch the quaint electronics wizard. In rigid parade rest, he stands before the table, reels off an obviously prepared speech which seems, from the mechanical intonation, memorized. No one from the other tables pays any attention as the chief explains softly but with quickness. "I didn't know my predecessor here. It was unfortunate, but I am certain we can pick up ourselves and continue to do a better than average job."

Stephan looks at me. His eyes dance. What's with this bird?

"I won't be around too much. I'll be in the Communications Center, where my skills, or rather, the training the Coast Guard has invested in me will more readily pay off." He brings his arms around, cups his hands by his belt as if glancing at invisible notes. "Bosun mate Malae will be be in charge.

If there are any problems, please feel free to come and see me. We will be getting to know each other better during the long voyage ahead. Are there any questions?" He drops his hands, ready to acknowledge any questioner.

Canino gets up, leans across the table, huge, black, invincible. Is he going to grab the new chief by the collar? George steps back. I think, the chief is about to extend his hand and shake, but Canino has picked up his metal tray. He holds it above eye-level and shouts at the mess line. "Shorty! There's too much rooster fuck in these eggs." It is as if the chief has never been there. I can see the chief recoil, contemplate an assertion of authority, then decide against it. He lamely looks back at the chow line. Shorty, in spic and span white hat, spic and span white T-shirt over a rolling gut, stands behind the griddle of his fifty frying eggs and slowly raises his right fist, then third finger, at Canino.

"As I said," the chief blurts out, "feel free any time to call on me, men." He turns and George leads him out.

The rest of the day is given over to soogeeing the small boat. The throb in my hand has subsided so that I can wipe and re-wipe the point of the bow. I imagine the lines in front of me strung toward the lighthouse. But just as I begin to re-form the whole scene of the accident, someone laughs, or Notari tells another atrocity story from his days on rescue work out of Atlantic City. The blood is hard to get off, but George insists we do not use scouring powder. Notari and Stephan discuss who should have first right of fondling women corpses.

Watley edges me aside from the bow. "Try working on the engine cover," he says. "It's full of little crevices."

Canino arrives with a hose and nozzle. And I spend the afternoon picking at the residue of the chief's blood on the engine cover. There is a brief interruption—just as I was seeing again his inverted body—when we cast off. George insists that I only watch.

At eight-thirty, I get a new bandage for my hand, then try to sleep till the watch starts. There are low lights on in the berthing area. On one corner on a rack, a game of cards, Hearts, is being played. Tonight's feature on the mess deck is *The World of Susie Wong*—a trade arranged in Rhode Island? Does some Caribbean-bound cutter now have our *One Hundred and One Dalmatians*? At eleven-thirty I am prodded awake. The watch stander scores a red flashlight beam on my eyes.

"Relieve the telephone talker in fifteen minutes. There's coffee on the mess deck."

"Un huh."

"You awake?"

"Yes. Yes."

"Sure?"

"Okay. In fifteen minutes."

Watley rolls over. His elbow barely misses my ear. "Have a nice time," he says with exaggerated sleepiness.

"Fuck you."

"Ah, that's not nice," he says, turns over and hoists the blanket over his head.

I sit up and forward, crouching, and rest the back of my neck against the rack overhead. I swallow, pick my nose. Never have the grey blankets looked warmer or more enticing—like dark mounds of furry softness, an envelope of safety. I watch the blanket over Watley's elbow go up and down slightly with his breathing.

When I get to the bridge and pass George on the starboard side, he grabs my arm, "You got any more pills?"

"Yeah, sure. I forgot'em, bring 'em later."

"Good. Cold mother tonight. Catch cold for sure."

I pull back the sliding door. There are two officers in the bridge, one with binoculars against the windows, and the other in a foul weather jacket and slumped against the door to the captain's cabin.

"Evening, sailor," the slumped one says.

I snap a salute, come to attention and mutter something about relieving the watch.

"Okay, okay. Done, done. I'm Ensign Ball. Ever been on a watch before?"

I think a few seconds. "No, sir."

"I thought so. Nothing to it. A snap, a real snap. This one's never been on a watch before, sir," Ball says to the officer still spying on the front deck.

Green light from the gyrocompass ripples on the bridge windows. When the officer with the binoculars does not acknowledge Ball's statement, the Ensign laughs to cover, and pushes me toward the telephone talker's headphone stand. "You relieved the telephone talker, so you'll be using these, relaying any message we might have to other places aboard. You know the procedure?"

I think again. "I think so."

"Good, good. Put on the phones. Stand here and be ready. In forty minutes you'll relieve the flying bridge, then the catwalk, then bosun mate of the watch, then the helm. Get it?"

"Yes, sir."

"A snap, a real snap," he adjusts the headphones for me, leans in, pulls one earphone aside and whispers, "Don't sweat it. You won't have one message. Believe me, this is the dullest watch going."

"Thanks, sir."

For a moment Ensign Ball seems to grasp I might not mean what I've said. He looks at me oddly.

I quickly repeat the thanks.

He smiles knowingly, gives me a cuff on the shoulder, turns back to the other officer. "This one's all squared away, sir."

The other officer lowers his binoculars, looks back at us. It is the Executive Officer. He nods at Ball, watches me. "You never stood a watch before, Spradlin?"

"Not on an icebreaker, sir."

"On what then?"

"A buoy tender. And on the boardwalk watch at Atlantic City, sir."

The Exec looks at Ball, then harrumphs, raises the binoculars. Ball winks at me, a lurid, greenish wink.

I fit the talker phones to my ears, letting the sputtering electronic cadence fade into silence, but immediately Ball tugs on my right earphone. "Where you from?"

I think, then say, "Michigan."

"Michigan, heh? Whereabouts?"

Has he caught on? "Ishpemming."

"Where's that?"

"Near Lansing."

"Is not."

I look at him dumbly.

"Is not," he repeats.

I begin to contemplate the punishment for lying to an officer. I almost feel the heat of bilge oil pouring down my sides.

"Is not," he says again. "I caught you there. Nailed ya! Nailed *you,* I did. I did. You reserves always trying to put us on. Now, where you from?" He cocks his head to the side in a tossing motion which indicates there was nothing serious in my deception. I think of another state but decide not to press things.

"I used to live in New Jersey."

"Okay," he says, adding, though not by saying, rather by the light in his eyes *now we're getting somewhere,* but then turns away. I swallow consciously, push the earphone back into place. The low sputtering drifts into soundlessness. I am held in a void watching the green reflection of Ball, the Exec., the helmsman, and my own sleepiness.

In the next thirty minutes, Ball says nothing to me. I stand entranced by the green glow of the bridge. Then, apparently at the precise moment,

Ball comes back over to me. He pulls aside the earphone again. "See, I told ya, there was nothing to it. Didn't get a message, did ya?"

"No, sir."

"Not one. Now, take those off and follow me."

I disentangled myself and followed Ball out through the sliding door. George is no longer there. "Now, look," Ball grabs hold a ladder welded to the outside wall of the bridge. "Climb up there and relieve that man."

I look up, see no one.

"He's up there, all right, and panting to get down if you want to know the truth. You get his foul weather gear. Got it?"

"Yes, sir."

"In about forty minutes, you'll be relieved."

"What am I supposed to do?"

"He'll tell you. Stand watch, report anything you can see."

"Anything?"

"And everything! Now get to it." Ball clamps me on the back.

As I get to the fifth rung, Ball shouts, "Michigan, my ass!"

Have I been sentenced to climb the beanstalk? At least Jack got somewhere. White ladder into the cold dark. I see Ball's hatless head turned up, watching me. I imagine him fifty stories below me, a tiny cusp on the red-lit deck outside the bridge. In truth the ladder is scarcely a storey high and there is plenty of light from a white running light mounted near the voice tube through which lookouts report back to the bridge.

I exchange remarks about the cold with the watch stander, take his coat, watch him descend, flip open the brass top of the voice tube and listen to the bridge. I can hear Ensign Ball saying, "This one's squared away, sir."

I close the cover, stare forward. There is a running light on the point of the bow, a tiny nimbus and nothing beyond it. I am not really aware the ship is moving. I feel only the cold and a slight wind. Forty minutes of nothing, not even Ball's banter. Where is George?

In the heavy foul weather jacket I feel like a strange panda trying to see in the dark. Only the bow light moves. There are two inert lanyards hanging on the railing I lean on. Forty minutes of this. I remember a training film about night scanning—about being an effective flying bridge watch stander. The quick rotation of the eyes, that was it. Settle on nothing, for if you let your eyes settle, you saw nothing. The glints of light were the key—return again and again to the little glints of light. I scan and re-scan beyond the bow. There are no glints of light. The ship moves gently, soundlessly, through grand darkness. I think about listening through the voice tube again, but what would it yield? Another Ball discovery of an errant home state? Or the regularity of crackling sputtering? I hoist the fur collar up. Not even a star.

There is a vague shuffling behind me. I crouch and wheel around, fully expecting a rush of the enemy. But there is only still, steady darkness. Is someone hiding? I begin to walk around the flying bridge, hand on the railing as a guide.

"George, you here?" I call out softly. That trickster Ball? "Who's here? I hear more shuffling, see nothing. The overhead lookout light is shielded against the stern, so at the point of pure night I know I am farthest from the voice tube. Gradually I see the stern light. Then the catwalk becomes visible, then the 01 deck. Shuffling again. The noise, I decide, is not on the flying bridge. I am invulnerable on my pinnacle. The shuffling is nearby, but a deck below me. I kneel down, lean out over the edge.

Twenty feet below, the stacked small boats in their davits materialize. Someone has folded back the canvas cover of the top boat. I just barely see it swing on its ropes as someone climbs in. I lean further out, shutting more light off, but hearing more clearly the churning of the screws and the swaying of the small boat, which appears to rock like a cork in the distant wake of the *Northwind.* "George," I start to say but trail off, for clearly it is George. I shift back slowly so as to be less noticeable should he look up.

He stands in the bow of the small boat, facing directly to port. Is he still thinking about blood on the engine cover? Apparently not, for he raises his arms in front of him, takes hold of invisible lines and begins to flail them up and down, as if beating long reins on the sea. Up and down go his arms. He puts his whole body into the flailing. Holding nothing, it seems he is holding the straps to the very tarpaulin of black sky. Again and again, he raises his arms up, snaps them down. Up. Down. Up. Down, as if to whale all consciousness out of whatever it is he imagines is held by the imagined lines. Up. Down. Up. Down. Faster and faster, arching higher, whipping his body like a snapped towel, he brings the lines down harder and harder. I shift further back, for even on the deck of the safe flying bridge pinnacle, I begin to feel pipes popping through my back.

Another Day: At morning coffee break I give George more Coricidin. His eyes water and he nods thanks, staring into his bakelite bowl.

"Cold last night, eh?"

He looks up, watches me. "Lot colder where we go. Woo whee!"

The rest of the day, Watley and I rearrange the paint locker, making sure the older cans get moved forward into position. Three times George comes to check on us, explaining that there should be no smoking in the paint locker. I sense he resents assigning us to the locker, but it is not clear why. On the third visit he is carrying a coffee mug held forward prominently.

"Chrissakes, George, you're the fucking chief already," Watley says.

Smiling, George puts the mug down, then flails his leg with his right hand, shouting, "Woo whee! You bet I am. You bet."

"The fucking chief already," Watley goes on. "You're gonna be the Exec before we get off here."

"Woo whee! He," George points at me, let's his finger rest against my chest, "he never see it. Off too soon."

"A chicken reserve," Watley says, "off way too soon."

George picks up his cup and turns serious. "You assigned to Officer's Country."

"What the hell for?" I ask.

"Better for you up there. You don't get so chummy down here. End up pulling each other off."

"Jesus," Watley says.

"Anyway," George continues, "it better for you. College educated and all."

"I dropped out."

"Besides, Ensign Ball like you."

"That half-wit."

"Woo whee! Woo whee! You report to Artiga first thing in the morning. Right after morning chow. You report there." George backs out of the locker. Watley laughs.

"It's good duty. You work alone. Nobody hassles you except Artiga who's scared to death all the time."

"But I was just getting to like it here."

That night the game of hearts goes on four racks away. I lie down, pick at the wiring holding the mattress a foot from my nose. Officer's Country. George must have seen me watching him.

Watley flops in on the other side. "Well, I guess I better write the old lady," he says, picking at the mattress above him.

"You married?"

"Sure."

"Really?"

"Yeah, really."

"Christ, how old are you?"

"Nineteen."

"Nineteen, and you're married?"

"Yeah. How old are you?"

"Twenty-eight."

Watley looks over at me. "Twenty-eight? Twenty-eight! You're a fucking antique!"

"Thanks."

"Jesus! How come you're still a seaman at twenty-eight?"

"I didn't do too well on my correspondence courses."

"Yeah!" He rolls off the rack, gets writing paper out of his footlocker. "I always tell her what a great time I'm having. How I'm getting laid and all. Terrific! Unreal!"

"I don't think I would like to stay here for six months."

"You know, neither would I." Watley laughs a strange wheezing laugh, then begins to write.

After a while I ask, "What's the flick tonight?"

"*101 Dalmatians.*"

"They got it back? That's really great. Really great!"

Watley looks up from his letter. He examines my eyes, searching for some sense of sarcasm. Apparently he finds none, for he says, "Yeah, it's one of my favorites, too."

I think, he is telling the truth. He sits on the other rack, head bent down and forward to avoid the upper bunk. He writes his wife and genuinely believes *101 Dalmatians* is a great film.

Later, while the Hearts game still goes on, Watley goes out. I lie semiawake, wrapped in a grey blanket, then drift directly into dreaming sleep. In old skivvies I summon up through the one-third light of the fantail a shimmering asphalt highway. A little girl, perhaps nine years old, in yellow pulls a wagon down the road. I see more and more clearly as she recedes—a yellow form on the chill black road. Then, out from the bottom of my view, stream the dogs. A ripple wave of 101 Dalmatians undulating down the road which seems to move under their white, spotted lurching. Like a wave of white blinking, they swarm after the little girl in yellow. She turns around to watch, doubtless unbelieving—horrified? She turns, yanks on the wagon, begins to run. She abandons the wagon which is inundated by the churning dogs. I hear panting and abruptly they draw around her. With low moaning they begin to lick away her clothes, slobbering. She begins to squirm against their licking. I sense her cries are excited, pleasing sentiments of attraction, not revulsion. The dogs swirl in tighter, licking harder. Pink lapping against pink skin. Continuous salivation, a spewing white froth, then a tearing away of flesh as they lick more furiously, revealing soft camel-colored interior flesh, like sponges oozing milk.

"Hey! We just passed Nova Scotia!" Someone yells from overhead.

Awake now, I think, *Nova Scotia,* a good sound to it. But beneath the blanket it is necessary to wipe off. And Watley has left his socks within reach on his rack.

Another day: Artiga assigns me to the officer's galley, where I work under the lone cook, a black second class named Pete.

"We do our meals. Then get it all squared away. Then we do it all over again. That's what we do," Pete says, staring at the grill. "7:30. Noon. 5:00. then we do it again and again. All the time we do it. For six months. Then we don't do it for a while."

"I see."

"Hell you do," he says looking at me, lips fixed in a weird, pursed smile.

"You're right," I add.

"Now, we secure from morning chow around 9:30. Open her up again around 11:15. Stay out of sight. Otherwise, you have to put in more time for George. Aw, what the hell," Pete says, "I don't give a shit what you do. But stay out of sight."

"I'll hide."

"Where?"

"I'll find a spot."

"You'll find a spot?"

"Sure."

"Sure." He sits down near the refrigerator, begins to read a fraying paperback entitled *Consenting Adults,* with soiled, curling pages.

"Where are you from?" I ask.

He doesn't look annoyed, "Syracuse."

"How long you in?"

He rocks back on the stool, looks at me and says, "Why don't you police up the wardroom."

"Right."

With a wire brush I clean off the green felt on the wardroom tables. Then, using a small yellow sponge, I eliminate the dust on the exposed pipes and the narrow woodwork. Using a grey sponge, I wipe off the black linoleum baseboard. Finally, I buff up the green linoleum floor.

"Take a break," Pete calls through the serving window of the galley.

Obediently, I walk forward into the small deck area in front of the Executive Officer's head, near the point of the bow. Through portholes I can see on either side, the blue-grey sea. I go out onto the port passageway. It is much colder, a light grey day with the air granite-cool. A vague outline of land appears white against the greyness. Below, the water weaves out without white-capping, rather like clear oil, heavy, odorless. I expect a polar bear to come by on an ice floe. Instead, I hear the starboard door open, close. A quick glance through the port door reveals the Executive Officer walking toward his lavatory. I go aft immediately, re-enter the wardroom and hustle into the galley.

Pete puts down *Consenting Adults.*

"The Exec's up forward," I say.

"Fuck him," Pete replies.

We prepare noon chow, then evening chow. I serve Ensign Ball, who looks up and says loudly, "Michigan, my ass!" At 6:30 we secure the galley. Pete props himself back on the stools, and locks again into *Consenting Adults*.

I go down to the mess deck and watch the first half of *101 Dalmatians*. But my little girl in yellow with the milk-oozing thighs does not appear, so I go back to the berthing area. Watley is getting dressed for his watch.

"I'm on eight-to-twelve tonight. How about bringing my pipe out to me when I'm on the catwalk."

"When's that?"

"About ten o'clock."

"You're not supposed to smoke on watch."

"You can smoke it, too. I'll only take a couple of drags. Couple's more than enough."

His eyes dance. He smiles, then pulls on his jumper, reaches under his pillow and puts the pipe in my hand. "Very good stuff," he says, controlling a laugh.

"Watley, have you ever ridden in a tandem?"

"A what?"

"A tandem, pulled by horses."

"What are you trying to say?" His voice drops and he crowds in, smelling of Right Guard. "What's a tandem? You got one? Where's it stashed?"

"You've never ridden a tandem, heh?"

"Come on. Come on, what's tandem. Look, this is really good hash." He pats the pipe. "It's good stuff."

"So we're going to smoke it on watch, eh?"

"Yeah, just a couple of hits."

"That's really cool, really cool."

"Listen, nothing's going to happen. I guarantee it. Nobody comes near the catwalk at ten o'clock. Not in this weather. Besides, just a couple of quick hits. Man, you float through those last two hours. This is great stuff. Better than any tandem." He pokes my shoulder, then looks around.

"Well, I'll keep it. If I'm awake, I'll come out."

Watley looks at me skeptically. "You'll come out with it, won't you?"

"If I'm awake."

"Well, be awake for Chrissake! This is quality!" And he bounds off.

I lie down on the rack, shift, pick at the mattress overhead. I wonder if the whole ship smokes. The stoned icebreaker. The game of Hearts begins. I turn over, face Watley's pillow and doze some. I try to summon my licking dogs, but only the asphalt highway appears. Just as the lovely yellow phantasm begins to take shape, I am aware of a certain lurching. There is swearing in the berthing area, and I feel, even in the semi-daze, that I have taken hold of the chain supporting the front left side of the rack. Every few moments, it seems, I am about to roll out, onto the deck. Evidently the game of Hearts stops.

"Jesus, Notari, don't puke in here." And I am fully awake, watching Notari race up the passageway toward the head. The berthing area feels colder.

"I gotta get some air," someone says.

Now the rolls are coming regularly, for we pitch first to one side, then the other. On the far wall near the exit to the first class quarters, there is a clinometer registering the degrees of the roll. I stare at it—21 degrees. I put a leg behind the pole at the end of the rack. It is like being on a swing.

Someone says, "What the hell did we run into?"

"Guess," comes an answer.

"I'm getting some air," another response.

I swallow to quiet the slosh in my stomach, the slosh in my head. I think, this is better than hash, this is really great. There is no way to control the rushes from side to side. Notari comes back in, white, drawn. He gets out of his work jacket and staggers back toward the air topside. Stephan, five racks away, hangs on to his chain, looks dazed, putty-white. Three more seamen rush out toward the head. Notari brings back a galvanized pail half full of water, sets it by the doorway, then obligingly pukes into it. The noise of the heaving drives Stephan out.

Notari faces the berthing area and shouts, "You gotta keep something in your stomach. You'll really be hurting if you dry heave. You gotta keep eating no matter how bad it tastes." He looks better for having saved us all.

I turn on my side, wonder how long it will be before the odor seeps across to me. Fresh air is the solution. I get up, crouch clutching the side of the rack. Then, as the pitch tosses me forward, I open the footlocker. On the return, the lid slams on my forearms, but I don't particularly feel it. The healing hand is deep into the locker, protected. On the next lurch, I yank out the turtleneck, boondockers—on the next, dungarees and work jacket, baseball cap. I sit on the floor and pull on clothing as the pitching permits.

"You getting air?" Notari calls out.

"Yes, absolutely."

"It's rougher than a bitch out there."

"No kidding."

"No shit. It's a real bitch out there. You better wear your life jacket."

"Right." I get up, lean in, and pull out Watley's pipe. What the hell, I think, push past Notari, noticing only for a second the slimy contents of what increasingly is his personal pail.

White water sprays into the passageway, which has open steps to the main deck. At least the catwalk, which is on the 01 deck, will be high and dry, I think. In the mess deck *101 Dalmatians* is still playing, but there are only two bodies on the floor watching. I go by more pails set out for immediate convenience. I go aft and receive the first shock. The sea has come level with the stern, yet the stern is falling. A swell will wash directly down on me. I almost dive back for the hatch into the fantail berthing area, when magically the water is gone. I lurch out on the railing, genuinely curious, to find the humpback of that swirling sea, when abruptly it rises to meet me again, rising higher and higher. I can almost pet it, and then, just as abruptly, drops away. The air is moist, as if a cloud were about the ship, but there is no direct rain. Plenty of spray, but no rain. I pull a life jacket out of a bin behind the steps to the catwalk, but putting it on requires that both arms be free and I am afraid to release my grip on the stanchion near the stairway. I solve the problem by wedging myself between the railings of the steps, and in a flurry near hysteria plunge arms through the proper loops. Spray washes at my feet and I spring up. Watley is shoved against the back wall of the CIC shack. He has hold of a chock with one hand and a life-ring mounted on the wall with the other. I rush at him, snag onto his foul weather jacket, spin off and grab the life-ring. A torrent of spray plumes past.

"Still want to smoke?" I shout.

Watley looks at me, fakes not hearing.

"Still want to do some?" I shout into his ear.

"Why not?" he answers.

"You sea sick?" I ask pulling the pipe out.

"No time for that, Jesus!"

Despite the sea wash and lurch there is a better perspective from the height of the 01 deck. I can tell the *Northwind* is actually oblique to the rolls, which appear to burst from internal pressure. The white lacing of the froth cannot contain the explosions.

"They'll never relieve me," Watley shouts.

"So what?"

"I could wash over here. My hands are getting cold. I can't even plug in the telephone." He points toward the socket mounted in a stanchion ten feet away at the edge of the catwalk.

"When you supposed to check in?"

"I don't know—long time ago. Jesus! Gimme a hit."

"You sure?"

"You brought it, didn't you?"

"Yes, I brought it."

"Well, come on."

"I don't have any matches." It doesn't seem possible that match could be successfully struck anyway.

Watley lets go of the chock, pulls a lighter out of his foul weather jacket. Water swirls over our feet. For a moment I feel the boondockers begin to slide. Watley pushes the lighter into my hand. "Come on, come on!" he shouts, grabbing again for the chock.

"Why don't we go inside?" I pound on the bulkhead of CIC.

"The chief's in there!"

The deck is clear of water. I wedge my feet down, press my back into the bulkhead, and bring the pipe up, light it. I can't imagine the lighter firing in the mist and spray, but the first drag is hot and not very sweet. "Where's the hash?"

"In the middle, in the middle. My turn." Watley grabs the pipe. Water surges over our shoes again. The *Northwind* lists further to port, then roars back. I pitch into Watley, who is still drawing on the pipe. "It's out. It's out. Gimme the lighter." He squats, curls almost into a fetal position in the threading water. Smoke comes out from him. Spray suddenly belches up on the starboard side. "Try it." He holds the pipe up to me, looking angelic and pleased. "Oh man, this is good stuff. Good stuff. Try it."

"You're a regular little head, aren't you?"

"Oh, yes. This is great. Hurry up before it goes out."

I think—not many people can claim to have smoked hash aboard ship during a hurricane. I take three deep drags. It is sweet, warm, like lowering a ten-watt bulb into your throat. Watley reaches up for the pipe. He takes it. More smoke bellows out. The ship steadies, the rolling swells seem to ease off. Can the stuff be that good? I get the pipe back—two more tokes. The spray again, this time lacing up the light sky on the port side, literally climbing up the air. The ship is turning. I expect the lace spray to fall on us like toppled drapery, but instead it climbs further straight up and falls back away into the water.

"What's happening?" Watley says, standing up. He pockets the pipe, clutches at the chock. "Wow! Try standing up. Whew! Try that, standing up."

"I *am* standing up."

"Well, try it. Try it, for Chrissakes! Too much! Unreal, unreal!"

Slosh comes down from in front of the CIC shack. Torrents on either side of us come rushing by, deeper and deeper. Has the whole ocean come over the bow? I expect the shack to move, be picked up, floodwashed over the catwalk and onto the fantail. As the water rises, it seems clearer, delightfully pure in its fierce descent. I kneel down, drop my right hand into the cascade, which bats my fist toward the stern. I pull the fist out, drop it again—out, in again—batted away, retrieved, plunged, yanked, retrieved.

"What the hell are you doing?"

I think, but cannot immediately say, finally shout, "Testing."

"Testing?"

Abruptly the slosh stops. The *Northwind's* stern rises, then the whole ship rolls to starboard. I fall into Watley. We tumble toward the railing. The ship lifts and one of those enormous mounds of sea collapses over us. It is the last instant before a wave breaks. I see the water arching; I think it will recede like the others. I actually turn my back to check the distance of the CIC shack. I imagine getting hold of the life ring hook, when the tent water falls, spinning us around, moving us out in front of the shack. Like dry sponges, we are slung amidship, sent spinning past the wench for the boats, then under the davits themselves. Though I am enclosed in water, knocked by it, I feel I can breathe—Ah! hash-grown gills! But there is no railing on the davits' side. We can go over, I think, yes, into the sea. Into the forever water. Yes, that's the place to try out new gills. The ship has to lift, but no! Only more water, grand tumblers of it pour down on us. I see Watley grab at the lines, at the small boats. He misses, slides like an otter under the boats. Over the lip. He hangs for a moment on the rail-less lip, bent around it, chest above, legs below, then is smacked over by a giant mallet of sea. My God, he is gone and I am spun around, about to follow him. I realize instantly that I have no gills, no chance at all. I flail wildly at imagined lines but am coasted to the lip, perhaps only a split second after Watley. I hang. I kick my legs, am washed, flipped back. I expect the long fall. Ah, floating into the sea. Hands up, Spradlin, watch through the water-sloshed lens the immense grey variety of sky. Ah, watch for the last time—the *Northwind* pulling away, bobbing white striped thing wallowing out of sound. The sea feels hard against my back, and I am standing in the passageway on the main deck square in front of the entrance to the head. Watley is standing beside me. The *Northwind* has rolled to starboard again. We have been washed out and tossed in. The passageway is wet but clear. We are higher than the spray, tilted up out of the torrent.

"Jesus," Watley coughs, "Jesus!"

I see him for the first time. In the head seamen are puking. Vomit streams at our feet. I suddenly grab Watley as the ship comes back to port, shove him into the head. The slosh comes boiling down from overhead.

"You were in the boat, weren't you, Andy. Weren't you?"

"What?"

"You were in the boat. You got out of the boat after the chief dropped. You got out afterwards, didn't you?"

"What?" he shouts, spitting water, trying to squirm away.

"You saw George, didn't you? He threw it into reverse, didn't he? Didn't he?"

"What? What?" He is nodding while protesting. Notari pukes into a urinal to our right.

"George put it into reverse, didn't he? Didn't he! He killed him, didn't he? Didn't he! Didn't he! You saw it, didn't you? Didn't you?"

Watley grabs at my wrists, yanks them off his sopping foul weather jacket. "Maybe," he shouts. "Now lemme go. Lemme go." Suddenly gaining strength, he shoves me aside, rushes out into the sea-spumed passageway and goes down below.

Another Day: "There's too much rooster fuck in these eggs," with a spatula I poke at the white surrounding the frying yokes.

Pete stands looking out of the serving window, watching Ensign Ball who, since he is the Officer of the Day, eats his breakfast late. Pete has allowed me to do the cooking. I watch Ensign Ball's eggs go dark at the edges. The hash browns on a separate part of the grill glisten with bacon fat. Grease for Ball, I think. Indeed, grease for Ball.

The sea has settled some, and the clinometer registered only 12 degree rolls this morning. The dishes are still strapped in.

"Lotta puking going on," Ball calls to Pete.

"Yes sir," Pete answers, scowling at my cooking.

"These kids never been in the North Atlantic before. Going to be real unhappy. 'Course, I never feel so good the first few days out. After that, though, I'm salt, old salt."

"Yes, sir." Peter says, taking the plate from me. He carries it out to the table.

"Ah, who cooked this?" Ball stares at the plate Pete has set down. I contemplate leaving. There is a silence.

Pete finally says, "I did."

Ball straightens up, "Did not."

"No, sir, I cooked it all right."

"Did not. Did not," Ball insists. I have come to the doorway. "Michigan did." Ball points at me.

I imagine rushing over and snapping Ball's finger off, but I nod at the floor, shuffle and actually say, "Ah, shucks."

"See! See!" Ball shouts, standing up. "I knew you didn't. Knew you didn't. He did. He did! Where you from, Michigan?" Ball continues.

"New Jersey."

"Learn to cook there?"

"Sure. Where else. . .sir?"

"Ah ha." Ball's eyes gleam. "Where else, eh, little snot nosed Jerseyite. Where else? I'll tell you where else, and I'll tell you what for, too. What for, What for!"

Pete looks around, scared. He frowns at me.

I shuffle more, kick at the glowing linoleum. "Aw shucks."

Ball sits down, says, "Michigan, my ass." Then without speaking again, not even to ask for coffee, he eats the breakfast, folds his napkin. He starts to leave, stops in the starboard door. "You know, that was really shitty," he says and goes out.

I clear the table—Pete goes back to *Consenting Adults.*

"Was he talking about my cooking?"

Pete looks up, shrugs. I buff the floor—an exciting enterprise since I have to maneuver as the ships rolls up and downhill. In lieu of evening chow, Pete makes me a giant salad. "It'll help," he says.

About 7:00 I get back to my rack. Watley is stretched out in his skivvies. "You got a watch tonight?" he asks, arm over his eyes.

"No. I'm on galley duty."

"Oh yeah, that's right. Lucky bastard."

"You're not on tonight, are you?"

"You shittin' me?"

"I don't believe so."

The arm comes away. "Not after last night. That was unreal." Watley sits up, cracks his head in the springs, flops back. "Unreal."

"Yeah, I thought we would go overboard."

"I thought I was overboard," Watley says. "Unreal!"

"Yes." I sit on the rack. Is the deck moving faster, has the sway increased? The clinometer, sure enough, registers 13 degrees. "You going to see the movie?"

"What is it?"

"*The World of Suzie Wong.*"

"Nah, I've seen it nine times already."

"There's still a lot to it."

Watley leans forward, looks at me. "Boy, are you unreal."

"I've felt that often enough."

"Fuck you. Why should I get horny lying around on the mess deck watching some hooker?"

"Okay. I was just asking."

"Well, I was just telling." He puts his arm over his eyes again.

"You could write your wife."

"Yeah, I better do that," he says, unmoving. "How come you're so interested what I could be doing?"

"Well, you see, Andy, since we both share the knowledge of a murder, I thought we might develop a relationship. And after we got to know each other better, then maybe we could decide what to do about the killing."

"What do you mean—do about it?"

"That's the question, all right."

"Look, I could write my old lady—a great, long, gushing letter. See. Unreal! I could come off just writing her, but right now, you know what she's doing? She's probably got a babysitter or her mother or her sister to come in, and she's down in front of Waffle House with her old high school crowd. Right now. So fuck it, see?"

"You seen George today?"

"At chow."

"How's his cold?"

"His cold is fine. . .."

"Okay, okay." I lie back. The yellow-dressed girl goes loping down the undulating plateau of creamy blackness and the white swirl chases her. But it is not sufficient. I turn over, "Look, did you say anything to George?"

Watley adjusts his arm, looks at me intently. "Say anything to him, what for?"

"Did you tell him we know?"

"Know what, for Chrissakes?"

"You were dazed, eh?" I think about putting his arm back over his eyes. "You were wet, cold, half drowned, dazed—you weren't thinking straight. You didn't know what you were saying, eh? Is that the way it is. You would have said anything just to get to a dry place, eh?" I think, it was like those water tortures Special Forces used to use. A little choking suffocation to clean the memory, purify the membrane of recollection. Then, obvious leading questions and admissions of guilt elicited themselves.

The game of Hearts ends with a perfect roll tossing the cards onto the deck. Notari comes in carrying two pails. He is pure white—a porcelain drapery of a person. The front pockets of his work shirt are stuffed with crackers. "I'm leaving these here," he says, turns and bolts back to the head.

Watley says, "I don't know what to do, what to think."

"About George?"

"No. Who gives a shit about George? About my goddamn cheating wife."

"I'm not interested in your wife."

"Well, you're just about the only one who isn't."

"I see. I see."

"All right, all right. I'll write her. I'll write her, now leave me alone." He pulls writing paper out of his footlocker, then turns on his side, his back to me.

"You don't think George killed him?" I whisper at Watley's back.

"I'm trying to write my wife," he answers just as softly.

"We both know he killed him, don't we?"

"I'm trying to write—"

"Okay. Okay." I put my arm over my eyes. The rocking motion becomes more noticeable, like riding a long slow swing. I trace a nifty parabola of ascent and wait for George with gleaming scimitar at the summit. Watley goes on writing his wife. Someone retches into Notari's pails. I hear someone opening the cellophane around five saltines. Just keep something in my stomach. The motion stabilizes me. In the bowl like movement, there is serenity and I start to doze.

"Christ, I can't write like this." Watley puts the pen and paper back into his footlocker, turns back to me. "You asleep?" he says, about ten inches from my ear. I smell Right Guard and concern.

"No."

"Don't see how anybody could sleep in this, anyway. I feel like puking."

"So puke."

"I didn't say anything to George. I'm not going to say anything to George, ever."

"I see."

He lies on his stomach, pokes at my head. "Are you?"

I bring my arm away from my eyes. "No. No. George would be the last person I'd want to talk about it to."

"It's over, right?"

"I suppose so."

"Yeah. Well, I know so. Now I'm gonna get some sleep." His elbow comes past the pole and into my shoulder.

"You just said nobody could sleep in this weather."

"Well, I'm gonna try."

"Do that."

"How come you're such a prick?" He arches up, leans over to me. For the first time, I notice his crew cut hair and the freckles on his face.

"You're just out of Cape May, aren't you?"

"Fuck you."

"You're nothing but a boot, a recruit. A boot."

"Fuck you," Watley says, putting his head down on his forearm. "You don't exactly qualify as an old salt," he adds, not lifting his head.

"That's precisely the point, boot. Or maybe you'd like some of the old salts around here?"

"I'm going to sleep."

"Good!" I say and bring my left fist down hard into the middle of his back.

He opens his eyes slowly, raises his head. I can see him start to smile. "That hurt something *awful*," he says, affecting a lisp. "Don't you evah do that again, you awful, mean fella." He turns on his side, offering his whole back. I think about hitting him harder but decide against it. I summon, instead, my 101 Dalmatians.

The midwatch standers getting up at 11:30 awaken me. The ship is rolling worse. But, magic of magics, I feel Pete's helpful salad begin to work. Don't lose this precious moment, precious urge, Spradlin, I think folding out of the rack. The linoleum is cold, shifting. I cannot find my socks. No time, Spradlin. I pull on the dungarees, put the work jacket over my T-shirt and hustle off barefoot to the head. The passageway is running sea water, and spray boils up as the *Northwind* dips and pulls. It is a rerun of last night. I expect for a moment to be lifted onto the 01 deck, yanked out of the passageway. Seamen are in the head, retching in the urinals and in the commodes. Notari, mystically white, is braced between two sinks, legs forward, boondockers splayed out. I rush past him, swearing on the far side for a vacant stall. Good old green ruffage, nature's remedy.

Leave it to farm peons for good old-fashioned solutions. Make a note, Spradlin—Give Pete a raise and a bonus. When you get back stateside, Spradlin send Pete the raunchiest paperback available. The end stall is empty. I rush in. The motion is fierce, and there are problems of balance, but just before midnight, hands shoved against the stall partitions, as if performing for safety's sake, a dreary isometric exercise, Spradlin, amid retching, cursing, puking, misery, happily, ecstatically, voids.

More Days: The storm passes and Spradlin, bantam weight and bouncy, rises to challenge the clean dawn, the icy chill winds outside of Officer's Country. I stand drinking the cold sunlight, watching through the wardroom porthole curling vapors off the officers' morning coffee. I dance through the day.

At noon I read in *Consenting Adults*: "She wondered why she had ever come to the city. What was it that drove her from Harretsville in the heart of the mid-west to this place so cold, so friendless, and so biting. For two days Dolly had been so attentive, so friendly, stopping by at odd hours, suggesting new places to see, new restaurants to try. And then, on that chilly afternoon in the balcony of that 88th Street theater, everything had come to such a grinding halt, wrenching her into a new view of herself, a new feeling about the deep longings in her body. Her body! That was it. She had never recognized her body until Dolly's silvery hands had traced out the constellations of pleasure across her stomach in the balcony. She had never met anyone like Dolly before."

Pete, taking the book away, says, "Buff up the wardroom."

At 5:00 I have heaping bowls of Pete's helpful salad. Just before securing I ask, "Look, how about letting me borrow the book? It's better than the movie."

Pete, slumped on the stool, raises his eyebrows. "The book stays here in the galley. It belongs here."

"Yeah, I can see that all right."

"What do I care? The book stays here. You can read it here."

"Okay. Okay."

"You can't take it out of here."

"Okay, okay. I'm not interested in taking it out."

"You want to read it now?"

"No. No."

"You can read it now, if you want, but here in the galley. That's where it belongs."

"Okay, I see. Jesus!"

Pete slumps down again. Sweat forms a small ellipse in the center of his T-shirt.

"I guess I'll lay below."

"You're secured," he answers, apparently still reading *Consenting Adults*.

I wonder where Dolly's fingers are now, and in the rack before Watley goes on watch, I imagine her coarse hands slowly exploring my loins. Instead of pursuing this vision to conclusion, I ask, "You see George today?"

"Sure," Watley answers. He tries on the knit watch cap. "He was feeding Notari, and working with Canino in the storage area."

"Working?"

"Well, they were up there."

"Okay." As Watley goes to the doorway, I add, "We're even."

He stops, takes off his watch cap. "What?" he asks.

"I said we're even."

"We are?"

"Sure."

He picks his nose. "How are we even?"

I hold up my socks, showing him the dried white-grey substance crinkling on them.

He blushes. "We're even," I repeat.

"Unreal," Watley says. "You beat off into my socks before?"

"Who else?"

"Unreal."

"Yes, but don't do it again."

"Well, don't leave your socks out."

"Shame on you."

Watley adjusts his watch cap, shouts, "Unreal!" and leaves.

I lie back—ah, sweet Dolly, fondle me. But no, it is the little girl in yellow, and a frenzy of dogs chasing her. Waves of dogs coming after her. I hold out to them all my government-issued and regulated socks, pliant, stable, and seawater soft.

Around 11:30 I get up and go to the recreation deck. George sits in a booth by the small stores cage. He drinks coffee.

"You on watch?" I ask.

"Nah—seen the picture before."

"How's the cold?"

"Plenty," he answers.

"Plenty?"

"Plenty."

I sit down. "When do we break ice?"

"'Nother week, maybe sooner. Pretty soon you'll see the floes. Woo whee! Some big mothers." He tries to rouse enthusiasm but fails.

"You want some more Coricidin?"

"Nah."

I hear yapping dogs and the white flashes along the mess deck floor are clear markers that Dalmatians are on the screen.

"What would have been the chief's job when we get to the ice?" I ask George clumsily.

He stares at his coffee. "Same as me."

"They won't let the E.T. take it over?"

"How can an E.T. do it?"

"I don't know."

"Well, he can't. I'll do it. I done it plenty times before. Plenty. Even if I don't make the hat."

"Make the hat?"

"Make chief."

"That is what you want? You want to make chief?"

"Sure. Woo whee! Then I bust your ass. Stand around all day — bust your ass. You'll see."

"Not my ass, George. I'm getting off here."

"Maybe, maybe."

Is there something ominous in his voice? He stirs the coffee with his finger. "They'll get me off, all right," I assert, watching him carefully. He nods his head. Does he believe it? Has Watley been talking?

"When you get off here, you got a nice place, eh?" His eyes flash. He smiles, then grabs my wrist. "Real nice, eh?"

"I suppose so." I think, a little girl in yellow named Dolly.

"You get some, eh?"

"Yes."

"Good," George smiles again, then laughs. "Woo whee! When you get some, you send some up here, eh?" He stands up, pats his crotch. "You send me some right here. You do it, else I come looking for you."

"With a marlin spike, eh?" I ask. George is backing away.

"Nah, no marlin spike. I just catch you when you not thinking so good." He brings his closed fists together, looks hard at me and snaps once more the invisible pencil which I see clearly enough is my neck.

Another Day: "Do you think I ought to talk to somebody about it?" I ask Pete, who has stopped reading *Consenting Adults.* "I mean, if you were positive something wasn't an accident, wouldn't you?"

"How do I know? Hell, no." He tosses the book aside. "Why don't you buff up the wardroom."

"What kind of answer is that?"

He looks surprised, then gathers in his book.

"I need some help." Immediately I think, do I really need help? Is that really the situation?

"Who don't?" Pete says.

I get the brass wire brush out, the dust pan, and begin to whisk off the green felt tables. Pete comes to the service window. "If I see something I shouldn't have seen, I forget I saw it. That's the best way."

"Just forget it?"

"Right, put it outta my mind. I put it in, and then I let it out and I make sure it stays out."

"Thanks."

"What do I care?" he says, retreating from the window.

"What if I said it had to do with an accident on board this ship. Right here, so that maybe you could be next."

"Or you, maybe," Pete answers from the galley.

"You? Me. What about me?" I come over to the window, "What about me?" I think about striking the right dramatic tone. Do George and Pete have something in mind for me?

Pete says, "Why not go through channels? Tell your chief about it. Have him say something for you."

"I'll do that," I say to Pete, who passes me (as a reward I suspect) *Consenting Adults.*

After we secure from noon chow, I read:

With gentle but firm pressure between her legs, Dolly was forcing her down off the back seat of the cab. Dizzy with sensations she had never felt before, she woozily watched the tall grey buildings flash past the car windows. 'Dolly please, Dolly, not. . .not, oh. . .oh. . ..oh.'

"Pete, this is crap."

"You wanted it," he says, taking the book back in.

"Maybe I'll see the chief."

"Sure, that's the best way—going through channels. That's always the best way. That's the way we do it—go through channels."

"You're repeating yourself."

"Sure, that's always the way."

The rest of the day I make periodic forays into Dolly's sensual world. The stimulation of it is all too real. Frozen air outside the wardroom helps. Before evening chow I actually do push-ups in the little recreation area near the Exec's head. I do them holding a sponge in my left hand, so that if anyone comes in, I can claim to be a prone industrious sogee-er But the squishing noise the sponge makes as I come down on it with my left palm does not add the right sort of distraction.

Instead of watching *The World of Suzie Wong,* I explain to Watley in vivid detail Dolly's antics.

"That's some fuck book," he says. We are sitting on the deck near our racks. The game of Hearts has started up.

"Yes, it had its moments."

"Unreal," Watley says quietly as if to underscore it. There is a pause, then Watley pokes me on the shoulder. "Wanna do some?"

"You still have that pipe?"

"Sure, Ready to go. Ready to go!"

"I don't think so. Last time wasn't too pleasant."

"It was a gas. Unreal! Come on."

"No. I don't think so."

"Come on! Ready to go! Unreal!"

"No." I get into the rack, pick at the overhead wiring.

"Okay," Watley says, "I'll just do a couple of hits here."

"You can't smoke in the berthing area."

"What are they going to do? Send me back? I mean, ice breaking—the worst duty in the Guard. Worse than the damn brig."

"Sometimes the way you say *Guard* has entirely too much affection in it."

"Fuck you." He puts the pipe away in his footlocker, strips down to his skivvies and gets into his rack.

I think about telling him what Pete said, but reject it. I can't imagine the E.T. will be much help either. Going through channels. The expedient solution which solves nothing. Merely keeps us moving as if toward a solution. How perfectly programmed has Pete been.

"You seen our new chief?" I ask Watley.

"Nah, he's always up in C.I.C. George's the chief now."

"Always in C.I.C.?"

"Yeah, always. He even eats noon chow up there."

"Thank you."

"Yeah, sure." He turns on his side.

I try to sleep and in the half daze of near sleep, in the heat of forearm on eyes and the mutterings of the game of Hearts, I imagine the *Northwind* has finally entered icy territory. I feel the ship moving soundlessly through sea steadily like canvas slit by the bow. Boulders of snow on the surface. Distorted triangles which glisten, sparkle like ornaments of chunks of quartz thrown over sea shells. Nothing but white, boulder-strewn flatness all around. It's possible to walk away from the ship, then walk back—for the pace is slow—slow tearing of the bow through canvas. Watley is sitting on one of those boulders. Sitting, pipe in mouth, nodding at the ship. Then he points the pipe stem to a dark lump on the icy surface, below his boulder. I walk off away from the 01 deck to see—to investigate his indicated find.

"Why, it's a penguin, a dead penguin," I say slowly, watching the brilliant faience of his boulder glisten. "Let's resurrect it."

"Unreal," he answers. "How'd you resurrect a dead penguin?"

"Prod it, I guess." I answer, for I no longer care. I kick the bloated penguin over. I expect to hear the buzzing of flies, expect to see the circling vultures, but of course neither occurs. "We could pick it up on the way back. No one eats frozen penguin."

"Right."

"Although some consider it a delicacy. Penguin on a stick for the thick tongues of the lifers."

"The lifers," he agrees. "For them penguin on a stick. Stick 'em with frozen penguin. Up theirs with a frozen penguin."

"Precisely."

Watley waves the pipe, then stands on the top of his snow boulder. He waves frenziedly at the ship and shouts, "Up theirs with a frozen penguin!"

I start my awkward walk back on the white canvas, noiselessly torn by the *Northwind*.

"Thanks for what?" Watley says, poking me.

"Huh?"

"Thank for what? For what? You said, 'thank you' For what?"

I think, but cannot remember. "Maybe for not resurrecting the penguin."

"Man, are you a freak. Unreal!" Watley says, turning back over.

I watch his legs—how smooth, downy sleek they are, like a girl's. I have a terrific, undulant, embarrassing urge to pet them.

More days: "Let me get this straight. You're actually saying that it was not accident. That the engines were reversed."

"Not reversed. Taken out of reverse, thrown forward so the lines would drop. Just at the right moment when the chief was over the pipes. He had to drop right into them."

"You saw him reverse the engines?"

"No. I heard the engines reverse. I was watching the chief. I heard the engines come out of gear—then go forward."

"But you didn't see him throw the lever forward?"

"No."

"How can you be so positive he threw it forward, then?"

"I heard it."

"Suppose the boat. Suppose the back, the stern," he corrects himself, eyeing me smiling, and I can see the intricacy of the possibility interests him. It must be like a circuit with a drop of misplaced solder. "The stern. Suppose the stern had come out of the water? Would that sound like the engine coming out of gear and going into forward?"

"I don't know. I don't think so. I've heard engines in forward and reverse. I can recognize it."

"There were waves, weren't there?"

"Of course."

"The stern could have come out of the water, or better yet, couldn't one of those waves have simply propelled the boat forward? Picked it up and hurled it enough forward so that the lines would come down?" he stares up from his metal tray. Dials, charts, clocks, switches, buttons, grids, oval glass viewers, swarm out of all four walls. His metal tray sits on the pale green felt of the card table, obviously older material cast off from the wardroom. He pats his hat beside the tray and then says, "It's not all very tight, is it? It's all too nebulous. It could have happened. But more likely it did not. Do you want me to speak to George about it?"

"No."

"Why not? It's, after all, a serious accusation, isn't it? I suppose if you accused me of murder, I'd like to know about it—have a chance to give my side. He ought to have that chance, shouldn't he?"

I think: why these questions, rather than some others? Is it a game for him? In cahoots with George? Merely a puzzle like some schematic diagram drawn in flesh that he wants to complicate by adding George's wiggling, woo-wheeing presence?

"I'd just as soon he didn't have a chance to kill me," I say.

"I see," he leans back. "Do you think he's out to get you?"

"Of course not, so long as he doesn't know I'm aware of what really happened."

"But if he knew, then he'd try to get you, eh?"

"It may sound a little paranoid."

"That's a good word to use. What does it mean?" He stops patting his hat, arches his eyes. I guess he's six years younger than me. Doubtless with a perfect record at E.T. school. A successful student, a curve setter, i.e., not knowing anything.

"Jesus."

"Pardon?"

I roll my lower lip over the upper. Finally I say, "Maybe I was wrong. Maybe I imagined it."

He smiles, the curve setter once more, brings his hands together. I expect a wash of fellow feeling, good old ingratiation. "You've got a long tour for a reserve, don't you?" He waits for an answer. I consider tipping the table over on him. I see him sprawled out under the edge of the table, the metal tray oozing its contents onto his baby face—zucchini puss. I long to have worn my boondockers—squash that vegetable flecked visage. "And I'm aware of the collective I.Q. of the deck force. Companionship must be difficult. . ."

"I'm sorry to have bothered you," I cut him off, exit quickly and almost slam the door.

All of Watley's hash is not enough. We sit in the head passing the pipe around the stall partition. Five tokes each are not enough, and then it is gone.

"Man, I'm floating," Watley says, "floating along. Scooped out. Ever get that scooped-out feeling? Like some big hairy arm with a soft scoop has come along and come right along, and—say." There is a pause. The *Northwind* tips a bit. "Say," he continues in evident surprise, "What was I going to say?"

As the *Northwind* rights itself, I am woozily tossed against the partition which feels spongy.

"What was I going to say?"

"About, about the scoop," I answer, but I have lost track of Watley's thought too.

"Man, this stuff is unreal! Too much! I'm really zonked." Watley says. I see his fingertips over the top of the partition.

"Are you just hanging there?"

"Just hanging, man, just hanging," Watley answers.

I pinch my nose, which feels larger than a grapefruit. My skin has acquired a creamy texture. I think, I'd better get out of here. The air outside is bracing, but not sobering. It is like slow razor slashes in my sinuses. Watley comes to the doorway. We are wearing work jackets and baseball caps—for a moment, on our way to the finals of a Little League tournament.

"Look at that sky," Watley shouts. "Unreal! Unreal!" He traces the horizon back and forth with his arm, muscling me out of the doorway.

There are bands of greyness, light at the meeting with the chippy sea, getting darker higher up. White chunks of ice form stepping stones to the edge of the world. I put both hands on the cold metal railing. I pick at the tin grill work beneath the piping—meticulous artistry by some lonesome steward's mate? A careful Filippino of twenty years prior?

Abruptly, Watley throws his pipe onto a passing floe. "I'm really getting into this ice scene, man. I'm really into it."

We watch the dark spot of pipe weave by on the bobbing floe. The *Northwind* goes slower. It is impossible to tell which is moving, the ship or the floes. The pipe moves soundlessly away.

"That was a good pipe."

"Yeah," Watley answers, "the best I ever owned, ever hope to own." He laughs, slaps the railing, then spreads his arms out wide. "Better to share it, don't you think?"

"Definitely."

"That's it. Definitely. Def—fin—it—lee. What a cool word! Def—fin—it—lee."

"The coolest word here."

"Yeah. Def—fin—it—lee. My mother used to use it. Can I go out now? Definitely not. Is it time for bed? Definitely. Wow. I think I could walk on these floes, man. They're right out there, within stepping distance."

He starts to get a leg over the railing. I watch him. Can he be serious? A deception of some kind, I decide, but then he is sitting on the rail. He kicks his right foot out, as if to grow it toward the nearest floe.

"Wait a minute. Wait!" I grab the back of his work jacket, just as the *Northwind* slams into something. The jolt tosses us both back into the passageway. Watley starts to giggle. The P.A. sputters, then George's voice shouts, "Deck force to the foc'sle. All deck forces to the foc'sle."

We sprint up the passageway, but it seems we are running through sand. The bow of the *Northwind* keeps rising.

"We hit a whale," Watley shouts. "A real whale, bigger than the ship for Chrissakes."

"I doubt it."

George comes down the outside ladder from the bridge. About twenty seamen are on the forecastle.

"Woo whee! Now we break some ice, baby. Now we earn our dough. Break out the five-pumps."

Operating the steam winch, Canino maneuvers two five-pumps up from below. The *Northwind's* bow eases higher. And as I get across to the starboard side, I see Watley's whale extends maybe four hundred feet out ahead.

"Why not steer around her, George?"

"We paid to break these mothers up. We do it now. Woo whee!" He directs the pump hoses over the side and steers the intake hose down below. The pumps turn over; 40 degree seawater churns into the bowels of the *Northwind*.

"We fill her up. Pop her through, break her right in half. Woo whee! The first one tells it all. Nice and clean, nice and clean voyage. Then nice breaking all the way. If she doesn't break easy, that's the way the rest goes too. All six months of it." George stands at the port side now, watching the choppy water suck into the hose.

"I don't care. I'm getting off."

"Sure! Makes no difference to you. 'Cept maybe we find one too hard to break, then we spend all winter here—high and dry."

The twenty seamen, once the hoses have been rigged, stand like twenty derelicts seeking work. I expect to see the chief materialize on the outside bridge, but nothing. The E.T. is doubtless deep into a tray of exotic food in the C.I.C. shack. The water torrents down into the bottom of the *Northwind*, but the bow has not moved at all. She still points up and out toward the darker grey above the horizon. To the port, free flowing water and chunks of ice/snow—Watley's pipe on one of them—and to the starboard, this canvas of ice stretched now almost to eyesight's limit.

"You ever been high and dry before, George?"

"Not since coupla years, when the old man let an Ensign run her up too high. We try blow torches to get her off. Didn't work. Woo whee. We were set for winter."

"What happened?"

"In the mid-watch, she caved in. Broke her in half and we were free again. Sound like the whole ship buckling. Woo whee!"

"The chief here then?"

George doesn't answer, shouts instead at a group of seamen instruct-ing them to arch the hose up before dropping it below. Useless instruction. Useless command. George moves away.

I feel that I am expanding as the *Northwind* absorbs more and more of the chill water. I blimp internally to the ship's swelling with sea. Watley may feel he's been floating. He wraps strands of lanyard tighter around the connection of hose to pump, but I feel weighted down, foot frozen, bottom heavy.

Pete appears on the bridge. Maybe the first breaking is significant for Pete never leaves his galley. He stands at the railing hunched up against the cold like a superintendent overseeing the foundation of a favorite project. Insanely, he is in a T-shirt.

It suddenly occurs to me: he has left the galley. He's not carrying the pocket book. In an instant I back away from the seamen, sprint up the steps, come into the rear of Officer's Country and hurry to the galley. *Consenting Adults* sits on the narrow counter between the grill and refrigerator. I put it into my shirt and slip back toward the steps.

I stop for water at the mess deck fountain, decide to hide the book in Watley's rack. Everything's so clear. The easy theft, the refreshing drink, the deft disposal. All ice-clear, smoothly accomplished. I actually hear the pre-cise switching of one event into another, one cause to one effect. Running through the starboard passage to return to the forecastle, I trip, sprawl near the head entrance. My arm goes under the impressive grill work. The pass-ing floes are some ten beet below, but I feel momentarily my hand gathering snow. I put my head down on the wet, cold deck. Ear freezes, eyes close, hand squeezes fragile air. Mouth gulps chill sea. I am totally relaxed, one with the *Northwind*.

I wonder, am I hurt? Why mustn't I move? Am I hurt? But it is not nec-essary to move for I feel, probably before anyone else aboard, the *Northwind* begin to move for me. The ship settles. Not much, but enough. The lethal intrusion. The opening wedge. I hear a creaking. Old steel giving out? New ice quaking? Then an increase of crackling—a growing, splintering, finally a crackling waterfall of shattering. And the bow drops. The bow drops like an anvil onto a feather cushion. Sprigs of ice tumble up in the air, plume out from the resonating explosion of the *Northwind's* freeing. The ship shud-ders. The sky goes white with bobbing flocks of sparkling snow. And face pressed against the deck, wet cold cheek laced to the worn steel of the pas-sageway, I think in the thundering breakthrough, I have the fuck-book to look forward to. I have the fuck-book to look forward to.

That night while Watley listens, Dolly explains, "Gordon Schumway, honey, is the biggest promoter this town has ever seen. To be invited to one of his parties, honey, you have arrived. Really arrived. You're in. Why, the things that go on at Schumway's, honey. Your little Midwestern eyes will bug right out of their sockets."

How many passages read aloud? How many repeated descriptions of how many stroking fingers, cupping hands, inserted members? How many mutual risings as I read over and again the golden passages. Watley, his back to me, shuffles his legs, pulls the blanket higher to avoid embarrassment.

When the berthing area lights go out, I wedge *Consenting Adults* between the mattress and the top of my footlocker. The red exit lights heats up a chill darkness. I turn toward Watley's back. I feel the bow rising, pulling up on the ice sheet, rising over the next slab. Watley turns toward me on his side now, his face barely a foot from mine. He sighs, semi-snores. The bow rises further, dumping us down toward the stern, sliding the racks against their chains. I touch Watley's shoulder.

I am primed by Schumway's party, dizzied by Dolly's spread contortions and her endlessly explained rhythm of absorption. Those enveloping thighs. Her kneading hands. I slide my hand down Watley's arm, reaching the lip of the blanket. I watch almost objectively my traveling finger tips and then I feel his hand against my chest. The bow rises further. George must begin soon packing the sea into the hold, the storing for the drop. My hand goes clumsily under the lip of the blanket. His hand goes further down my chest. His eyes are closed and his breathing is studiedly regular, the sleep pattern prevailing. I think, child of unconscious murder. My hand reaches the top of his left hip and I move it, curiously into his groin. His hand comes down below my navel, rubs against what Dolly would call "my rig." My rigid rig and panting for release. I reach through the wide vent of his government-regulated boxer shorts and take hold of him. We begin a mutual motion. He feels thinner than I would have expected. Do I strike him that way? No way to tell. His eyes are relaxed closed and he preserves the sleep aura flawlessly. I watch his face closely. I expect to see him blink, arch an eyebrow, grimace at our ministrations. But nothing. Nothing save studied ignorance. Closed-eye unconsciousness.

"Open your eyes, Watley," I say softly, then repeat. "Open your eyes, Watley. Open your fucking eyes." His acted bliss of sleep-inertia is unendurable. I stop, cuff him on the side of the face, swivel loose of his grasp on me. "Open your fucking eyes, Watley. Goddamn it. See what's going on. Open your fucking eyes!" I am shouting at him now, punching at his face. "You're a lousy actor, you little bastard. Open your fucking eyes. Open 'em up! Look? Look, for Chrissakes, look! Don't give me that crap of 'eh I was dazed or drunk or water-logged. How can I tell what was going on.' Don't give me that crap. Open your fucking eyes!"

"Huh? Huh?" Watley says, raising his arms to fend off my fists.

"Don't give me that unconscious crap. Don't give it to me, you lousy acting bastard. See. See. Go on, look!" I am screaming at him now, hurling a tight right fist as hard as I can into his shoulder, his neck, his forearm-protected face. He rolls away, backs off the rack onto the deck. But in lush anger, I am determined not to let him get away. I lunge through the poles onto his rack, then flop down on top of him.

"You saw him kill him, didn't you, Watley? Didn't you? Admit it. Admit it!" I cannot shout any louder. I have hold of Watley's neck—trying to slam his head down on the steel deck. His eyes roll in moist terror.

"For Chrissakes, what's goin on?" he shouts, bridging to get relief from the slamming I try to carry out. "What's a matter. Cut it out. Cut it out!"

"Knock off the grab ass," voices from the berthing area. I hear the convergence of voices, feet on the deck. They rush toward me.

"He killed him, didn't he, Watley? Didn't he!" I shout, repeating and repeating, as pillows, arms, legs, thrust shoulders, knock me away. I am kicked in the stomach, the thigh, pinned to the deck. Before the final body crush, before the pure immobility of body weight settles, I think: will they believe we were asleep? Will they buy the nightmare excuse?

More days: The door opens about four inches. "Ah, Michigan, what's up?"

"I wondered if I might speak to you, sir."

"Now?"

"Yes, sir."

"I'm making tapes," he keeps the door firmly at its four inch admittance level.

"It's reasonably critical."

"Is, huh?"

"Yes, sir."

He pauses, look directly into my eyes. "Well, all right. Come on in."

There is a Luftansa poster of Bavaria, a poster of London and a large Kodak print of Yosemite National Park on the three white washed walls. On the desk where a tiny Panasonic recorder shows a red recording light, there is a brown plaster cast of praying hands.

"Sending thoughts to the wife and daughter. They like my descriptions of snow and ice."

"Sending them?"

"On the mail copter. Maybe you could add something to them—details about your life in Michigan, for example."

"I wanted to talk to you about a killing."

Ensign Ball smiles, stops the tiny tape recorder. "You and your buddy, the other reserve, getting, along? Want a new rack?"

"No. I don't want a new rack. "

"You don't? I don't want you killing him."

"I'm not talking about killing him."

"Look, guys jack each other off on icebreakers all the time."

"Glad to hear it."

"I don't think you are."

"I'm talking about an actual murder. George killed the chief. He threw the motors into forward, moved the boat deliberately. He dropped the lines. He deliberately sent the chief into the pipes. He murdered him. I saw it. He butchered a man—he killed the chief. Watley was in the boat with me. He saw it too. The other reserve Watley."

"Your rackmate."

"He has the next rack."

"You saw it all?"

"Yes. Saw it all." I lie.

Ball puts the recorder into the top desk drawer. The *Northwind* bow drops. The crunch of broken ice echoes out from her side. Chips flash past the porthole on the starboard side.

"Level again," Ball observes, watching me. "You want to talk about it."

"I just did."

"I don't mean about the 'murder.'" He exaggerates the sound of *murder*.

"That's all I came here to talk about. I want to make sure charges get filed."

"George been hard-assing you, eh?"

"I never see George. I work up here under Pete."

"And why bring Watley into it? What have you got against him, eh? He's just a kid. He's not getting off, you know. He's here for the duration. He's not leaving on the mail copter in a couple of days."

"Couple of days?"

"Sure. Day after tomorrow."

"It's not due for another week."

"Due Friday," he answers, smiling. He goes over to the rack, sits down on the edge. Enviably thick officer's mattress. "You ever hear of being breaker-happy?"

I look at the praying hands.

"Happens to everybody, sooner or later, everybody. Some sooner than others. You get a little nuts just sitting around in a ship for six months. Hell. Hell, look at what I'm doing. Sending snow descriptions home to my wife and kid. No need for that, stateside."

There is a substantial affection in his tone of "stateside." I see him polishing a maroon sedan in the shade of a grey suburb, beneath a silver beech tree. I think about picking up the praying hands, cracking him across the temple with them.

"Why don't you hang on for a couple more days. Till Friday. When you get back stateside, when you've thought about it for a while, then go ahead. Did you really see it? Or did you just think you'd seen it? Why do you really want to get Watley into it.? Questions like that. No problems. Then if you still think you know what happened, then go ahead."

"How?"

"At District. Governor's Island."

"How come the copter's coming early?"

"Is not. Is not."

"Is so. Is so, sir." I try to mimick his inflections.

He rolls his head back. "Michigan, you're a fucking troublemaker. I've seen 'em and seen 'em. I was just like you."

"You weren't."

He gets up off the bed. Thick mattress reshapes itself. I expect to see him whip a knife out, or throw a quick left, maybe butt me in the chest. For the first time I think he is really mad.

"You're just a scroungey seaman," he says softly. Over his shoulder I see old London's lights seem to come on in sparkling color. "I could bust your ass into the bilges from now until the copter comes. Like that, eh?"

"Would not. Would not." I step closer to him. He is shorter, very stocky.

"Are you nuts?" he shouts. "Are you nuts?"

"I want to see the Exec, or the Captain."

"Get out of here. Get out," he nudges me on the chest. I reach for the praying hands. He nudges me harder away from the desk. Stiff shoulder prod with unexpected torque behind it. "That's an order, you scroungey seaman. Get out!" He bats me toward the door, out into the passageway.

"I want to see the Exec."

"I'm going to book you." He slams the door.

In a daze I go back down to the berthing area, sprawl on my rack. Empty rows of racks. I think about sleeping. Pete will never report my absence, and who would roust me out of the rack? I feel I can fall asleep immediately. But the P.A. erupts.

"Seaman Spradlin, lay to the mess deck. Seaman Spradlin, lay to the mess deck. To the mess deck, on the double."

I try to think, where could I be and not hear this? Evidently nowhere except, of course, Officer's Country, but Ball must have spoken directly with Pete. No escape.

George is smiling, laughing. He stands by a tray of garlic pickles. "Woo whee! What you do to Ball? Woo whee! He really pissed. Burned up. Really pissed. Look, John, you get into your scroungiest dungarees and T-shirt. Your tennis shoes. It's really shitty in the bilges." Did he learn "scroungey" from Ball?

"Great. The bilges, what for?"

"This came straight down from the Exec. What you do to Ball?"

I stare at George, briefly flirt with telling exactly the charge I made, but the dark splotches on his face stop me. They seem to dance in anticipation of a fiendish confession. He is ready for an accusation. Probably he has worked out nine contingency plans, from denial to another murder. Does he know?

"Fuck it," I reply.

"Woo whee. You better get changed. Ball come down here himself to make sure you in."

"Fuck it. I'm no snipe."

"Now you are. See a lot of engines. Twenty hours."

Enough until Friday. "How you know this came from the Exec?"

George hands me the Extra Instruction sheet. I think: that takes care of everybody. The Exec's signature is perfectly slanted, perfectly spaced and legible.

There is a small group to bid me farewell into the bilges: George, Canino, two anonymous snipes in sweated T-shirts. The engines throb, pinging, roaring. There is no use talking. George hands me a bucket full of rags, points at the sprawl of pipes below. He gets down on his knees, makes an exaggerated wiping motion, points at the pipes which suddenly seem like a section of intestine through the open hatch. George moves toward the opening. I start down the ladder. Should I wave? Do they close the hatch? Is it twenty straight hours, or a little break for chow? It is too late to ask these questions.

I smile up at them. Canino smiles back. Though the clatter is too monstrous to hear, I see, feel, George shout, "Woo whee!" Then a pipe to my left makes a swinging motion, comes into my shoulder, searing it. I smell the T-shirt burn, and I leap to the right off the ladder into a foot of warm water. The hatch cover comes down.

The clatter is less, but still deafening. Then the lights go out. A moment of pure terror. The water sloshes hotly. My shoulder seems on fire. I try to stand but imagine more swinging pipes. I crouch, then kneel into the slosh. Oil fumes are overwhelming. A match would detonate the place. The lights come on. Although pipes, copper, or chrome, or grey painted, snake all over the crawl space, only a few of them are overhead: one near the ladder, two at the other end, moving hydraulically. I cannot decide whether that is the stern or the bow. The place is steaming hot. Sweat boils out of my forehead, forearms. I am glistening like the overheard chrome turn valves, which move up and down a total of four inches. I imagine them smashing into my head. The lights go out again. Absolute dark. Stupid and careless of me not to use the light to find a place. Stupid, Spradlin. Stupid. And the noise. Some way to overcome the noise. With remarkable clarity, I see the bootcamp rifle instructor walking quickly up and down the line, or rather I see his ear plugs. The flesh colored plugs dance past the prone gunners. I shred a rag from the bucket and fashion two noise tamers, fitting and shoving them into my ears. How the noise hollows away. I *feel* the clattering, a series of dark reverberations in a dark canyon, but I *hear* it less.

Somehow, ears plugged, I seem less vulnerable. The water is soaking upwards from my ankles, reaching higher levels on the dungarees. How can that be? Does the whole place get filled? George's final assignment? Out like a rat in the bilges? Yes. I should try the hatch cover. I crawl back toward the ladder. Just as I am about to grab the first rung, I notice that the water level has receded. Of course! The bow is rising and the water slops toward the stern. Further forward will be high and dry, until the *Northwind* breaks through. There will be a slosh torrent and the process repeats . The perfect resting place would be, therefore, somewhere in the middle. Nifty deduction, Spradlin.

I struggle away from the ladder. The lights come back on. A little touch of the subway in the old arctic. The bow is still rising. I move beyond the ladder. I am now convinced the mid-bilge area is still forward. I climb onto four huge pipes about eight inches in diameter mounted on an ascending oblique. The last one, as I rest my shoulder against it, turns out to be 2000 degrees Farenheit. I roll hysterically away from it. Gordon Schumway laughs: you weren't quite prepared for that one. You should have been. Ecstasy was, how shall we say it, quite something else. The other three pipes are grimy but dry and cooler. The water moves below me. I dangle four fingers in the dark soup.

Okay, survival one: a place dry enough to avoid the water. Survival two: coming up, twenty hours without meals, without sleep, without water, without, ah, excremental relief. The lights go out. I imagine sweet Dolly in the dark speaking to me, but, alas, the clattering bears her voice away. Her soundless ministrations are not sufficient. I cannot arrange my back comfortably. She drifts away. Survival three: the proper vengeance. Concentrate on the proper vengeance. Is that the key to survival two?

I pull up my bucket of rags. I expect the hatch to open, and I am ready to take up pretend cleaning, scrubbing, but it seems mere enclosure will satisfy all authorities. My being in the bilge is sufficient. No task, then, beyond survival. Oil fumes induce nausea, don't they? Had I heard that in some training film years before? "On oil fires the use of fog, low or high velocity fog, or the use of foam is essential. Water streams will merely aggravate the problem." I struggled, then as now, to stay awake. How much more comfortable was the old bootcamp classroom chair than these pipes. And one particular 2nd class petty officer had refined the sleep-disturbing, sleep-annihilating threats: "You guys will stay awake in this class or. . . ." There followed, every session, a new threat—galley duty, extra instruction, liberty denied, hanging around on the weekend, endless close-order drill, push-ups. The threats were more interesting than his prepared lecture on low velocity fog, and I took elaborate notes on the threats. Categorizing them: the nameless cosmic threat: "I don't wear the crow for nothing and I can pull rank fast;" the mundane specific threat: "You 'll stand on one foot till you puke." The list was impressive. He never mentioned the bilges; their terror passed from boot to boot, recruit to recruit, as the ultimate refinement of torture, the threat too grand for threatening. Enjoy, savor it, Spradlin. See into it. Roll, slosh with it. Wallow through the wet end of it. And now in the hollow reverberation I shout, "Light!" But the command is lost in the heat, in the sweating, all-fumed dark.

"Lights!" I shout again. No one responded. They are doubtless thumbing calendars of Bavaria in the engine room—views of beer halls and forested mountains, between gauge watching and thermometer reading, bell listening. "Lights!" I shout once more from my prone position, and the lights this time do come on.

"*It's a nice long way to run to get a hatful of water. I mean ta bring it back here.*" The 2nd class intones. "*I mean it would be quite a feat. Nobody ever does it right the first time. Do they?*"

I think—they never do. Not even Gordon Schumway. Not even deft-fingered Dolly. Enjoy the lights. The bow drops. Even over the shatter of piston-ram and crank-turn, I can hear the splintering of the ice. The water rushes forward.

Steam spurts up as the water reaches previously dry pipes beyond my feet. Make a note, Spradlin, should you leave the lair, the three pipes protection center with its fourth, quite heated remainder, should you leave the lair, there are other, hotter pipes approximately three and one half feet beyond you going north. Ah, yes, north. Remember the hot going before, the searing after. Sear it in mind. But now, only to rest. Survival two, accomplished by celebration of the past, is it not so? A firm feeling that each moment gone is one less to plow through. The endurance block is melting in the oil-fumed, heat-fired day, now night, as the lights go out again. Survival three comes of itself—the product of meditation and the random, thoughtless touching of

2000 degree pipes. Steam ahead and behind. Survival three comes right out of the situation. I imagine the chrome valves in their imprisoned dance—up and down, their four inch lunge, their four inch retract. "Woo whee!" shout the valves. "Honey, your New Jersey eyes will bug out of your New Jersey head when I tell you what I have in mind."

Speak Dolly.

I will close my eyes to listen. I will still the rambling clatter of the bilge, siphon off the noise into those reservoirs yet unacknowledged. Speak, sweet Dolly, speak.

"I came down the dock with a valise, can you believe it? A damn valise full of corn candy and Pamparin. It was to be a hell of a party. But Gordon took the play away from me."

Put away the valise, honey. You've got all the instruments right before you. All you need is to use them. All the instruments, Spradlin. Use them. All you need is to time it right. I simulate sleep by going over and over again the proper timing.

At the ninth hour, a miracle happens. Sandwiches, sealed in thick plastic, come down into the bilge. I see Pete's face for an instant in the opened hatch. And at the fifteenth, cellophane cupcakes from Stephan. I piss across the pipes. Urine is no match for oil. At the seventeenth I begin to puke . But there are no crackers from Notari. It makes no difference. The timing is right. I understand the task. If the copter is on time, then dozens of dry-heaves, acres of them, can't dull the edge I've grown.

Last Day: Stephan and Canino haul me out. Only in the engine room do I realize I reek of vomit.

"Man, get a shower," Canino says turning away.

Stephan cuffs me on the shoulder. "Ya set a record."

I do not answer, merely plod to the head. In violation of the rules, I take a double sea shower. Then Canino and Stephan help me pack.

"How hot down there is it?" Stephan asks, but I go on stuffing the skivvies into the seabag.

"Here, man, lemme do that." Canino takes out the skivvies, then puts in my boondockers, work jacket, a ditty bag of dirty laundry.

"It's very hot. Very unpleasant," I say to Stephan. I watch them, zombie-like.

"The Exec's a prick," Stephan says.

"Yes."

"Well, you're getting off this soon. That's something. We got four more months of this shit."

Canino folds in the dungarees and cambray shirts. Five extra hats never worn.

"Where's George," I ask.

Stephan looks at Canino. Do they know? Have they understood? I expect no reply or mock-thug evasions. But Canino says, "George's up in the storage area, repairing rain gear."

"Look, finish the packing for me, will you? I want to talk to George for a minute."

"The copter's due right now," Stephan answers.

"I know. I know. But I just want to say something to George." I get into my dress, departure uniform. "I'll be right back."

"Right back, hell! You better meet us on the o1 deck. The chief wants you there."

"The chief?"

"That E.T.," Stephan corrects Canino.

"Oh. Hey, where's Watley? With George?"

"Watley's got your old job."

"No shit."

"Yeah, He's working with Pete. The reserves always draw Officer's Country."

"Well, tell him to look out for Ensign Ball." I step away from them, take the passageway past the head to the main deck storage hatch. I lean in. Do I look like the chief against the grey ice sky? One light burns, a dangling bulb. I see George, holding a torn yellow slicker.

"I'm coming down. I'm coming down." I shout, hoping he won't greet me with a marlin spike. But he steadily patches the coat. A small G.E. iron sits upright on a table beside him.

"Plenty hot, eh? Woo whee!" He points below decks to the bilges.

"You said it, George. Lots cooler here."

"Lots."

"You said it, George," my voice goes slower and he looks up, adjusts the slicker across his knees.

"Copter here?" George says.

"No. Where does it land?"

"Land? Woo whee! You are some reserve. It can't land. Drops a line. They strap you in. Then up. Up." He motions, gets up himself, puts aside the slicker. "Yank you right in."

Armless Spradlin swings across the sky over stacked rain gear.

"You killed him, didn't you, George?" I speak smoothly enough—like more small talk before departure.

He smiles, reaches for the lacing needle.

"I don't care, George. I'm getting off. This is my last tour anyway. I'm getting discharged. I don't care. I thought I did, but I don't."

He picks up the needle, bronze colored and thick as a knitting needle. For a moment I feel it go into my eye.

"What you going to do? Stick me with it? I'm trying to tell you, George. I'm not a threat to you. I heard the motors reverse, but I didn't see anything, and I don't care."

"I hear the copter. You better get to the boat deck."

"He was a prick, wasn't he?"

George nods, working the dull point of the lacer into his left palm, as if testing his limit of pain.

"I'm no threat to you, George. I didn't see anything. They'd never believe me. I know. I tried."

The needle wobbles in his palm.

"I'm not interested in telling them again. Besides, I didn't see anything. You can't be a witness if you didn't see anything. And I don't care. I wanted you to know that."

"Woo whee, that copter gonna take the stack off this ship." He stops working the needle, gestures with it toward the ladder.

"But somebody did see, George. Somebody was a witness. I'm getting off, and I don't care. He's still on and he cares. He's a real threat, George. He means to turn you in. And he saw it. Actually saw it."

With his left hand George pulls out his lower lip. His eyes widen.

"You better get Watley before he gets to the Exec. That's if you want my advice." I start sideways up the ladder. I feel terribly vulnerable. He could bury the needle in my side anywhere. The best I could do would be to kick him away. But he is solidly attached to his spot in front of the rain gear, mired in yellow slicker reflection.

"He saw it, George, for Chrissakes. He saw it. He'll tell. You better get him, George, when he's not thinking."

I vault through the hatch.

"Seaman Spradlin, lay to the boat deck on the double."

George starts up the lader. I turn, run to the steps down from the bridge. The air is clear, grey but clear, stainless steel sky. The copter's hovering tosses up a fierce wind on the bridge. I lunge over the stanchions directly onto the boat deck. Canino has disconnected the mail sack, and then fixed my seabag on to be reeled up. I watch the bobbing ascent. Overhead the copter glistens, its blades a mirror wheel smack in the center of the grey sky.

George bounds over the stanchions. I move behind Canino. The E.T. comes out of his shack. He carries the brown envelope of orders.

Stephan helps me on with my pea jacket.

"Where's Watley?" I ask.

"Working with Pete."

"Tell him goodbye."

Stephan smiles, as if sharing something wry and embarrassing.

"Fuck you."

Stephan laughs. The line comes back down. Canino snares it.

"I'm scared shitless," I shout.

"Who wouldn't be?"

But there is a harness this time, a brilliant pink harness which locks under my arms, around my legs. George comes up to me. Does he have the needle? Canino signals for a hoist. I lock my arms in front. The pea jacket feels thick, wonderfully thick. George reaches up. I start to back shuffle, but the first yank drags me up toward the davits.

George suddenly shouts, "He saw?"

I nod furiously, wheeling about to make sure I can kick away from the boats. The second yank is longer, more direct, hauling me free of all superstructure.

"He saw," George repeats.

"Kill him, George. Kill him," I holler back, nodding and nodding.

The third yank comes in a rush, whipping me beyond the *Northwind*, out over the sea which appears dropped away into the center of the earth.

I kick out my legs as if climbing on the air. The *Northwind* turns below me, a somber buff-colored toy in the white of ice and black of sea. I begin a wonderful parabola swing as the copter apparently moves away from the ship. The harness cuts into my shoulders. For a moment I imagine the pink straps unsocketing my arms, which fall flip-flopping like feathers into the water. Oh, armless Spradlin, frozen above the sea. But the pain prevents full, imaginative flight. The drop now is awesome. Were the line to snap now. Ah, that would be a plunge indeed. Nothing to do but turn away, look up, and savor the suddenly affable sky.

The Gondola of Desire

PART I

The End of the Plague

What Donna expected of Venice: soft sunlight, still water, foul smells, beige-pastel buildings shedding their color, canals unstirred like black/green wax floating/surrounding everything (including her best fantasies). What she got: shuddering wind, pails of rainwater thudding into the thick glass doors of Marco Polo airport; pools of rippling water in the sullen cement of the docks leading to gangways of scummy ash planks supremely slippery. And wind that tried to lift her through moist greyness.

And no Claudio to meet her. So a choice. She could go to the Lido, to his apartment and retrieve a key from his wife, or she could risk a bus to the railway station, St. Lucia, then a walk down the Strada Nuova to the alleged apartment where presumably her roommates would be waiting with an extra key. But roommates were unknown and undependable, and she understood that Claudio's wife, Julee–an American from Connecticut, was always home. Surely that was the better bet. Besides, there was a ferry waiting with "To Lido" hanging on the side.

2.

"Of course he didn't meet you," Julee said. "Good Christ, Claudio never meets anyone. He actually thinks it's better that way. Students have to be self-reliant from the moment they set foot in Venice. That's how he thinks.

If you can't read the signs, if you can't speak Italian, then why did you come here? That's the way he thinks. He doesn't say that, but, believe me, that's the way he thinks. He's a Venetian–did you know there are only about 3 million of them in all of history. Aren't you thrilled? Jesus! Who wouldn't be? Go to the frige. And get me a Popelmo. It's the only thing I can drink in my condition," she laughed and pointed to her slightly bulging mid-section.

"Popelmo?"

"Two liter bottle, green, maybe lime green, but darker. Top shelf. Just bring it."

When Donna tried pouring Popelmo into the blue plastic goblet Julee kept on the rattan end table at the edge of the beige couch, Julee took the big bottle away. "I tee up my own drives and I pour my own Popelmo," she laughed, slopping some of the light green liquid over the edge and onto the dark brown lacquered cane of the table top. "Once, Claudio actually ignored meeting his major professor, if you can believe it. Still, he's always extremely lucky. When the poor fellow got here, about four hours later, he was winded, lugging two giant bags, but he actually thanked Claudio for not being there—'taught me how to survive here right out of the box ,' he said full of good cheer that, A: He'd made it to this dump. And B: Learned you can't depend on Claudio. But of course you have to. Just the relationship he likes. You better believe it. I'm still hoping he'll find some willing Venetian honey, so I can go back to Maryland. We didn't plan this child. I told him I wasn't ready, but did I mention he doesn't listen? Maybe you don't want to hear all this?"

"I don't mind."

"A ringing affirmation of my penchant for self-revelation. Want some Popelmo yourself? And if you say yes, that commits you to getting more for me at Standa near the boat docks before you go over."

"I don't want any, thanks." Donna answered.

"You're a quick study, and that means he'll want to sleep with you soon. Before Redentore, so look out. It's not that I mind. Believe me, I don't, but if you do, you have to commit to taking care of the bambina–yes it's a girl. Will you do that? And I mean stay here and let me go back to Maryland. I'm tired of his macho bullshit."

The phrase lingered in the rainy afternoon through the open screen-less giant windows. And to steer away from surprising embarrassment, Julee asked, "What's your dig?"

"The Lazaretto."

"You bring bug spray?"

"Yes."

"Heavy, really heavy on the Deet, I hope."

"I don't know."

"Well you'll learn fast enough on the Lazaretto. I expect he's planning for you to sleep there."

"Yes."

"Jesus! In what? Tents? There's not even toilets there. Did you know that?"

"Claudio said it would be somewhat primitive."

"Oh that's him all right. Somewhat primitive. Jesus! I love it. Somewhat primitive. Sums him up, you know that? Somewhat primitive. Oh, I thought it was so, so Italian, so captivating once. He can be suave, you know, skillfully hiding that ego the size of Cleveland–that scheming mind. It's all very Venetian, you know. He'll tell you that, as he sticks you for whatever it is that he wants. And he'll stick you, all right." She let the phrase linger in the humid air. "But all you came for was a key, right?"

Just before releasing the key ring with its dangling tag, Julee said, "And as a junior archeologist, you're dying to dig, right? It means everything to you, right?"

"It's better than another summer with my folks in New Hampshire," Donna answered.

3.

The vaporetto from Lido to Rialto took thirty minutes and even in the grey, spraying rain Donna still deliberately chose the right rear fantail seat unprotected from the elements. From that vantage point she could see the colonnades of trees, almost a thousand strong on the eastern edge of Venice, St. Elena, as if God, she imagined, stored up dark greenery against its absence in the rest of Venice . The tree flood ran abruptly against the enormous parked yachts and ended behind an over-mammoth cruise liner, ten decks high, discharging its umbrellaed masses on the embankment beyond the entrance to the old Arsenal. The black-bulbed umbrellas waddled slowly through the rain, up Riva deghli Schavione toward San Marco square.

By leaning out beyond her railing she could see the campanile spearing above the square and marred by scaffolding on two sides. Repair work undermined the effect she thought, but had proved useful to the demonstrators some weeks before, who scaled the pipework to proclaim the New Republic of Venice, the most serene independent entity to detach itself from the Italian state. Amid huzzahs and laughter from the crowd in the square, the revolutionaries were all arrested and incarcerated west of Verona. Their assault weapon had been a yellow rubber amphibian landing craft driven directly out of the lagoon onto the flagments of San Marco, and discharging its ten "Soldiers of Venetian Independence" with bull horns to scale the scaffolding. "It was more fun than Carnivale" Claudio had said in lecture back in Boston. "And for a moment Venice the supreme city state seemed to proclaim its dominance over the Adriatic, but, alas, not for long. The Carabineri quickly rounded the rebels up."

"And where are they now?" a student asked.

"Waiting for you to rescue them and restore Venice to its former prestige." Claudio answered. "You get your chance in just three weeks. And you'll need my help. My connections. My translations. They won't come cheap. You'll work harder than you've ever worked in your brief lives. But you'll love doing it. In work, liberation!"

"Do we have to wear brown shirts?"

"He made the trains run on time," Claudio answered, as if to discourage occasional rumors that his father had worked for, benefited from, Mussolini. "If brown shirts make you work harder, then wear brown shirts. Actually, no one will care. . . . You think I'm funning you? There's no interest in fascism now in Venice. Too many visitors. Maybe 20 million this year alone. Think about it. Two New York Cities passing through. Two New Yorks."

It seemed one New York already filled the mini campo down from the north side of the Rialto Bridge. Bodies wedged into the street, eddying around the three ATM machines that studded the perimeter. Bodies sitting on the edge of the statue in the center, bodies resting against the glass of shops. Donna found her way finally through the mob and slipped into the archway of an alley that led apparently nowhere. Yes, there was, just as Julee had described it, a dark red door which her giant key opened, leading to a narrow hall at the end of which was a tiny three-person elevator behind a sliding metal grid. The lift took her to what seemed to be a fourth floor. The grid on that level was oily and grimy and marked her soft hand, as she yanked in to one side. Claudio stood in the doorway, watching her.

"You're strong enough," he said, smiling.

"And dirty too," she added.

"Actually quite clean. Tourism requires no smoke stacks. The grit is all on Murano, maybe. That would be interesting to measure—another project: collect data on the particulates in the air in the Rialto versus, say, the edge of Cannaregio. No handling dirt. No trenches. Should I switch you?"

"I thought you said you'd meet me."

"I don't think I promised. And now you know how to get to the Lido and to here. Independence is knowledge." He smiled again. "I had a chance to talk with Tito about the dig and that's the most important thing."

"Apparently."

"It truly is. You'll get that as soon as you start in the trench." He leaned against the door jamb as if trying to press his back against the wood to lessen the protrusion of his stomach. His mustache had thickened since she'd seen him Boston, or so she thought, and it seemed he was heftier, though not fat, but the web belt was cinched too tightly so that some of the dark blue sport shirt lapped the buckle. His relaxed legs were crossed displaying one of his tan boat shoes blatantly. Parts of his hair were prematurely grey although she was certain he was still in his thirties. There was a soft spoken relentless lilt to his voice, as if inviting everyone to hushed conversation. He tended to fix on you as you spoke, and that was disturbing to her, but at the same time enveloping and beguiling.

"Can I see the apartment?" she asked moving toward him.

"I guess you're old enough," he answered smiling.

An oddly accented voice came from inside the apartment, "Yes, she's quite old enough. We all are. Welcome to Rialto where the crowd never disperses and you can hear the ATM machines all night long. I'm Shilpa." A tall Indian girl in blue jeans and a black T shirt with some English across the front proclaiming: *Let's Sports Violent All The Day Long!* walked toward her. "I got this in Osaka. It's perfect for this crowded, silly place." She paused and said, "I mean both this apartment and the campo."

Claudio pulled Donna's bags in from the elevator which was buzzing since somebody down below needed it. "I see you didn't take my advice about packing," he said.

"You didn't meet me," Donna answered.

"I promise to meet you at the office tomorrow at 9:00 for a cappuccino. That's my apology."

"The term doesn't start until Monday," Shilpa said.

"So you both can come. It will be expensive but worth it," Claudio said. "Now unpack and buy some trinkets by the bridge. And study your map of the Lazaretto."

"Your wife needs more Popelmo." Donna said interested to see how he would take the statement.

"She doesn't," he answered smiling, and letting the definitiveness of the assertion linger above the crowd noises. It seemed he was checking her response to his decisiveness, but then added, "There's a case of the stuff on the back stairway. She forgets that."

"Important information," Donna said.

"What's Popelmo?" Shilpa asked.

"A very dangerous drug, worse than a spritz." Claudio answered. "Better stick to spritzes or Prosecco. See you tomorrow." He took the stairs down.

4.

In the morning they took a vaporetto to Claudio's office— only one stop away from Rialto, it would have been faster to walk, but Shilpa insisted the view on the canal in the earliest morning was transfixing. Empty and icy smooth the canal stretched behind them with buildings like enormous clothes lines of colorful laundry hanging on both sides of the water. No sounds beyond the gentle insistent chug of the vaporetto's engine. Only a few commuters on board, a stray seagull overhead and the morning sun dappling the stacked cargo at the Rialto market. Only an occasional cargo boat with its T-shirted cargo man straddling the rudder control and smoking as his thighs guided the vessel away from the vaporetto. Donna thought, who would not want to paint this scene? Enshrine this scene in some permanent memory. Wouldn't traders from east and west imagine they had stumbled upon a civilization at another plateau of development, a nest of artistry beyond all duplication, or even conception? Or was this only an imitation of Istanbul?

Claudio's office was more prosaic. On the first floor with bookcases on crates to survive the periodic flooding. Reams of student project reports in tortoise shell cardboard bindings, acres of CDs dutifully recording miles of data: canal sewage changes over time, outdoor art listings with prioritized recommendations for restoration including detailed task analyses, even cost estimates per date of the project, fotos of the extant flagstaffs in Venice, and well-heads, leaning towers, docks, bridges, tie-up spots, violated parking spaces, past hunting lodges on near-islands in the lagoon; feasibility studies for kiosks with tourist information, data bases of all boats in Venice, studies of foundation damage caused by motorized boat traffic in the canals; and, lately, archeological studies of remote islands. Claudio and Tito, in particular, seemed intent on proving that Romans and Etruscans were first in Venice, long before fleeing barbarians—perhaps proving that Venice actually sired Rome, and, as the original founder should be again the center of Europe, as well as the best bridge to Asia minor.

Over a small hot cup of cappuccino Claudio explained that recently in a foray through Venice's archives (he was good friends with one of the archivists) he had actually handled the letter of 1212 from the King of England requesting four ships is built for the crusade to Jerusalem. "The actual King's seal was at the bottom of the parchment," he said, eyes gleaming, and with an immensely self-pleased smile. "But we've no time to lose. Since you're early, we can sprint to the boat leaving for the Lazaretto."

"We're not dressed for digging," Shilpa insisted.

"We're not digging, just learning. You'll see what you need to do." He finished his drink in a single gulp. He led them through winding calli to the outside, to the Fondamenta Nuove, and down to the boat dock opposite San Michele, the cemetery island. He signaled the boat captain, a friend from childhood days, he said later, to wait as he guided Donna and Shilpa on.

5.

"You only get 12 years there," Claudio pointed to the neat hedges of the cemetery island.

"Then what?" Shilpa said.

"Then they dig you up and take you away. Who knows, maybe somewhere out in the Adriatic–sometimes the water there does seem fleshy and boney." Claudio smiled. "On the other hand the 12 years are very good ones, very neat ones, very pretty ones. And maybe Wagner is wandering about."

The vaporetto rounded the end of Saint Elena and tracked south along the western edge of the Lido. In the expanse of the lagoon, the sky grew bluer and bolder, shimmering above the waters that lightly misted in the distance. "The lagoon is deep only in certain spots, sometimes only four or five feet down, but over 300 square miles, if you were to sail it all around, or row it." Claudio said, in lecture mode. "But the Lazaretto is near the south end of the Lido, not tucked away in the lagoon. I once thought about building a bridge over to it, but of course that's not feasible. Not really feasible, but certainly imaginable. I like to think of things that aren't really feasible. Sometimes they become so. Don't you think?" he said staring at Donna.

She didn't answer, turned away to savor the distant mist and the pervasive blueness, and the heat boiling up from the vaporetto's hull slicing through the green/blue sea.

Soon enough the Lazaretto came into view, a few board boat docks stuck out into the lagoon and attached to them a series of flat lands full of scrub pine, shrubbery and hay fields apparently. There was one building, hangar-like, with a tin roof and faded red wooden sides.

There were narrow horizontal windows just below the roof line, the full length of the building.

About midway down the dock there were two car batteries with wires attached over the dock's edge and into the water. "We're testing whether some kind of sea water electrolysis will add substance to Istrian stones under water. Maybe electrically we can strengthen Venetian foundations." Claudio explained.

"You're not serious," Shilpa said.

"Oh, it's worth a shot," Claudio replied. "I'm not saying it's the most advanced technology, but it's worth a try. Besides you can see some build-up. I could pull up a block for you."

"Don't," Shipa said.

"Yes, let's not be confused by evidence. Facts are always troubling," Claudio answered.

"I'll wait for the Salute to be elevated a few feet, before I'll accept your electrolysis." Shilpa said.

"The church of the Miracoli is sinking," Claudio countered. "Wouldn't you do anything to prop it up?"

"All Venice is sinking," Donna said. "Or the water is rising."

"And car batteries won't help," Shilpa added.

"Venetian technology could build a galleon in three days," Claudio said. "Every three days, and in the Veneto trees suitable for keels were numbered and cultivated. Numbered for inspection and eventual use. That's what's meant by Venetian craftsmanship. Rebuilding Istrian stone is only another example."

"Proof you're a Venetian, is that it?"

"Absolutely."

When they were inside the building two students, Rolf and Pierre, joined them but initially said little. Claudio poured lemonade for the group and holding their paper cups they updated him on the dig.

Prompted by Claudio they told her there had been a Franciscan church on the site but it had fallen away when the brothers moved to a different island and built a more magnificent monastery. But someone in the archives had discovered those early monks built their church over another church, a much earlier Byzantine one, and there had been speculation that the Byzantine church itself rested on top of some Etruscan or Roman temple. Only digging could provide the evidence. And a national Italian archeological club took up the task with enthusiasm. But after two summers of weekend digging, gave up the ghost. The heat and mosquitoes won, although the Sunday mid-day pasta and seafood meals had been memorable, and watered red wine overflowed.

Everyone went outside to observe the carefully marked trenches.

Lines of string criss-crossed the 100 foot dirt patch; rectangles had been strung out and there were kneeling pads at certain corners of the string work.

"There's nothing here," Pierre said, in khaki shorts and a faded green T shirt stained with sweat. "We need to move the site another thirty feet away toward the back."

"Why?" Claudio asked.

"I think the shore line has changed in the last five hundred years–the map is wrong."

"Luciano was a meticulous map maker." Claudio countered.

"But he can't hold the tides back," Pierre said.

"Thirty feet is too much. Maybe we should move ten or twelve feet back, not thirty. We'd move off the target. Incremental moving. I've told you that before."

"But the water line has changed a lot."

"And you know that because you have three hundred year old maps to superimpose on the oldest, is that it? Or does Google not go back that far?"

"I don't know." Pierre said.

"Map Info might," Rolf said.

"It doesn't," Claudio said. "Move it back 15 feet and dig another two levels down. I'll be sending you three more trench workers, next Thursday."

"Before Redentore?" Pierre asked.

"Yes," Claudio smiled, "before Redentore. Thursday comes before Saturday."

"We're negotiating a boat, a cargo boat, for the celebration."

"Good luck with that. Bring all the cash you can find. "

"I know," Pierre said. "We'll have enough."

"You can never have enough for Luigino," Claudio said. "Unless you can find him a girl. Then he'll settle for a fixed price, if he thinks the girl will like him. Will you like him, Donna?"

"Only if he meets me at the airport," Donna answered.

"Ah very good," Claudio said. "I'll speak to Luigino. But you won't have to join his cargo boat. You can come on my smaller and more maneuverable one."

"What are you talking about?" Shilpa asked.

"The biggest festival in Venice during the summer," Pierre said. "Redentore–celebrating the end of the plague, back in the 16th century. Party boats up and down the Grand Canal, all the grappa you can drink, all the watermelon you can eat, and fireworks for almost an hour at midnight. The digging team is renting Luigino's cargo boat. At midnight all the boats tie off each other and fill the lagoon from San Marco over to Maggiore."

"And a special boat bridge for 24 hours from Zattere over to Guidecca, so that you can walk across the sea–the only time during the year. "Claudio said. "A marvel of Venetian boat engineering."

"The boats Wellington used to defeat Napoleon at Waterloo were all built in India, did you know that?" Shilpa said.

"I'm impressed," Claudio said. "I'm very impressed."

6.

When the return vaporetto docked opposite San Michele, Claudio said goodbye to Shilpa and guided Donna inside the restaurant, Algiubagio, across from the dock. "They make the best spritz in Venice," he said to her then ordered two. "It's a drink you can only get in Venice. No place in Italy understands what the drink consists of–an apple liquor, Aperol, and white wine and carbonation (sometimes Prosecco for both) and two olives on a stick and a disk of orange, or maybe a lemon peel. Magic!" he said with emphasis. He took hold of her elbow in a grip that suggested affection, as well as control, guiding her closer into the bar.

The spritz, golden orange in the evening, red sky billowing beyond San Michele, quickly diminished whatever truculence had been in the gesture. The first olive was succulent, soft and mesmerizing as she probed for the pit.

"Let the second soak a while," Claudio said smiling. "Let it soak and then flick it around a while in your mouth. Savor it."

She was aware he was looking into her eyes, but she deflected that by staring at the swirl of magical orange in the spritz. For just a moment she thought she was seeing double as the second spritz was set down beside the first.

"I'm not sure I can handle two," she said.

"Oh, you can. It's not the alcohol. It's the color, and the evening, you might not be able to handle. We'll get something to eat outside beside the dock. This place makes the best "pesto con naomi" in Venice."

She tackled the second spritz when they were at the dockside table.

Claudio said, "We'll listen carefully to the little lapping water right here, and we'll twirl our pesto with elegant competence and we'll sip our spritzes and perhaps drink some Chianti with the pasta and then, then—who knows what will happen. Certainly a traghetto to the other side and maybe a walk down to look at Wagner's favorite painting, followed by some gelato at my favorite spot near the Frari. And then who knows? Whatever you'd like."

"I'm still stuck on the olives," Donna said.

"Fine, we'll get more olives," Claudio answered. And soon enough two more spritzes arrived, along with a bottle of Chianti. Then staring out at San Michele Claudio said." It's important to be able to stand on the traghetto. If you have to sit down in the gondola everyone will know you're not Italian. Only foreigners sit. If you want to pass for a native you have to stand, ignoring the unbalance across the canal. Can you do that?"

"You want me to appear Italian?" Donna said.

"Of course! Who wouldn't want to?" he laughed.

But on the traghetto he took hold of her elbows and steadied her pulling her into him so that she took on his balance. "Initially it takes help to be Venetian," he said quietly. "Besides there is real danger. The last traghetto is usually packed and very unstable." As if recognition of his voice the gondola lurched a bit, swayed over to the left and then righted itself beyond the center line. In mid canal, waves from a passing vaporetto set the gondola rocking again. She eased back into him and he spread his legs to pull her buttocks in tighter to him. She closed her eyes and imagined the scene as if on a subway with others pushing into her too, but she knew the gondola was not that full. His hands released her upper arms and encircled her completely, locking his fingers together. The air, the spritzes, the cool evening breeze and the slosh of the canal wash played with her imagination again, but not a subway, something more majestic, ingratiating, captivating. It seemed a distant string orchestra was toying with some Vivaldi, or maybe Marcello. A mild adagio wafting in the canal currents.

And then there was a jersey- striped gondolier reaching out to take her out of Claudio's encirclement, pulling her upwards toward some firmer ground, surer footing. Momentary unbalance forcing compensation for the canal rock, Claudio's closeness. A wave of nausea at once fearful and delicious flooded into her.

"I need to sit down," she said.

"The Frari's very nearby," he answered pulling at her, tugging at her through dark calli, until they reached the bridge and steps into the little campo before the Frari. He locked an arm around her and whispered, "You can hear vespers, which means we can pretend to be Catholic and look at the painting for free."

"Pretend?" she said slowly.

"Of course," he answered, "unless you want to part with Euros. Do you?"

"I don't have any."

"Then just stick out your tongue for the Eucharist. And no wine."

Taking her arm, Claudio steered her right by the formidable gentlemen apparently able to discern cheating tourists from earnest believers. Claudio waved him off with panache and palpable piety.

The Frari was truly dark. She sensed mausoleums to her left and right and swerved around one with elaborate statuary directly in their path. Male voices chanting in lulling tones from the choir's elaborately carved benches framing the view to the altar, and beyond the altar, towering above the altar cross was Titian's immense painting. Stretching beyond the width of the altar and proceeding upwards as if to meld into the ultimate overhead archway linked, apparently, to the celestial sphere itself, the painting was segmented into three sections stacked on high.

The lowest section depicted disciples, men only, she noted, in brilliant colors with arms extended, gesturing toward, perhaps beseeching, the ascending Mary, the mother of God being inducted whole and inviolate into the realm of the almighty, her swirling, flowing crimson, fire-red gown catapulting her upwards, her arms extended toward the third section—God himself, a male head on a black cape across the painting's top. Godhead as darkness and bearded compassion, oddly truncated into some remnant as if shot out from one's own most hidden psyche and sheathed in darkness like a giant ink blot. Why would she be seeking such darkness and dank absorbency? Perhaps because just below the Lord was a nebula of golden light, a brightness as if the sun itself resided somewhere under the darkness of God's truncation, tied above the light by a young angel on the right and a baby cherubim on the left. The light between Mary and God was so transporting as if to suggest a suffusion of such power as to suction in all counter-will.

The cloud on which Mary stood was apparently transported upwards by a myriad of cherubim, angelic babies curled in, and through, and below, the billows.

"Depending on the light, I counted 27 of the babies," Claudio whispered. "But my students thought God was a giant bat."

"God as bat," Donna repeated, smiling.

Mary's gown was so gorgeously twisted as to suggest she was beginning to twirl on the ascent, and the dark green/black shawl whipped across the redness in her assumption. The saints below seemed to be beckoning her back. "Are they beseeching her to return to be with them? "Donna asked.

Claudio turned to her and whispered again, since the priest was saying something at the altar, "Some Venetians think they are pushing her away. Good riddance to the virgin mother."

Donna took up the thought, "And the way she is holding her hands extended to God she's saying please free me from this bevy of baby penises."

"Exactly," Claudio said. "Or maybe those extended palms of hers are saying, push me back among the earthly saints, out of the light and into delicious, adult flesh." He paused and then said with a peculiar solemnity, "We mustn't banter before such artistry. We should only kneel and let its incredible energy sweep us upwards."

"Such impressive piety," she answered, too quickly she thought.

But Claudio had slipped down off the pew and was kneeling on the grey cushion he had unhooked and placed on the worn marble floor.

7.

Redentore celebrations began around 11:00 a.m. on Saturday but took on a more serious, aggressive tone by 2:00 p.m. Cargo boats, emptied of wares, now held folding chairs around the inboard engine cover, and gradually the seats filled. Candelabras appeared on the makeshift table tops, and mounds of watermelon, fried chicken, grilled fish, platters of salad and antipasto. Vaporettos skirted to the side of the Grand Canal and soon enough stopped altogether as the cargo boat parties flooded up and back the waterway. If palaces along the canal had upper balconies or open windows, they filled with heads to cheer on the revelry. And after an hour of drizzle the Venetian sky cleared, a mild stenciled blue with wisps/lines of silver grey clouds. Even the waters seemed to lighten a bit, achieving a green/black that suggested below the oily surface some cleansing wash from the Adriatic had somehow drifted through the lagoon. Conflicting recorded music played across the canal surface, matching the coloring of the oil scum, but then were immediately furrowed by the crowded wakes of the rollicking cargo boats.

Luigino's boat took on Claudio's students from the vacant plaza that usually held the Rialto fish and vegetable market. Claudio tucked his small boat behind Luigino's and motioned to Donna.

"You won't regret missing Luigino's bigger party. A lot of students end up peeing off the boat. Ours will be more refined," Claudio said, extending his left arm up to Donna. But she fixed on the much larger fellow who suddenly lurched forward from the tiny boat's stern.

For a moment he had been draped over the boat's 5 horsepower outboard motor and in her delight at avoiding Luigino's frolic, Donna had assumed the fellow was actually part of the motor. He had a large, rubbery face, some extra chins, and an extra narrow roll of stomach visible through a stretched banlon blue shirt.

"I'm Hugh Frendell," he said quietly, holding his right hand up to her. "Vacuum Sewers."

"What?" Donna asked far too quickly she realized.

"My firm makes vacuum sewers. Precisely what Venice needs." He eased her down onto the seat beside Claudio. "I come every Redentore, and Claudio takes me out on his boat. It's terrific, if it doesn't rain. Perhaps the best fireworks, certainly in all of Europe, maybe among all industrial countries. I'm thinking the Chinese must have something superior. They invented this kind of celebration, so you'd imagine they'd have the latest wrinkles, but maybe not."

Did Hugh's presence mean the end of romance? It would be like Claudio to forget about prior engagements, annual promises.

"Vacuum sewers?" Donna asked as the boat drifted back into the Grand Canal.

"Piped to central facility on the mainland, near the Mestre port. Currently the big hotels use a constant tanker service emptying waste kept in bins in their basements. Only residents use the original pipes to the canals, which often are corroded and leaking into the substructures anyway. Vacuum would be the most up-to-date facility, and Venice from its earliest days led the way in waste disposal. In the 12th century the city was the healthiest place in Europe, solid-waste wise. Why not again?"

Claudio, having heard the pitch before passed Donna a jug of Julia Grappa, and a narrow green plastic cup. "Pour a few fingers" he instructed, as if to compensate for Hugh's incantation.

"Why not again?" Donna echoed, drinking the grappa down in a single, hot, searing, choking swallow.

Claudio guided the small boat into the middle of the canal and suddenly there were cargo boats filled with revelers on either side. The pace of patrol dramatically slowed as they got toward the low end of the canal. Boats clogged the waterway under the Academia bridge and by the Salute church it seemed you could simply walk across boats to reach the island of San Giorgio Maggiore in the bay opposite San Marco. Gradually the tying off linked the boats together, but there was still enough wiggle room for Claudio to guide his small boat out further off shore from San Marco.

"We want to be right under the display, with bits of cardboard from the explosions coming directly down on us. That's the perfect spot to get the full effect." Claudio said.

"Some of the cardboard is quite hot," Hugh said. "Some of these people actually put up umbrellas to keep the debris off them. They tend to get quite excited, because the display is really quite first rate. Amazing. But most people, especially here, are like this," Hugh traced and undulating curve in the air, up and down with his right hand, "but I'm like this," he traced a straight slow moving line. Isn't that right, Claudio?"

"Hugh doesn't get ruffled," Claudio agreed. "He's steady, very steady."

"Yes, I'm very steady." Hugh concurred, redrawing the horizontal line in the air.

"So now we eat watermelon and drink grappa, and in a while the fireworks will redeem every boring moment." Claudio said. "Hugh, keep the bowline handy. Somebody will want to tie off. Just pass it to them. I'll link back here." Claudio poured himself another three ounces of grappa. He sat back down beside Donna. "Some day I'll take you to Bassano for the best grappa in Italy. You can choose from hundreds. There's a bar at the end of the bridge that has the best stock in the country. I'll make you a grappa connoisseur. Everything's better with grappa. Everything!"

"Even the fireworks?" she answered.

"Even you," he laughed, then leaned forward to pass a cup of grappa to Hugh.

"Afterwards we'll go over to the Lido and watch the sunrise."

"Not with me," Hugh said. "You can drop me off at St. Elena."

So, Donna thought, some of the evening will be Hugh-less.

But as if to play with her anxiety, Claudio said," You'll miss the best part—the orange fireworks can't match the sun's coming up."

"I agree on the spectrum, but there's no appreciation if you're asleep. My sleep after 1 a.m. is automatic."

"Steady and inevitable," Donna whispered. "Very steady." She sucked the tip of a small triangle of watermelon, one of many tossed onto a doubled paper platter.

"Orange is the distinctive coloring I remember here from the past. Unbelievable weeping willow trees of orange branches dropping down over you, as if the forest was on fire in the sky. Cascade after cascade of orange lines arching over everything and then bits of paper and cardboard filtering down. And each year more extravagant than the last. More orange, more weeping willows, more central bangs. It's all a matter of expenditure. This Redentore it's rumored they spent over a million Euros." Hugh said. "Weeping willows of orange. Explosions descending slowly. Unbelievable."

Donna finished her grappa and lolled against Claudio, eventually able to close her eyes and rock sweetly with the lolling boat. She whispered, "You should record him for Venetian publicity. Redentore with Frendell. Hugh and the fireworks beyond all imagining."

"Drink up," Claudio answered, pouring her another.

"It may be necessary to have a gravity fed section of the piping to Mestre. We may need to elevate a collection station," Hugh said.

"Before or after the fireworks?" Donna said.

"We'll let the Venetian officials decide that," Hugh answered, chuckling and apparently immensely pleased with his response.

Donna finished the grappa, then ate another triangle of watermelon.

"Maybe on top of the car park at Ferro Via," Hugh continued. "That's plenty high enough."

"Too high," Claudio said.

"Perhaps," Hugh answered, offering his bowline to a larger inboard boat whose smiling Captain looped the line around a cleat, and offered a bottle of grappa to Hugh.

"Take a swig," Claudio directed.

"I'm not a grappa fan," Hugh said.

"Take a swig. Don't be rude. We might need his bathroom."

Hugh hoisted the bottle then passed it to Claudio and Donna, determined, apparently, that if he had to follow orders, so did they.

When the bottle made its way back to the Captain, he, too, took a swig.

"So much for shared trench mouth," Hugh said, then thanked the fellow, who continued to smile widely.

8.

As the darkness thickened overhead, even as the gentle orangeness of boat lights increased on the water line, Claudio leaned forward and brought out two thin blue pillows which he put on the bottom of the boat in front of the seat. He lowered himself onto one of the pillows and motioned for Donna to join him. When she did, he slid further toward the bow and put his legs over the starboard edge of the boat. She did likewise over the port side.

They could then rest part of their shoulders and neck on the empty boat seat, and stare straight up for the fireworks. More grappa eased the pain of the position, as did periodic sleep and mild nuzzling.

The first rocket scratched a brilliant white trail on ascent through the black sky, and then puffed into an orange cascade.

"Ah," Hugh shouted, "the first weeping willow and always the best."

And the luminous orange tracery wept into branches out of branches that fitted a cap over the boats, just as the thunderclap and shuddering of its explosion filtered down through the light.

Claudio said, "Orgasmal!" and toasted the opening volley. "Tchin! Tchin!"

Abruptly four more rockets soared upwards. Two were simple white flash bombs, noisemakers, but the two others scattered purple streamers that suddenly ignited into mini stars of redness, almost concurrent with their rifle-fire sounds, and then faded instantly.

"An opening superior to last year's," Hugh said, "and time for the parasol."

Donna swiveled to see him open a very small purple umbrella, just as bits of burnt cardboard drifted down out of the darkness, clicking as they hit the assembled, captive boats. A dozen more rockets screeched aloft, whistling and hissing as they ascended. Detonations scattered a confetti of lights—reds, oranges, blues, green and streamers of yellow, culminating in yet more silver detonations. The scent of burning filled the cloudy air and flecks of blackened cardboard tumbled across the assembled boats. As the detonations escalated so did the shouting from the boats.

"Primal," Hugh said, "absolutely primal! An invitation to one's origins."

Claudio draped his arm around Donna and rolled his eyes at the commentary from the stern.

She understood Hugh's declarations were a kind of license to go further into intimate contact toward outright desire.

Hugh said, "And what do we have here? A loving couple's exploratory embrace? How appropriate in Venice, in the most gala night of all."

"Be quiet, Hugh." Claudio said, turning and kissing Donna with slow, tentative fervor, his tongue just playing with the tip of her lips. Overhead a lattice of orange light seemed to clamp her into the crook of his tightening arm, and she felt his left leg slowly fall onto, then over, her right one. He swiveled up to push his tongue deeper through her lips. His knee nudged further up her leg, gently pressuring her thighs and pelvis. His tongue went further into her mouth, and that exploration rinsed with grappa and cascading light overhead seemed spectacularly beyond regulation, a flow that simply cut a channel through the painful darkness, then illumination, then profound clatter. Whatever occurred surely nothing could consummate given the fat observer in the stern doubtless about to make some inane commentary on whatever it was he saw via explosions of light. And that possibility of commentary liberated her to test the limits of Hugh's receptivity. Could she drive him off the boat? Send him screaming toward the Arsenale, bounding across the tied-off boats, leaping deftly from deck to deck until he plunged into the crowds sitting on the riva? How much witnessing would catapult him to shore? Time to see, so she let Claudio roll further on top of her, let his tongue probe the most sensitive back part of the roof of her mouth, let his knee move circularly across her pelvis only to be replaced by Claudio's cupped right hand massaging what the knee had softened and melted.

"Time to check out the facilities next door," Hugh said, rocking the boat as he stood up, turned, stepped on his seat and launched himself onto the deck of the adjacent yacht, an agile move indeed requiring him to step over the thin chain looping along the port side of the yacht, a foot off the deck.

"Toilet? Toilet?" Hugh shouted to the patrons lying on the deck. The beefy Captain sat upright and pointed toward a brass banister in the yacht's center. Hugh disappeared down apparent steps by the banister.

Donna felt Claudio ease off a bit working his hand, but lolling on his hardness pressing her above his hand.

When in memory she sorted through what ensued, she never quite accepted or embraced each time's assembly of ordered events. Except she always accepted that, yes, she was kissing and embracing Claudio in the wet bottom of the tiny boat, and the sky overhead was raging with billows of color and tracings of silver, detonations of delight. And there was a delirious scent of watermelon and grappa all pervasive in their mouths as the kisses grew more fervent, more exploratory. And the boozy rapture was surely filmic, an echo of the end of "To Catch a Thief "and like a movie not exactly, at least in the boat setting, capable of full realization. Moreover, there was the possibility of the reappearance of Vacuum Sewers man. Thus lust was unconditional having been truncated from the start. Or so it seemed. She was aware of loosened clothing, clutching arms, harder pushing. And always orange overhead explosions.

At some point the boat was untethered at the stern—was Hugh wildly gesticulating from the deck of the yacht as the boat drifted beyond leaping distance? It was impossible to say, given the grappa and the illumined sky, the falling burning cardboard. And then Claudio was off of her, releasing the boat at the bow. He deftly stepped aft, started the engine and soon enough they were slowly churning through the remaining boats—cinders still spiraling down.

From the blue cushion she asked, "What's going on? Where are we going?"

"A spot at the end of St. Elena. You'll like it," Claudio answered, pre-occupied.

"But the display isn't over."

"The best is over."

"And Hugh?"

"He'll be fine. He'll be very fine."

"Good. We don't have to worry about him."

Claudio said, "I don't think we were ever worrying about him." He drove the boat up on a narrow tongue of beach about five hundred feet beyond the St. Elena boat stop. The sand path extended back into a several large mangrove bushes. He rocked and stopped the engine, leaped out into the water and pushed the boat further up the beach path.

"Come on," he called grabbing her hand and pulling her out of the boat.

She liked being hauled out of the boat, although it seemed the path was rocking back and forth into the bushes. "It's weaving," she said, fighting back a giggle. Were the Virgin Mary's hands seeking a grasp or pushing the heavy bat away? Donna couldn't tell and the quandary seemed more and more comical. Wonderfully liberating and laughable.

"What's going on?" Claudio said, flopping her down and landing half on top of her. The sand was unexpectedly hard, though still undulating, and wet. Cold and wet through the back of her blouse. But that, too, seemed funny.

"Everything's moving, swaying," she said, still giggling.

He stifled the chuckling by kissing her, hard–tongue searching. "Calm down," he said. "Move with me, please."

She swiveled under him, took hold of the back of his head, nuzzled his left ear and whispered, "Vacuum sewers. . . . take me, oh, vacuum sewers. Vacuum sewers!" She relaxed back, hair on the cold wet sand and surrendered utterly to whatever was going to happen, all the while laughing, a sharp, half-smothered cackle.

But if delivery had been handed over, in the aftermath of distant gigantic detonation, she heard a ringing in Claudio's pocket. And instantly he was bolt upright, and fumbling at his side. The cell phone snapped open and there were despite distant orange billows, clouds of Italian phrases drifting down on her like sexual embers.

"It's Tito," Claudio said. "He's at the site. They've found something."

9.

When, at summer's end, she returned the keys to the Lido apartment, Julee said, "So he threw you over for a brick. Not even a Roman brick, a Byzantine brick! Jesus! Maybe the only error the great Tito ever made. Claudio told me all about it. Pretty funny. There you were, the loving couple. . . Just about condom time. And Tito summoned him. He'd found a true Roman connection. Proof positive linking Venice and Rome. A brick, a fucking brick. And where was my little honey who was going to deliver me, get me back home? Oh, where was she? In a mangrove. I could have told you. He's great at warming you up and walking out. He's the world's best vibrator salesman. So get me some Popelmo."

"I wasn't in the mangrove. I went to the Lazaretto with him."

"Ah, ever the good student! I don't care. I don't care. You left me here with him. All for a mistaken brick."

"The brick was dirt covered. You couldn't tell without scraping it carefully or dunking it in warm water, but no one wanted to do that in the darkness. Even with lanterns it seemed washing it would risk everything. "

"Risk everything?" Julee said, softly. "That's a laugh. I could show you a thing or two about risking everything. He threw you over for a brick."

"The dimensions seemed right, seemed Roman, not even Etruscan."

"Oh please, " Julee said, "spare me. I was counting on you and I've been let down again. I lost out to a brick, a mistaken brick. *Maria virgine!*"

And it was the very Italian lilt Julee gave to that exclamation that seemed to sanction Donna's departure, seemed to speed her on, like the mother of God, fleeing male menaces below, even as she aspired to, or thwarted, the omnipotent bat above.

PART II

Mostly, it was the Schioppettino

At Arco's, a Venetian standup sandwich place straight off Calle del Botteri and not far from the Rialto Market boat stop, Claudio handed Hugh a small white- slathered bruschetta. Hugh thought: Italian Rondele? as he muscled his way deeper into the crush of standees crowding toward the glass encased, and very high counter— a long way from Waterbury, Connecticut.

"Wine?" Claudio asked, still holding his position against the glass case.

"Sure." Hugh answered, taking a skeptical bite at the bruschetta.

Soon enough over the restive crowd Claudio handed Hugh a half glass of wine. "You're gonna like this."

Hugh took a slow swallow, letting the smooth blackberry taste swell in his mouth and then the almost magical peppery aftertaste startle through his throat/nose/brain. "Hehn, great stuff!" he exclaimed, "What is it?"

Claudio smiled and leaned toward him, "Schioppettino, a name even better than its flavor. Truly fine. From Fuili, near Slovenia."

"Remarkable," Hugh concurred. "Really."

"Yeah, the peppery aftertaste is terrific."

"More than terrific. Can I get a bottle of it?"

"I'll ask——you really like it?"

"Think about what I asked you. The answer's clear enough."

While Claudio swiveled back to the counter, Hugh turned away and studied the short blond woman in gray capri pants near the wooden shelf next to the glass entry door. Her back was to him, but from the orange tote bag she carried and the lovely controlled roll her hair made just tickling her shoulders and the back of her neck, he was pretty sure she was Agnes of ISMAR, a hydrographic company in the Arsenale.

Hugh finished the Schioppettino and in the quick pepper glow of that swallow (he'd skipped breakfast) a wave of celebration about Venice washed through him. He remembered reading some art critic's comment that every time the fellow came to Venice he had immediately to kneel down and thank God that such a place existed on the planet. It was true enough, how could one imagine that simply walking through a dark sorteportego would lead to Arco's glass door and the sweet, pliant backside of Agnes of ISMAR? On each trip to Venice Hugh felt himself relax, reach new plateaus of self-satisfaction or at least new releases from self-consciousness. Since he didn't know Italian, what damage could the language do him? Not knowing anything being discussed delighted him somehow or seemed to seat him in a private kayak on a rio beyond reproach. Outside conversation about his overweight form, his crushable LL Bean rain hat, his Lands End stormer raincoat with confusing pockets, his rigid posture and smug way he tucked his chins into his neck when describing his reasons for being in Venice— overheard judgmental Italian babble he knew was impenetrable and therefore dismissible, more than dismissible, actually enjoyable in the way anyone might enjoy some Southeast Asian kickball sport the rules of which were unfathomable. The way limbs played the game was all that mattered and Agnes of ISMAR had splendid limbs.

Over his shoulder Claudio passed another half glass of Schioppettino. "He'll sell us a case but only at his price, since the next batch isn't due in till May."

"And his price?" Hugh asked, still staring at Agnes.

"Twenty five dollars per bottle."

Hugh clamped his front teeth over the left side of his lower lip and furiously spun the memory disk. There was one Venetian phrase Claudio had taught him–a question that enabled you to dispute an excessive bill with particularly disarming effectiveness. A question so local that the Venetian you sprung it on would immediately recognize a compatriot entirely worthy of a recalculated invoice. But Hugh wasn't comfortable pronouncing the words. . He took another long swallow and in the blossoming pepper fumes summoned up, " Ma go roto qualcossa?" (Did I break something?)

Claudio said, "Perfecto! You've actually learned something from me."

"I'm a very steady student, very even person. But I'm very selective in the lessons I learn."

Claudio laughed and said, "I'll give it a try. He'll come down some, I'm pretty sure of that."

"If he'll come down to twenty dollars a bottle, I'll take the case." Hugh said with some grandiosity, imagining he could easily write the expenditure off as a business necessity, and wondering about that, even as he temporarily stopped Claudio from turning back to the counter, "That's a twenty percent discount." He smiled and felt masterful mathematically if not linguistically. "A standard discount in the states, for a case."

In the flush of that mastery he moved directly on Agnes, calling out her name softly but insistently, "Agnes, Agnes."

She stopped eating her sandwich, turned, contemplating him with a brow scrunch that requested further information.

"Hugh Frendell, Vacuum Sewers," he said, with a peppery smile.

"Oh yeah, you're the Vacuum Sewers guy," she answered. "What are you doing way up here?"

"I could ask you the same question, but I wouldn't." Hugh answered, swallowing the rest of his bruschetta.

Agnes eyed him a bit and said, "You're a funny one, all right."

"Funny laughable or funny peculiar?"

"Both."

"Have you tried the Schioppettino?" Hugh held out a glass, and, surprisingly, she quickly took hold of it. More than a sip followed.

"Pretty good," she said. "A little bite at the end."

"The only way to go," Hugh added smiling with what he hoped seemed a suave leer.

"A hundred Euros minimum," Agnes said, looking directly into Hugh's eyes.

The cool, soft solicitation and certainty of her tone moved him a half step back. He wasn't quite sure he'd heard correctly. ISMAR ran computer models of lagoon behavior that helped Centro Maree, the Venetian weather/tide service, predict high water for the city. ISMAR didn't seem the place for a hooker home base. Hugh imagined she might know her way around algorithms as well as whips, chains, and handcuffs. That intrigued him.

"What do you do at ISMAR?" Hugh asked.

"I do damn well, thank you." Agnes answered, watching to see Hugh's reaction.

"We all do well, after all, we're all in Venice, drinking Schioppettino."

"Not all of us."

"Oh, of course, let me get you glass of your own."

"Don't bother, I'll finish yours. It's a terrific wine," she said quietly, taking the glass from him again.

Claudio arrived with two more glasses in one hand and a tray holding prosciutto and cheese in the other hand.

Hugh took his glass and then whispered to Agnes, "Did you say a hundred Euros?"

"I did."

"Is that for an hour or a night?"

"It's sure as hell not for a night."

"Agnes of ISMAR, you amaze me."

"Venice eats money."

"I'm not at all experienced with commercial bedroom activities."

"I gathered as much. So let's just have Schioppettino."

"I'm in the process of getting a case."

"I'm impressed and I'm available to help you dispose of it."

"I'm not too happy with 'dispose.'"

"You're absolutely right. Let's go with 'consume it'—isn't that better?"

"Maybe, 'entomb it,' is preferable." Hugh smiled insanely suddenly jolted into liveliness by an elevated edge of banter, he'd never heretofore tried. "Agnes of ISMAR will you go down to the pit with me?"

"The pit is two hundred fifty Euros," she replied, chuckling. "Just about a case of Schioppettino."

2.

The 1 p.m. crowd thinned rather quickly and the released space seemed to dovetail with Claudio's wife Julee's entrance, who came through the glass door just as Claudio called out that a case was waiting for them in the kitchen. The little glimpse of sky beyond the sortoportego had turned a lovely afternoon grey color and Hugh smiled imagining how the pastels of the myriad palaces would mark their slow ride down the Grand Canal, a parade of muted flares in the October chill. He was never happier than in his favorite Venetian spot: one of the seven green plastic chairs mounted on the fantail of most vaporetti. There he could stretch out his arm over the back of the next seat, imagining some beguiled friend sitting beside him, even Agnes of ISMAR , and smell the mucid scent of Venice, part petroleum, part imagined gardenias tinged, amazingly, with the distant fumes of watery human excrement.

But that rotten reverie Julee demolished by announcing, "I got Alberto to bring me over in the boat, Claudio. And it's ours for the rest of the day. He has to go to Mestre. It's out back in the rio."

Julee was wearing a very leopard skin long scarf around a thigh length brown leather jacket, matching her high leather boots. And what appeared to Hugh to be black jodhpurs leggings. Her face as always for him was fixed in a kind of frozen toothy smile that conveyed a certain distant desperation and hostility. The desperation, Hugh imagined, first attracted Claudio, and the hostility he assumed had long since sent him elsewhere. Hugh supposed that Claudio's ISMAR connection also encompassed Agnes at one time.

"I see everyone's drinking but me," Julee said

"We are indeed. And it's Schioppettino and I believe your husband will immediately get you a glass—perhaps a whole bottle." Hugh answered.

"There's a case waiting for us in the kitchen," Claudio added, giving his glass to Julee.

"No greater love hath a husband than he gives his wife his Schioppettino," Hugh said.

"No greater love," Julee echoed, downing the remainder of the drink. "Let's get the case on board and be gone. I don't like to eat standing up. It's too Italian."

Hugh thought–I'm not Italian and then he remembered how quickly Claudio and Julee could spend his money and how automatically, almost unconsciously. But in the warmth of the Schioppettino, in the glow of Venice's soft light, a little rapacity by friends seemed positively appropriate. Hugh recalled a conversation with an elderly pensione owner over a morning cappucino in which the fellow lamented how the Venetian daily newspaper reported with extraordinary elan the previous day's highest paid luncheon meal, as if it were an American baseball statistic tracked by innumerable cheering fans. "Imagine," he said, "celebrating how two Japanese businessmen paid over six hundred dollars for lunch on the Lido. It can't go on too much longer." Still lamenting the fleecing the Japanese suffered, the owner nonetheless offered to invoice "whatever price you'd like for spending the night here. I assume you get reimbursed in America. I'll write the invoice for the amount you tell me. The actual price is, say, sixty-five dollars."

Hugh mused: 250 Euros for Agnes for what? Discussions of piping routes from Venice to Mestre? But she hadn't any piping connections (spreading a smile on Hugh's face) did she?

Maybe Lagoon flows would need to be assessed if piping followed the bridge to the mainland?

Surely the IRS would buy that? Better, yet, accept that.

"My God! What are you dreaming about?" Julee interrupted him. "They need your card for the Schioppettino."

"Yes, indeed," Hugh answered. "I'm the Vacuum Sewers, Visa man, aren't I?"

"Just give him the card," Julee said, pushing softly at Hugh's grey cardigan.

"I never move precipitously," Hugh said, slowly extracting the Capital One card from his wallet.

"That's a joyous thing in a man," Agnes said, as they passed out of the kitchen area into a lane of stones lining the rio behind Arco.

Claudio carried the case to the boat. And as they all settled in, Claudio started the motor, while industrious Agnes worked a corkscrew into the first Schioppettino out of the case.

She examined the cork and then tossed it between slats on the deck. Julee brought waxed cups out of her large handbag, and Agnes seemed to overfill them almost to their curled edging. As Claudio eased off the wall Agnes staggered a bit and the wine slurped over the edges of the cups resting on the small table between the narrow benches lining the small boat; pepper fumes rose quickly beyond the sea smell of the rio. Hugh thought about licking the table surface. Instead, Agnes sipped a quarter inch from off the cups to prevent further overflow. Julee quickly took one and handed it to Claudio safely at the wheel, then took one herself. Hugh finished his and poured himself another just as the wobbly boat reached the Grand Canal. Surprising sun flecks off the dark green water sparkled around them as they turned past the closing Rialto market. Already cocktail tables were being set up replacing the disassembling grocery platforms.

"I used to love drinking Prosecco there," Hugh said motioning toward the collapsing market.

"But, Schioppettino is far better," Julee answered.

Claudio slowed the boat as they eased under the Rialto bridge.

Agnes, pointing to the scrawled black markings on the cement, said, "I wonder what the graffiti says."

"It says the city doesn't have the funds to clean any of Venice up. That's what it says," Julee shouted as if to test the echoing quality of the bridge. "Perhaps we could ask our Chinese tourists," she went on gesturing toward the packed gondola going in the other direction with its apparent soloist hunched over and fiddling with his noiseless boombox.

"One day, Venice will have a Disney like passport system and it will include a forty minute gondola ride complete with crooning tenor, delivering 'Nessun Dorma.'"

"No, one day, you'll need a snorkel to visit Venice," Claudio said speeding the boat up again.

"Once the vacuum sewer system is in place, it can easily be switched to general drainage. That's a point we need to make with Central Maree." Hugh said, evenly, feeling as if he had been slowly spread over the soft flecked Grand Canal, a mantle or perhaps a grey frosting over the sea.

"They know all that," Claudio called him back. "We need a different argument altogether."

"Well, I'm sure you'll find one," Hugh said, smiling at the columns of City Hall slipping by.

"Are you going to throw up?" Agnes asked him.

"Only if you want me to," Hugh answered, giving the top of her very pliant shoulder a squeeze.

"Jesus," she sighed. "Let's pour another." And she did as they rounded the bend off the San Samuele boat stop, with a view now of the Academia bridge. Hugh closed his eyes, took a long breath and then opened them again confident he'd see the grandest sight in Venice—parts of San Salute church intersected by the bridge so that it seemed the noble grey/white dome protruded out of the heavy wooden lattice work of the arching canal overpass. In the cloudy grey picture Hugh imagined the waving tourists could turn and mount the dome directly, bounding beyond the two hundred yards of canal separating the edifices. It was a lunatic vision Hugh understood, but a captivating one–with enough Schioppettino wafting over water distances seemed appealingly plausible.

"Take my hand, Agnes of ISMAR," Hugh said quietly, but she apparently did not hear. And standing together they passed under the Academia Bridge past the boat stops, past the Peggy Gugenheim's truncated museum and past, sadly, the empty boat stop of the Salute itself and on into the fuller, roiled bay waters between San Marco piazza, and the island San Giorgio Maggiore.

Claudio revved the motor a bit to settle the boat across the swells, but it was clear only the most experienced Venetian could avoid sitting down and Agnes, Hugh and Julee plopped on the bench seats. The wine cups on the platform toppled.

"No worries, " Hugh suddenly shouted. "We've got at least ten more bottles."

3.

Hugh had noticed that Claudio always took a sort of reverential stance when he steered a boat into the narrow channel leading to the immense Arsenale harbor, as if the wide still pond for ship construction had opened history itself for examination. Why did the hundreds of ship builders frenziedly at work on three galleons at a time need to harken to his vacuum sewerage dreams? His imagined piping back to Mestre surely must have seemed puny compared to their dazzling labors guaranteeing that the crusades would continue for a hundred years and untold lives butchered. Overnight we could supply the King of England a galleon to pursue his Savior's honor in the Levant, and you come to us with pvc piping and an argument that sucking our dregs to the mainland would improve our health? "I know it's shamful and embarrassing, but it's what I do," Hugh said to Agnes, as the air turned suave and supple in the ripple-less Arsenale water. He loomed large against the grey/gold sky. She looked at him and then said, "I mentioned, didn't I, that I'm not interested in what you do."

"Only what I can pay," Hugh answered. "Venetians are always looking for, looking for *tagente*," he finally remembered.

"I'm not Venetian, actually don't understand it. I'm from Padua, and Jersey City."

That revelation forced Hugh to look more carefully at her. There was a certain insouciance to her eyes out from that leathery darkened skin. He imagined in Jersey City the sun seldom shined so she spent most of her time in sunstruck Padua. Finally after thinking further about how that tanned skin might look totally uncovered he asked, "From which country are you exiled?"

"I'm at home everywhere," she laughed. "That's what no one can understand. How at home I am."

Claudio cut the engine and tied off on a cleat opposite the massive metal door to ISMAR's offices. They occupied about a quarter of the four storey high building whose tin roof sheltered, 600 years before, the grid work of galleon-making. Were the phantom builders, glue splattered and tar stained, scrambling overhead watching the computer screens and the nifty post modern artistic touches arranged now in the building housing only cubicles and meeting rooms with iridescent Formica-topped tables or faux leather veneered chairs, tiny printers humming, coffee makers perking along so that white board charts could track lagoon flows traced out by improvised algorithms?

Perhaps the only sustaining legacy from Venice's flowering was a certain saturnity about foreigners moving throughout the property–and courtesans always within Venice's roadways of numbered stones.. Was Agnes Casanova's chosen, and content with Casanova's memory, since Hugh could not afford the going rate? Agnes gathered up two unopened bottles of Schioppettino, and the party shifted inside.

Almost immediately the group confronted a steep metal stairway of hammered tin. To the right, improbably, stood a giant stuffed Polar bear, brilliantly white and apparently powdered with a lilac scent. Hugh was struck dumb by the juxtaposition–Venice's wealth he understood might encompass such indulgences, but Agnes explained: "ISMAR has a station in the arctic. It's a gift from the natives there."

"I don't believe it," Hugh said.

Claudio answered, "Good. No one at ISMAR cares whether you believe it or not. The main thing is that you can ride it, lean against it, fornicate under it. And it will never reveal anything."

"Jesus," Julee said. "So let's get to the room and party on." She took hold of Hugh's hand pulling him up the stairway. "I'm dying to know more about vacuum sewers, and how they will save Venice."

Hugh was aware that it was direct thrust at separating him from Agnes, and he wondered if she and Claudio were playing some well rehearsed game of switching partners. If that were the case he imagined he needed to go along, for no other reason than to observe more closely the tango moves as they unfolded. Besides, he evidently didn't have the ticket to access Agnes. Schioppettino said "Simon says go along," he thought reclining in the sweet peppery arms of bonhomie and feeling how cool and soft was Julee's yanking hand. Schioppettino says, catch up with Julee, get close enough to put an arm around her narrow waist and lean into her as if falling into the harshly lit room with its giant cold grey table and its fifteen aluminum chairs. Schioppettino says, contemplate leaning her over that table, kicking aside two chairs and then mouthing her face in a fake silly laughter of dysbalance and apparent dysfunction. But Hugh remembered he was a even flow person abjuring highs and lows, dependable, predictable, and in a trice swiftly flowing to Mestre. The sturdy old Hugh said slowly, evenly, "You want the five minute or the forty minute explanation of Vacuum S ewers?"

"I want the one that makes a person swoon with vacuum longing, with gorgeous furry sucking."

Hugh blinked, finally said, "Forty minutes, plenty of hydrodynamic foreplay."

Julee laughed and then plunged forward kissing him sloppily on the upper lip and lower nose.

Hugh thought, this is Claudio's wife, Claudio, my contact and entry to the Venetian account. One must not trifle with power. It is necessary and beneficial to begin denial with the most enveloping challenge. Out of such denial comes, at length, achievement, fruition, purposeful focus, but as she licked him again and again, he knew his fingernails were slipping off the edge of the bar. Soon enough he knew he'd have to cross that bridge of sighs, down onto the sweet polished tiles of the conference room where he'd explain the linkage of gravity feed with generated suction requiring ever narrower pipings out along the Zatterre beyond the parking garage well behind Ferro Via and onto to Mestre via the sleek low and lowering bridge to the mainland. And at the mainland pumping station and purification plant he'd find her sumptuously red nail polished toes deliciously thrust into his mouth. "Julee, Julee," mouthed into her ear, "You're sacred goods, unavailable to overweight Americans."

"Fuck you," she answered with overpowering sweetness.

"Not here, not now," he panted.

"He doesn't control my life. Doesn't control my choices. You better understand that. He sure as hell does. Why can't you?"

"I'm a slow but steady learner. Instinctively I'm an engineer of safer circumstances and more predictable environment." Hugh thought: why am I talking this way?

"I can show you the curvature of the egg containing you. We can peck our way out," she answered.

Involuntarily Hugh started laughing and they separated; she sat up on the formica table, he backed away and pushed against the entrance door jamb.

"Claudio will bring us fresh, fat worms," she continued. "You'll have to strain to get them. Can you strain?"

"I cannot." Hugh continued laughing. He eyed the two bottles of Schioppettino beside her. "I. . . .I . . . I didn't bring a corkscrew."

Without speaking Julee reached into her tiny silver handbag and tossed a chrome collapsed corkscrew on the table top. Hugh rushed to it, opened it, carved the first wine bottle metal capping away, deeply drove the screw into the cork and with indelicate crankings finally got the cork out. He offered the bottle to her and she swilled it directly. He followed and when half was gone they paused to reboot romance.

"It's hardly that I don't want to. I want to more than anything," Hugh said.

"I know. I know. Little Stacy, is that right?, and the kids give you pause. Jesus, the paws they give you, little teddy bear."

"Not Stacy, Jenean."

"Jesus. Let me guess: a little hefty and wearing shifts."

"Not far wrong. Nothing of your style."

"About as clear an invitation as I'm likely to get, to go back outside and celebrate family solidarity." She took another long swallow from the bottle. "Just as well. This room reeks of fidelity, the worst smell on the planet."

4.

As they went back down the metal stairway, it became evident that Claudio had Agnes pinioned against the stuffed polar bear. She leaned back on the bear and using her palms, gently took hold of his arms, stanchions on either side of her shoulders.. There was welcoming surprise in her expression, and it seemed she was actually interested in his soft conversation. Hugh imagined Claudio whispered of the Venetian planning for future ship construction—actually numbering the oak trees in the Veneto and then bending the choice ones from their earliest moments toward becoming the spines of galleons. It was lately Claudio's fondest recitation and one Hugh thought emphasized Venetian tenacity and long term planning—surely harbingers of the city government's evident fascination with his sewerage proposals. Still, the city planners had not really committed, Hugh remembered. Perhaps he and Claudio struck some kind of humorous pose, Mutt and Jeff, obese American and the soft spoken bilingual agent threatening their Venetian certitude, their unconscious affirmation of imperial dominance. More likely the city fathers were weighing Claudio's future importance against the present favor of a contract. Hugh understood they sensed Claudio's abilities and connections. He couldn't be dismissed, or so it seemed. But still they had not indicated much interest in the novelty of Hugh's firm. Maybe Claudio was not the ideal partner—just the available one, and how could Hugh choose another anyway? Hugh was confused between the City sanitation department and a corporation called INSULA, charged with dredging the canals, and clearing the sewerage from the city's waterways. They had never made a presentation to INSULA and maybe that accounted for the City's reluctance. Yes, that was the way to proceed.

"Jesus, the tireless rutter wants to take her against the mangy bear," Julee said, turning back to him. She finished the bottle and tossed it down against Claudio's arched and lowering back. "You're such a shield," she said loudly as Claudio looked around with apparent anger.

"I didn't do it," Hugh shouted. "I had nothing to do with it."

"He did," Julee countered. "He's so jealous–you know how jealous he is. Jesus, such a jealous little son of a bitch."

Claudio laughed and shook his head, then resumed dialogue with a giddily smiling Agnes of ISMAR..

Was there a script somewhere being played out, this time, as times before, Hugh wondered. And if so, of what did the last acts consist? Dizzily he sorted out fantasies, but nothing seemed persuasive. Was it operatic clutching and hurling over the parapet, or sweet succumbing to malaise and fever before fading strings?

When they were outside, the sunlight muted in overhead golden greyness, Julee said, "I know what he wants. He wants to take her underneath the bear. We did it against the beast," she emphasized "we." "And up close the beast is smelly as hell. That lilac lavender scent comes from powder they toss on the bear, as if it were a French shower or something. But he wants to try it underneath the bear. He begged me to try it under the bear. There's an absence of hair there. Just like a damn football or something."

"You've been under the bear?"

"You bet. I'm game for under the bear, at least now I am."

"Agnes is a hooker."

"Not when she's on Schioppettino, and we all are, aren't we?"

"And you've brought the corkscrew?"

"Of course, I don't leave the Lido without it."

"Then, give it to me."

He quickly opened the second bottle and Julee said, "There's more on the boat."

"I like the way you keep count."

"Do I ever."

"Let's dangle our legs in the fragrant water of the Arsenale," Hugh said, sitting down on the rough concrete edge. The water line was about four inches below his shoes. He thought about reeling his legs back up, and taking his shoes and socks off, then stretching down further to disturb the rancid sea. But that seems excessive effort, as the Schioppettino settled into him, compounding a silly satiety that flowed through all his imagined limbs. How softly sweet was the Venetian grey/golden sky, how calm the Arsenale's water, how glowing Julee's tan arms, how impressively powerful her dark brown, well-oiled boots.

"Whenever I come to ISMAR and look at this empty Arsenale water I like to think of a new Venice emerging from below this water line, rising up, reasserting itself the La Serenissima once more," Hugh said, repeating a line he'd heard from Claudio.

"That's tiresome," Julee said. "And I've heard it a dozen times before. Try something more inventive."

"But I actually believe it, and I believe Vacuum Sewers can lead the way."

"Maybe under the bear he can impregnate her. That's his heart's longing, you know."

"We couldn't handle the big hotels. They'd still have to have their own septic barges and haul everyday, but at the very least we could make the old canal flows suddenly brilliantly modern again, deflecting a lot of the waste to a plant in Mestre."

"So much pressure for a bambino, you couldn't imagine how much, could you?"

"Pressure is the key and gravity feed so that pumping stations don't have to siphon off too much energy, generating too much cost."

"Why don't you shut the fuck up?"

Hugh abruptly stopped staring at the water line which seemed to be getting higher and turned to her. "Why do you talk that way?"

"Why do you think that way? Jesus!"

"I think that way, because that's what I do, what I am. I'm not Venetian wallowing in my past. It's what I am and if that's not good enough for you, that's fine with me. I can search out other contracts. I got a contract for two train stations in Bridgeport just before I flew over here. Two damn galleons for the King of Bridgeport." Hugh laughed, and the phrase seemed to float out over the still Arsenale water. On the far side a neon blue sign flicked on spelling out "Thetis." Hugh took a long swill from the bottle, and then set it clinking on the concrete. "Okay, I get it. I get it. Vacuum Sewers isn't going to rescue Venice, since it needs no rescue, and Claudio's not going to get the bambino of his longing."

"Of his parents' longing," Julee said.

"Venice is disappointment. I get it. You come with hopes and you drown."

"In sewerage," Julee said gathering up the bottle for a long swallow.

Just then the klaxons went off from ten church bell towers all over Venice.

"An emergency or what?" Hugh shouted.

"Shhsss." Julee commanded. "We have to listen for the tones. Each change of tone means another 10 cms of water above normal. Listen now, listen closely—it tells our future."

"Not likely," Hugh said, taking back the bottle.

The first electronic tone lasted 10 seconds and was followed by a second higher 10 second tone, and then a third and then a fourth.

Claudio burst out of ISMAR's huge metal door. "We'd better take the boat back to Cannaregio now. Plenty of high water on the way."

"Like a tsunami?" Hugh asked.

"No," Julee answered, "just a slow rising of everything. You couldn't possibly vacuum it away."

"Was it really four tones?"

"It was."

"Forty centimeters?"

"Yes."

"That's not so deep."

"Depends on what 'normal' is."

"I'm not going to ask."

"If you have to ask, you aren't. . . ."

"Are you coming to the boat or not?" Claudio asked, pulling the bow line in and jumping on board.

"How do I get home from the boat yard?" Hugh asked.

"You don't. The vaporetti will stop, or at least some of them," Claudio answered. "We'll have to wait it out. Maybe five hours, maybe less, if they got it wrong."

"In the boat yard?"

"I suppose. In that section of Cannaregio most places close in the afternoon."

"So what's my choice?" Hugh asked.

"You could probably walk home before the water got too high."

'Walking's always faster in Venice," Julee said, drinking another swallow of Schioppettino.

Hugh heard that as her desire to get rid of him. And that seemed entirely defensible to him. Things had, he decided, turned around quickly— perhaps a natural intervention but more likely the little group had found out how boring he was. Self-effacing to perfect deracination. A wave of delicious melancholia washed over Hugh who saw himself, like Lord Byron, swimming in the Grand Canal to reach his apartment on the top floor (historically the servants' quarters, of course) in campo San Maurizio. There was Hugh, buffed out of his natural penguin shape, and cleanly stroking the filthy sea as if to purify it with each forward glide, pausing only every three hundred feet to vomit his diminishing innards into the scummy water. Hugh cresting the dappled canal reaching his oar-slapped hands toward the rescuing edges of gondolas filled with laughing patrons, who insisted on abandoning the faux Byron to his watery grave.

Hugh couldn't decide whether it was his slumping sitting, or an unconscious attempt at leg elongation that made the Arsenale pond gently lap the sole of his right shoe, that Timberland waterproof model he had so thoughtfully selected as perfect for Venice in high water season.

5.

When Agnes came out of the metal door, she quickly latched onto Julee and both leapt on to Claudio's boat. "I'll walk," Hugh said loudly, pulling his wet Timberland out back onto the concrete. "I know the way –up the riva and through San Marco. Piece of cake."

"They'll be putting the planks up," Claudio said, slowly spinning the boat into an arc away from ISMAR. "You can use them if the water's getting high, but remember its more than a step up."

"Don't strain," Julee added, smiling. "And they're called *passarelle*. Remember, step way up."

Hugh shouted to Claudio, "Think about a presentation to INSULA." But he apparently didn't hear or at least didn't reply, heading now toward the other exit of the Arsenale, to the backside of Venice along the Fondamenta Nuove.

Almost immediately grey silence came over the Arsenale harbor. Hugh realized no one was about, as if news of high water had gotten around much earlier and alert Venetians had taken the day off. Or, he wondered, more likely no one worked much in the abandoned shipyard. Surely no workmen came clammoring out to build passarelle planking around the swelling pond. Let the lagoon reclaim the Arsenale, then, Hugh said to himself, as he hurried toward the riva along the lagoon's opening toward San Giorgio Maggiore island. If the water got high enough the Arsenale would be a natural spillway to the backside.

To the east the giant trees of St. Elena would withstand any flooding and hold the island until receding occurred. In a burst of elegant joy Hugh realized he could probably climb the trees of St. Elena and outlast the flood, should it be necessary. He imagined himself two thirds of the way up one of the giant Tilia trees watching the slow rising sea overflowing the bell towers of Venice, eventually smothering even the electronic tones, as if Neptune had tossed his accordion into the on-rushing Adriatic.

Laughing and half stumbling Hugh turned west and started along the riva toward San Marco. Up a tree Frendell, suddenly delighting in nature's triumph over Venetian pretension. Was that why he felt so good? Throttled by the notion that, yes, some force, some undercurrent beyond all stopping would burst over Venice and envelope its smug self-satisfaction. Actually barrel over Claudio's enviable sense that whatever happened Venice would endure with or without vacuum sewerage.

Hugh suddenly wished Julee were with him, not so much for her company as for her stash of Schioppettino. He wanted another round to keep his lurching unsteady and his pace leisurely stumbling in sweet strides of triumph over nature's growing threat. But the little shops were closing. Everywhere plywood boards were being set against their doors. Shopkeepers believed that water would not circulate around the layers. Idiots. Idiots who doubtless felt the tides would keep the canals clean as they were in the 14th century. Smug idiots.

In a little while he could see the water washing over the lip of the riva and the vaporetto stops posted as closed . Workmen were in fact putting up the planking, but no one as yet bothered to climb up. The water hadn't reached the passarelles, and Hugh sensed it would take not only a semi leap to get on the boards, but essentially careful calculated balancing to move along them. Delay of their use made perfect sense to him, but it also seemed possible that permanent passarelles could provide on their undersides, splendid sites for vacuum pipings. Would this ingenious Venetian simple device to facilitate personal movement become something more spectacular in the imagined resuscitation of La Serenissima?

The passage down off the first bridge led naturally to a small leap onto the planking which proved a bit spongy—maybe, Hugh wondered, from his own Schioppettino's sogginess? He thought of the several remaining bottles on the boat, and understood Julee would drink his rightful share. That, after all, was her compensation for fending off bambino imposition, and relentless Italian patriarchy. He was alone on the passarelle; everyone else still stepped swiftly on the stones–ah the numbered stones he remembered, each one labelled, itemized on their undersides so that any could be lifted up and precisely returned to their exact placement after any repairs were finished. Evidence of a Venetian sense that whatever happened the city would remain and precisely in its remembered places. And the screwy way that numbering took form visibly on the buildings by sestiere in one continuous line that recognized new construction only by adding a letter to the number that existed forever it seemed in Venice's archival frozenness.

Hugh stopped at the second bridge to watch the water sloshing beyond the edges of the riva, then resumed his passarelle stomping, noting that as he got closer to San Marco, adjacent parallel plankings appeared, even though surprisingly there were no crowds to use them. Most people still could walk on the stones. But as the Bridge of Sighs came into view off to the right it seemed more water appeared on the stones, and more people joined him on the plankings. He'd heard that San Marco was, in fact, the lowest portion of the city and the flooding consequently would be worse there. And sure enough as he reached the twin pillars beyond the Doge's Palace water had reached the one foot level on the draining slope of San Marco piazza.

He'd have to stay on the planking all the way to the archway corridor on the east side of the plaza, past Florian's few remaining tables on the plaza's stones. Only one table was occupied–four fellows, shirts off, shoes, socks, pants piled on the table top, laughing at the rising water, actually toasting it with lager in wine glasses. They motioned for more liquor from the lone waiter who had donned thigh high rubber boots and seemed amused to bring them more food and drink.

"When it reaches the table top, we'll run away. We've got a pool when that will be. Want some of the action, mate?" the stoutest of the contingent called out to Hugh who lingered watching from Florian's third doorway.

"You understand if it gets higher over your feet and legs, you'll have to go to the hospital," Hugh said, smiling and at the same time admiring their casualness.

"No worries, mate," the fellow answered. "We've got a bloody nurse with us."

"A lot of pigeon shit comes up when, when the water gets higher," Hugh said, helpfully, he hoped.

"There's pigeon shit everywhere, mate. Everywhere. We're stepping it all the time. All the time."

"True enough, lads," Hugh said feeling suddenly very Aussie. "Enjoy your pint." He wondered as he turned away whether he should have said, "Tinny," though neither descriptor applied to the wine/lager glasses.

They said something, but Hugh was fixed on the distant planking beyond the end of the piazza. It seemed water might actually reach over those passarelle. Hugh sped up, aware that wet marble could become very slippery. Why was he always sprinting in Venice, worried that the next bridge might reveal one more beyond, worried that the vaporetto would clang its shuttering gate and drift off the boat dock before he could flash his pass at the sensor and thus earn the right to get aboard, worried that the glut of tourists would make his preferred route impossible, angry that the couple with the stroller took forever to bang it up over the crucial bridge.

Heavier rain began coming down and a weird wind rushed through the narrow exit out of the piazza near the Correr Museum. On the wet boards Hugh carefully picked his way past the posh stores near San Marco, past the several ATMs, the handbag shops, over a large bridge just after St. Moise church, and then onto narrower passarelle now only a few inches above the rising water flooding the streets.

By the time he reached Santa Maria del Giglio's campo the bottom of his pants was wet, as water sloshed over the passarelle allowing him onto the first bridge to San Maurizio. He stood and stared down the narrow passage to the Giglio boatstop, entirely planked so that passengers hauling their luggage had to pull it along the boards and awakwardly fit it around others trying to get to the vaporetto. The biggest clog-up occurred midway up the narrow lane at the start of the Best Western Hotel, an irony Hugh found amusing. He crossed onto the bridge and pressed toward the next entry to San Maurizio. At the end of that passageway the passarelle ended. The campo was under at least a foot of water. Tourists were apparently trapped on the steps of the well-head in the center of the campo. Some of them in near panic had begun to take off their shoes and socks, contemplating walking through the slop to reach where they intended, but the water continued swelling slowly upward. Only the most knowledgeable tone savant would have known the peak was about to occur.

Hugh slogged through the brackish flood, already planning to launder his socks and pants, and thinking about using a hair dryer on his allegedly waterproof Timberland shoes.

6.

His key for the outside door never worked the first time in. He'd come to understand that a particular karma was necessary for the tumblers to fall and the lock to loosen. Belly breathing helped, but he suspected standing in water altered everything, so breath control did not turn the trick. Besides he had a sudden and feverish desire to urinate, and, inexplicably, an urge to vomit. That was worrisome indeed, since even if the lock yielded there were still four flights of concave marble stairs to climb.

With the key in the lock he pulled back on the door handle and turned the key only to encounter immediate and overwhelming resistance. Come on, come on! he said quietly to the door. —Indulge me, just this once. . .yield this once. But no.

He let go, turned to watch the disrobing well-head dwellers, let his arms relax and then turned back to insert the key again. Magically the door fell away from his slow precise pressure on the key. At last!

He strode through the slosh beyond the mailboxes and ascended above the rivuleting rush, taking two, some times three, steps at a bound. On the second landing he swiveled into the railing at the corner and vomited so that the mess poured down the open stairwell. He crumbled downward as if to join the shards falling ever so slowly, it seemed, to the brackish water below. He thought: Venice is reclaiming my insides, scrapping them out, making sure nothing enjoyable remained. All was to be Schioppettino-rinsed. He recognized and regretted that. It's always the last bottle that does maximum damage, he thought—the last and most delicious bottle. But regrets about Schioppettino gave way to a more ominous sense that something was pressing on his chest. Initially only a faint pressure, so little that, relieved by vomiting, Hugh was able to stand and resume climbing. At his door he regretted again that there was no landing-—the steps just terminated at his door and he had to balance on two steps to fit his key to the lock. He blinked as if squeezing his eyes shut would turn off the pressure on his chest. He massaged the area with his right hand as he worked the key with his left. The door swung back and he dumped forward onto the cold but somehow welcoming terrazzo-like floor, his home.

Surely things would be better now. He swiveled onto his back, massaged his chest again and began to realize that the pushing down on his chest was signaling something far more dangerous. He got to his knees and crawled to the half bath near the front door. There was a providential bottle of St. Joseph aspirin on the edge of the sink. He'd left it there after a headache four days ago. He had worried that the aspirin was so obviously old style American that the Farmacia where he'd bought it probably had kept it around for over a decade. He assumed the old pills were ineffective, just inert powder, but two had worked, and now he quickly put four into his mouth, turned the faucet on and leaned over to get water to wash them down. But swallowing apparently only triggered another vomiting response. He belched into the toilet and immediately took four more aspirins. These stayed down, but the pressure only got worse. He imagined someone was piling bowling balls on spinning saucer whose pivot was centered on his chest. Kneeling again he managed to get his phone out of his trousers. He called Claudio.

"I think I'm having a heart attack. I know I'm having one."

"Are you at home?"

"Of course I'm home. I couldn't be where it would be convenient could I?"

"I'll get the ambulance boat, but it will take some time. Can you rest?"

"Maybe, but the anxiety is pretty damn epic."

"I'll get Mrs. Deste to come up and stay with you. Just sit and wait. Don't do anything. Just rest. The boat will come, but it will have to take a longer route, since the bridges now are too low. The high water. Do you understand that?"

"Do I what?" Hugh answered, trying to breathe more steadily but the pressure seemed to be collapsing his lungs.

"Mrs. Deste will come up. And I'll meet you at the hospital. Just rest. Think quiet thoughts, but Hugh can I ask you a question?"

"What?"

"Hugh, if something should happen. I don't think it will, but if something should happen, could I have your Timberland shoes?"

"Only if you pay 100 euros to the estate."

"That's too much. You know a euro is worth a good deal more than a dollar now."

"Get the boat, please."

"Mrs. Deste is coming. The boat is coming."

"I've left the door open. I can't close it."

"That's great. Not to worry. Everything will be fine. Even Agnes is nodding."

Hugh imagined them drinking another bottle at the boat club. I should have gone with them, and had I done so, this never would have happened.

Or if it had happened how much better off I would have been than now on my own.

A sentiment Hugh regretted the minute Mrs. Deste came calling through his door. He remembered she spoke no English, he spoke no Italian. On a landing three weeks ago they had tried something in French but it had proved impossible.

She nodded at him. He pointed to his chest and grimaced.

She said, in an irritatingly knowing way, a patronizing way, "Infarto!"

I'm not farting, Hugh imagined as a reply, suddenly dragged back into sixth grade and the bullying that followed his occasion passing gas. Instead, he nodded and acknowledged, "Infarto!"

He slumped on the couch in the reception room and she sat opposite him in a overlarge lawson chair upholstered in a magenta print. Like the angel of death, Hugh thought.

Rather than attempt fractured French conversation, she merely looked carefully around her as if evaluating the holdings in the apartment. They sat in observing silence for almost twenty minutes, when, blessedly, four orange vested ambulance boat personnel arrived dragging a large wooden stretcher behind them.

The largest fellow among them carried a portable EKG kit. Hastily they attached sensors to Hugh and then the fellow said, in surprisingly fluent English. "It shows you're not having a heart attack, but we're going to take you to the hospital anyway. Sometimes these things don't register properly."

"I'm feeling better," Hugh said.

"But we're still going to take you to the hospital." The fellow motioned to the stretcher and Hugh slumped aboard, and was strapped in.

As the group started down the stairs, straining visibly at the load and easing their knee high rubber boots into the slippery marble steps, Hugh noticed the stout fellow in animated conversation with Mrs. Deste. When they all reached the campo and fitted Hugh into a wheel chair with suspicious wooden wheels and eased him through the receding waters, he called out to the fellow, asking him what Mrs. Deste had said.

"She wanted to know what you paid in rent for the apartment."

Hugh thought, ah, a true Venetian. "And what did you tell her?"

"I said about three thousand euros, but she thought that wasn't right. Is it?"

"I truly don't know. As a dying man, I don't know." That shut down the conversation.

Because the water was still high and the passarelle at Giglio so narrow, they wheeled on to San Marco Vallaresso where it became evident Hugh needed to walk to the boat rather than attempt a stretcher or wheelchair transfer.

The boat ride, when he later thought about it, seemed uneventful to Hugh. Uneventful and long, since apparently they went around St. Elena along the backside of Venice to the hospital, Four more assistants waited on the dock. They gathered him onto a more heavily padded gurney and then things began to haze over. He heard their voices but couldn't follow any of their conversations; he felt himself lifting off the gurney, slowly magically drifting upward and he was aware at some point of a very slender man in weirdly clinging patent-leather slippers, motioning in various directions and speaking ever so softly in ways that made the assistants snap to, and follow his directives quickly. Once when they were getting him off the gurney he suddenly doubled over and he noticed a peculiar calm settling in, an almost delicious feeling of well being, as if he had been intoxicated beyond even the sweet fellow feeling of the second or perhaps third bottle of Schioppettino––a poignant drifting upwards and an all-bathing mood of elevation, as if some gorgeous Schubert melody had suddenly wafted through all elements of his body and, in response those sinues, tissues, muscles simply followed the music in soft patterns above whatever was happening wherever it happened underneath the sound.

The sound softened and doubled back on itself and it seemed he could see the ligaments knitting themselves back into his body.

"Mr. Hugh! Mr. Hugh," he heard a voice shouting. "Have we lost you? Mr. Hugh, can you hear me? Can you?"

7.

He was on a weirdly high bed and Claudio and Agnes were standing near his pillow. They appeared to be leaning in as if listening to something he was saying, but he knew he was saying nothing. Instead he heard the tapping of slippers in the corridor and he was sure the dainty man directing everything was nearby. Pay attention to the dainty man—he felt certain of that—but he was only nearby, not in the room.

Claudio's phone went off, and Claudio turned away to take the call. Agnes pressed in closer. She leaned over and Hugh thought she smelled of Schioppettino but he didn't know if it was wine's scent or something inside his mouth that prompted the pepper smell.

"You have two stints," Agnes said.

He squinted uncomprehending.

"In America they call them 'stents' but 'stints' here. And you have two." She repeated "Two," rather loudly.

Was she drunk? And why was there a round port hole in the sliding steel door to his room?

Was that the dainty man's face in the porthole?

"We sloshed our way all the way over here from the boat club. It wasn't that far, actually. And in fact the fondamenta nuove was not so flooded by the time we came down here."

Hugh listened carefully to her voice, so compelling and soft, surrounding him in a fragile cloud of comfort. It seemed he was swimming slowly, thoughtfully, through the nimbus of her immense care. Was that truly it? Did she really care? He fixed on the way her eyes looked as she said 'stints' as if the foreignness of the sound would require extra solicitation and gradual immersion in a new language of concern. Her wonderful linguistic stroking made the concept slip easily into his mind. Some part of you now would be artificial, she seemed to be saying, a coiled infinitely flexible and thin steel mini tunnel through which the stream of your living would swiftly pass.

Yes, that was it, "swiftly passing." He reached out to her. At least his right hand reached up to find her fingers. How softly and solicitous they seemed, how tenderly they gripped his pudgy palm, then intertwined with his fingers in the kindest invitation he could imagine. He squeezed her hand harder to get her attention that seemed to have wandered in Claudio's direction.

"Agnes," he said, "Agnes of ISMAR, you're not really a hooker are you?" He tried to ask but he was not sure his words actually formed and were received.

"Oh, but I am. And I'm here to save you from your anxieties and your despair."

"I'm not despairing. I'm holding your hand, and I'm not despairing."

"See? That's why I'm here holding your hand."

"But you're not really a hooker, are you? I mean it was just a sort of joke, wasn't it?"

"You want to believe that. And if you want to believe that, then I'm here to reassure you."

"What does that mean?"

"It means I care about you. Do you believe that?"

Why, Hugh thought, should I believe that, since he knew very few people cared about him. Venice surely didn't care. That had been clear enough from his first visit, only to be reinforced on his second, third and fourth visits. Claudio it seemed perfectly mirrored the city's leisurely dismissal of his technology, his imagined resurrection of the city's innovative leadership.

And if Claudio didn't care, then the enterprise was doomed. No stint could keep it from swiftly passing. Swiftly passing.

Hugh was aware that the technician shouting, "Mr. Hugh!" was summoning him back from somewhere, somewhere ferociously interesting, liltingly engrossing. An experience so softly, so sweetly egging him onwards by simply repeating and repeating a litany of celebration and affirmation, as if slipping him easily onto a cloud toboggan and launching it through infinite cotton candy. He remembered thinking, if this is death, wow, let's get more of it. Envelop me more, oh such aimiable lightness. But the technician–Hugh remembered someone calling him Roberto– kept calling him back. "Mr. Hugh! Mr. Hugh!" And while summoning him back Roberto was simultaneously pushing his fist into Hugh's upper thigh, punching it down and holding it down for a twenty seconds, then releasing, then punching down again.

"I hear in America they just put a sandbag on the area and leave it for some hours. To close the wound, but here we're more systematic. Punching it down and releasing it works better."

"How long do you do it for?" Hugh remembered asking.

"About an hour."

Hugh thought so this fellow punches my inner right thigh about three inches from my groin and for an hour we make conversation in some language neither of us feels comfortable. Endless examination of the reasons behind Venice's escalating real estate prices even as its population declined. Considerations whether extra virgin olive oil was truly "extra." Relivings of high waters in history. And always the weird punching pressure and the nodding in and out of consciousness. And always, Agnes nearby with a 5 by 8 inch card on her lovely chest with the simple notation 100 Euros written on it. And on the fourth day, her whispered summons––enough to tear him loose from the lilting lovely nimbus of his imagined succumbing—, a faint moist whisper in his ear–her sweet enveloping closeness literally lifting from one reverie to a better one—"Schioppettino, I still have three bottles."

PART III

Deliverance in the Contarini Chapel

By the fourth day after Hugh Frendell's heart attack, his mentor in Italy, his translator, his business partner, his only friend in Venice, Claudio, stopped coming to Hugh's private room at Ospedale Civile on the Fondamenta Nuove. Instead, he sent a college student named Donna, who, she said, had been recruited to an archeological dig on the Lazaretto in the Venetian lagoon, 300 square miles of slightly misting, grey/green, still water.

Her very focused approach to this new assignment interested Hugh. For a while he decided she had consciously adopted a stern reproachful stance–a clipped directedness that would shape him up and ship him out in jig time. But he eventually convinced himself that it was only a pose; her natural sweetness, her almost uncontrollable care he imagined lurked like capped lava beneath the lid of barked orders and immediate shock at his stumbling compliance. Their initial exchange set the pattern:

"I'm most appreciative of your coming, and I hope Claudio hasn't threatened you with failing on the dig unless you relieved him here."

"Nah, nothing like that. He couldn't, you know. He only thinks he might be able to. I'm so over him."

"Well, I know how boring this must be for someone your age–"

"I'm older than you think."

"I'm sure you are. I'm not too sharp in my present condition."

"You're sharp enough I guess."

"Well, thanks for that. And what do think of Venice?"

"You know they're not going to let you out of here until you produce a well-formed turd—to their sick liking."

There was a rather lengthy pause in which Hugh decided Donna sounded very much like his own daughter in high school. There was a familiar calculated affront in her choice of the word, 'turd'—a testing of the boundaries that at once amused and irritated him. He admired Claudio for sending him a cross between Nurse Rachet and Paris Hilton or some other figure large in what he imagined was the collegiate world. Donna seemed more instinctively kind than his daughter, or was it that she had become more focused recently?

To savor the comparison Hugh answered in kind: "And are you the arbiter of 'well formed'?"

"Nah. One of them is. I'm just sayin.'"

Hugh wondered if the easy diffidence of her expressions was generational or particular? "Some say health is a matter of visioning, imagining wellness. I guess I'll envision a well- formed turd."

"You do that and we're out of here pronto. And Dr. Risica told Claudio you need light exercise, constant light exercise."

"I like the adjective 'light'" Hugh said.

"And I have two places for your exercise."

"But only after a well-formed turd."

"Of course, but they'll only give you one more day for that."

"Really? Then what?"

"You enter 'enema territory.'" Donna laughed, too loudly. And then, as if to undercut her embarrassing mirth, she added, "Claudio said your wife isn't coming over."

"That's right. She has obligations in Waterbury." Did the phrase sound deceitful, Hugh wondered? "Jenean works full time and we have a daughter finishing high school—maybe only a year or two younger than you." Then responding to her apparent disappointment about the high school analogy Hugh said, "And given our scatological conversational turn I suppose Claudio has told you about our plan."

"You mean the vacuum sewers stuff? He mentioned that."

"I hope more than mentioned it. We have a major presentation to Centro Maree coming up, despite my problems. The contract could save Venice."

"Everybody wants to save Venice."

"Piping to Mestre, to a plant there could make the canals gleam again. Don't you believe that?"

Donna answered. "You're supposed to take a short walk now, so let's get you up."

Hugh was happy to take her arm as he slipped off the surprisingly high bed. And they walked in the gleaming orange titled corridor with its view of San Michele island beyond the nurses' station. "You only get 12 years on that island," Hugh said.

"I know. Claudio tells all Americans that. He likes nothing more than to tell us about his Venice. It gets cold soon enough, doesn't it?"

"I appreciate the information," Hugh said delighting in her grip on his left arm.

"Next year I hope he has better factoids," she said.

Did that mean she was coming back again next summer?

"I've noticed that a number of students who say unkind things about Claudio, nonetheless end up coming back each summer for more." Hugh said, as they stopped before two huge buff-colored doors.

"We have to go back," Donna said, pointing back to his room. "We can't overdo it, can we?"

"I don't think we're overdoing it."

"Not what you think. I'm jes sayin.'"

"I don't mind going back," he said. "But I worry the nurses don't like me. I've given them some grief."

"Did you bad mouth them?"

"No. I'm not like that."

"I'm thinking you're always considerate."

"Yes, that's me. Considerate and affectionate."

"I doubt that. Men your age aren't considerate, or affectionate."

"I'm better than Claudio," Hugh said, enjoying the comparison forming in his mind.

"That's no trick. Everyone's better than Claudio. He's only interested in telling you about Venice. Saving Venice. That's all he talks about. He thinks an old Byzantine brick is more interesting than a live human being."

"I suppose that's natural for an archeologist."

"Heh! He's no archeologist. His dig manners are terrible. Tomorrow we'll go to Ca'd' Oro for the Etruscan exhibit. And then to Claudio's favorite church, Madonna dell' Orto."

Hugh paused, wondering if Dr. Risica or Claudio had set up the itinerary. Finally he said, "I can't wait."

She looked carefully into his eyes and then said, "But first, a well-formed turd."

2.

When she arrived in the morning Hugh was already dressed and stuffing his hospital gown into a laundry bag. She eyed him and said quickly, "Congratulations. So they're letting you out."

"Yes, don't ask." Hugh answered.

"I'm thinking a slow stroll over to Ca'd' Oro beats taking a boat all the way around."

"Good enough, so long as we can stop at a Pharmacy and get my prescriptions filled."

She nodded but Hugh went on, in not quite convincing exasperation, "Dr. Risica says I get to take drugs for the rest of my life. The rest of my life. I can't say I like the phrase."

"It's just a 'morning handful.' My father has been doing it for years. Nothing to worry about."

"I like the phrase, 'nothing to worry about' It speaks to a man in my condition."

When she didn't answer, he said. "Sometimes I can feel the stints moving."

"They're stents, and Dr. Risica says they don't move, can't move. You shouldn't worry about that."

"Oh, I understand the science, the medicine of them. I get that, but I still have feelings. It's okay to have feelings of being threatened, isn't it?"

"Not necessary."

"Okay not necessary. But not going away either. Surely Dr. Risica can grasp that."

"I could talk to him about it."

"Please don't. I'd rather just have the feelings."

"That's weird."

"Weird or not, it's what's happening."

When they had exited the back of the hospital, away from the campo at San Giovanni et Paolo, it seemed she pressed ahead toward Ca' d' Oro so as to keep him at a difficult pace. Was that the simple lurch of her youth, or had Risica told her to keep pressing him? When they reached the open square at Saint Apostoli he slumped into a conveniently empty metal chair and table and called out to her. "We need to pause here."

She turned back, "Here? Why here?"

"I need to rest."

"Are you feeling bad? Chest pains?"

"No. Just tired, wilting. Let's have a spritz."

"What's a spritz?"

"You've been a month in Venice and you're asking that question?"

"Yeah, what is it?"

The drinks arrived, orange and glowing in the early afternoon sunshine. "Aperol, an apple liquor and Prosecco, with some olives, or maybe with a disk of orange, sometimes made with cheap white wine and selzer, but the sturdier stuff has Prosecco. A spritz is unique to Venice, or so Claudio thinks. All Claudios think. You drink them slowly, achingly, and stones under foot get softer. The numbered stones melt. The stents stop moving."

"You just feel sorry for yourself."

"Probably," Hugh said, letting the icy liquid loll in his mouth around the hard olive, salty in the wash. "The Prosecco hardly fizzes, assaulted by the liquor. On a good afternoon, like this one, I can imagine just opening a vein and letting the spritz slip in, directly into my brain."

He closed his eyes, felt stilts inside fall away. "It's better than a Vacuum Sewers contract signing in a beige-carpeted lawyer's office in Bridgeport." He hoped a sewers contract in Bridgeport would somehow impress her, but soon enough he realized the idiocy of that estimate. He'd have to try a different tack.

"And do you know why, mysteriously, I settled in Waterbury? What keeps me pinioned to Waterbury like some giant preying mantis impaled on an orange gold tee? Do you?"

She laughed guardedly.

"Because Waterbury has the tallest bell tower in Connecticut. Better than any Venetian bell tower, though this place is littered with them. In Waterbury you can squint at it, and you'd swear you could smell the lagoon."

"I love the lagoon," she answered, "sometimes it's like a cookie sheet."

"I don't think so," he said.

"Okay not, then. But I want to see the Etruscan exhibit. Rolfe was on a dig near Viccio and he says they found a helmet there last summer. They're still determining its age."

"Lovely for Rolfe. Should I know him?"

"No. Definitely not. He's on the Lazaretto dig. And he hasn't showered since he got here."

Hugh thought, perhaps someone enamored of a 'well-formed turd' might be enchanted by the pheromones of sweat. It heartened him he was not sweating from the walk so far; he remembered epic sweats before the heart attack. Anxious sweats pouring down his sides, down from his forehead and a vague nausea roiling around as if testing the doorways of his intestines, looking frantically for an exit. He remembered the casual way his daughter would run into him in the house and simply observe: "Dad, take a shower." With no more emphasis or investment than as if she had said, "The bus is running late."

That was the key question, Hugh thought, "is the bus truly running late?" He remembered in elementary school sitting quietly in seventh period waiting for the clock to click over to the final exit moment, which was always extended if the buses were running late. If the orange line of busses wasn't in place, there could be no end of the day.

"Did you notice near Claudio's office the elementary school playground contained within the building? A stone playground big enough for a modest soccer game, with the kids running back and forth, back and forth in that contained campo slightly larger than a half tennis court?"

"I could hear them, but I never saw them." Donna answered. "We need to keep moving."

"I wonder why," Hugh said. "Why not sit here all day? I could get us some Schioppettino Have you ever tried it?"

"Do you drink or eat it?"

"You imbibe it. You fill up your calves with it. You pour it slowly into your forearms and the most empty places of your brain. Lately I've a lot of those."

"Ah, feeling sorry for yourself again. That settles it. We'll move along and at a good pace. Dr. Risica said it was important not to surrender to lassitude."

"Is that the word he used?"

"Of course. It's a nifty word, 'lassitude.'"

"Indeed, the key word it seems to me."

"Of course not. There are no key words."

"Only key actions."

"I don't think so. There are only key feelings."

Yes, thought Hugh, key feelings like the ones I'm feeling now to take this svelte nurse companion in my arms and swirl back across Apostoli square and down the steps toward the Rialto bridge and then up into the Venetian grey blue sky with swart circling pigeons dripping ill-formed turds onto the numbered stones below. "So lead on. Lead on." He got up, remembered to leave the small change for their waiter. Sudden bars of sunlight flooded onto the square denting the umbrellas ringing the campo. But soon enough they were back among narrow walkways through buildings and over bridges until suddenly they were in the narrowest passageway leading to Ca' d' Oro on the Grand Canal. And as they entered Hugh felt a sudden familiar sweating. He put fifty euros in her hand and asked her to buy the tickets while he sat on a wooden bench.

"Rolfe's helmet is on the third floor, one over the *piano nobile*. The walk up will do you good."

"I doubt it."

"No. Come on. Press yourself. You can sit later."

It did seem to Hugh that someone was indeed pressing him, flattening him out, ironing him opaque against a too high board covered in a silver-metallic cloth. He remembered his daughter's stern tirade against the way he had errantly (apparently, very apparently) hung her jeans with the seams matching. "What were you thinking?" she demanded. "Nobody wears jeans with that kind of crease. Nobody does. Nobody."

3.

At the third level Hugh said, "You go ahead. I'll sit here a while. No one uses these stairs anyway. I'll be fine here, resting. You go ahead and come back and tell me about it."

"But Dr. Risica said–"

"Fuck Dr. Risica." It surprised Hugh how strident he sounded. He almost checked, looking around to see if he had offended anyone.

"Well, I really wanted to see the Etruscan relics–"

"I don't think 'relics' is the right word. Better is 'artifacts.'"

"Suit yourself. I'll be back in a jiff."

He'd never heard his daughter use "jiff." He slumped down on the tough rubber tread lining the concave marble step. He could feel the ridges through his trousers, and his knees rose too high for much comfort. He rocked back to ease his breathing which seemed constricted. Golden sunlight flooded into the stairwell from long narrow windows above and below him. He used his left palm to push sweat off his forehead. Abandoned on the steps. Venice had a way of dismissing pretenders. You came here to sell us something, but Venice answered: "We are not about purchase." Oh, but you really are, Hugh thought. You really are.

Anxiety and stress are the natural enemies of the heart, he'd read somewhere in the brochures they'd handed him about heart disease after the stints went in. The nurses seemed delighted to find an audience for the wilted English texts. Anxiety and stress and anger——perhaps most of all anger--all enemies of recovery. No, not recovery, just *elongation* of whatever time remained, he decided. Taken daily the medicines will alter the architecture of the heart, yielding more time, Dr. Risica explained in the softest voice imaginable. I will *elongate* my life, Hugh repeated quietly, as instructed by the burly nun he imagined had come twice to his room. I will *elongate* my life. But to what end? More vacuum sewer piping in Bridgeport or throughout Fairfield county?

Elongation after all was a piping term. There was even a formula—so much elongation beyond gravity feed required an additional hydraulic assist. Yes, of course, down the line the stints would require a pacemaker, and anon, after the pacemaker failed, additional pounding, shocking attempted resurrection. And then eventually nothing more than easy slippage into the lagoon, like the slow billowing red or green powder he had Claudio's students introduce into the toilets of Venice to track where the sewerage went. Flush the colored water and run to the canal to see where it exited, if it exited at all, where, after exit, the currents bore the markings, if they carried, out into the lagoon. You could spin high above the lagoon and see the red/green spirals dissipate among the thin mist of the lagoon's grey/green surface.

Perhaps wisps of color worked magically beyond the Lido into the Adriatic.

"Are you ill?" came a soft voice from above.

"Maybe," Hugh heard himself answer, too tired to elaborate.

"Perhaps you'd like to rest. We have a room on the first floor, for that. It's air conditioned. There's an elevator very nearby you–you could take it. I'll show you how to use it."

"Yes."

And she was on the step above him, helping him get to his feet. She had a whistle on a leather lanyard around her neck. She wore a tailored Navy blue uniform, blazer and skirt and in her left hand was a long rectangular cordless telephone. Just as Donna had, she took his left arm at the elbow and steered him into the creaking, cranking elevator.

They rode in silence to the first floor, exited left and into a tall-ceilinged room and then she deposited him on a maroon velvet couch.

"I'll bring you some water and find your daughter and tell her where you are."

"She'll figure it out," Hugh said suddenly more tired than ever. But the attendant had gone.

And Hugh slumped a bit, dipping his head against his chest for sleep.

Donna awakened him: "There wasn't any helmet, so Rolfe was right about them trying to date it somewhere else in Italy. But it would have been nice to see it here. You didn't drink your water."

True enough, the translucent cup was sitting on the end table beside the couch.

"So we can press on to Madonna dell 'Orto."

"I don't think so. I can get the *vaporetto* here and go back to Giglio and home."

"No. You need to press on, a walk to Madonna dell 'Orto is what Dr. Risica suggested and Claudio said I've got to do what Dr. Risica wants."

"I'm beginning to see a conspiracy."

"Nah, only interest in keeping you alive."

"For what?"

"So you can see your wife and daughter again."

When Hugh didn't react, Donna went on, "Or maybe just Madonna dell 'Orto. It's supposed to be quite beautiful and there's Tintoretto paintings inside."

Hugh sighed and finally said, "I've seen Scuola San Rocco–that's enough Tintoretto for a life-time."

"Aw come on. We'll try the walk. If it's too much, we can get a *vaporetto*."

Hugh felt more than a pang at the expression "we" can do whatever. By what decree should it be "we" now? He was not an invalid. How could it be he was following directives from this child? By what strings was he being pulled? He wondered if Venice imposed a mask of compliance on longer-term visitors–something akin to those Carnival masks sold at a hundred instant shops in the *calli* everywhere in the city. Daily you will walk on nothing but stone, smell nothing but eerie sea and petroleum, human excrement, see only shimmering reflections below dripping laundry, and hear propeller churn, shouted greetings, and seagull moans, eat nothing but pale pasta and endless San Erasmo tomatoes. And yet there was a self beneath the mask that rejoiced in being *here*, sampling *hereness* that included sitting in stunned silence before paintings that tossed one magnificent mantle after another over the ever prosaic *now*.

The *now* that recognized an incomparable *then*–so immeasurably greater than the prosaic *now* that celebrated being able to grasp the infinitely greater *then*. That was Venice's thrall: an opening to the infinitely greater *then* — a *then* that transcended the tourist-garroted, putridity-saturated *now*, but somehow was knotted together so that the one generated the other and vice versa. Hugh understood he was not the putridity liberator, the solid waste redeemer he had dreamed of being. *Then*, after all, precluded *now*. And for an instant he recast his role in the paradise of *then*. What was he, if not the most advanced technology of *now*, just as the canals were the most advanced sewerage system of *then*. Why wasn't he recognized as the *Doge* of this day? Had he thrown in with a dubious partner, the Claudio who excited a nimbus of suspicion wherever he went?

They exited Ca' d' Oro and slowly went up the Strada Nuova, the wide straightest street in Venice, Austria's clearest legacy to the occupied Serene Republic, at the end of the 18th century. In the open air Hugh breathed more easily, and the sweating lessened. Still he had the feeling that nausea was waiting, impatient for a random stimulus. Coiled and about to strike. Hugh tried belly breathing, drawing in slowly to a seven count exhaling quietly through a partially opened mouth to another seven count. Then repetition. Donna forged ahead of him, turning occasionally to summon him up to her. At the second bridge to the north side of Venice the airport tower visible across the lagoon and, improbably, the jagged Alps beyond, he asked for a rest.

They sat on a pew that had been set out in the *calle*, since the small church nearby was undergoing renovations. Hugh slumped toward the left. Sweat again came out of his forehead. And nausea swept through his torso, only subsiding as it reached the depth of his throat. Instead of retching he curl-growled thick mucus upwards and then forced back down in willful swallowing. He turned away to hide the ferocity of the effort.

"We have only one more bridge to the church," she said cheerily. "And inside it will be cooland pinkish, or so the guidebooks say."

"Oh joy," he answered, still struggling with excess saliva.

"My dad used to use a lot of sarcasm, but the doctor said it only increased his stress, so he trained himself out of it."

"I bet you were a big help there."

"Actually I wasn't around that much. He did it by himself. My mom said so." She paused to assess his reaction, he imagined, but then continued, "She was impressed. She never thought he had much self-discipline."

"So it was blessings all around."

"He might have thought that, but he wouldn't say that now—maybe wouldn't even have thought that. Let's go."

Hugh stood up and immediately felt dizzy. The Istrian stone of the final bridge felt coldly reassuring, steadying. They emerged at last into the small campo before Madonna Dell 'Orto.

The sunlight flooded onto the scaffolding at the front of the gothic facade of the church.

More restorations, Hugh thought, Venice's lame emblem of vitality. He imagined a bamboo scaffolding was being slowly erected around him, pressing in, obstructing his view of the carved statues atop the church, pressing further in, cutting off his air. He heard the thong straps lashing the poles together tighten, in a squeaking rhythm that approached waltz time.

"I'm not sure I can actually go in," he said. "Or if I go in I'll need to sit a while, really quickly. I'll need to sit."

"Of course. No problem. No worries. I'm sure there's a chapel right at the entrance. The Contarini Chapel, right on the left. Maybe you can lie on his tomb."

After a while and in the wondrous orange/pink light of the church's interior–light flooding off the embedded glass globes in the brickwork of the myriad high arches, he said, "I don't think so. I just need to sit."

"I wasn't being serious. Couldn't you tell that?"

"I can't tell much. My stomach hurts and sometimes I think I'm not breathing."

"Jesus! Why didn't you tell me?"

"I just did."

"Should I call Claudio?"

"Maybe if we just sit for a while, a long while, maybe it won't be necessary."

Hugh slumped in a pew and began looking at the massive painting over the chapel's altar.

It was dark but gradually he was drawn to the white center of the painting–a young girl with a radiant white halo around her head. "What's the painting?" he said with a dark, gravelly voice that seemed not his own, but some sort of pebbled water moaning out of him.

"I don't know."

"Find out."

"How?"

"The guide book, a brochure, something they sell at the entrance."

"There's no one there."

"Get the brochure–there has to be one. Get it."

"I think I better call Claudio."

"He won't answer. Just get the guidebook." Hugh recognized his own rising discontent, even as chest pain escalated.

She came back with a brown burnished brochure. "It's by Tintoretto, The Miracle of Saint Agnes."

"Agnes?"

"Yes. Agnes. She's bringing the Roman procurator's son back to life. He died because he accused her of being a prostitute."

"Of course he did."

"He dragged her to a brothel and tried to rape her, but God struck him dead."

"Of course he did."

"But his father begged her to save him and she did. She asked God to spare him and he did."

"Of course he did. And of course you led me here to see this," he gestured toward the painting. "I was supposed to see this painting, and Venice wanted me to see the clearest view of Agnes of ISMAR."

"I don't know what you're saying."

"I'm jes sayin'" Hugh mocked Donna's intonations. "Tell me more about the painting."

She read silently and then said, "The top part of painting is special. Those are angels, men and women in swirling blue. But you can't see them very well."

But as if on command sunlight from the pink, orange golden central aisle shifted toward the chapel and flooded across the painting, so that the top segment in unbelievable blue motion, clothing rippling over the exposed gorgeous angelic flesh tones in the sky, with tiny cherub heads peeking from the top-most nave seemed to beckon to Agnes' sparkling below, embodying what she must have visioned as a heaven suffused with bodily delights. Or perhaps only his rapturous longing–Hugh's and presumably the painter's. The angels were fully adult, male and female, yet swaddled in undulating blue gossamer fabric—glimpses of lush flesh splayed out in the heavenly vault.

There was an enormous dark shadow like a massive pillar down the right side of the painting. When the sunlight hit it, maybe there was a face or two in the darkness, Hugh couldn't tell, but the brilliant ochre scarlet of the Roman procurator's flowing gown fed into his hand held out imploring Agnes.

I should have known, Hugh thought. Oh Agnes, I should have known. Forgive me, Agnes. You were such an innocent child, joking with this vulnerable old man, who took the bait and foraged with it in thickets of reverie, utterly unaware of your gentility, your goodness, your celestial blessings. Only feasting on the imagined softness, the delicate softness, of your deliciously perfumed flesh. Forgive me, Agnes. Only now do I see the luminous innocence of your wondrous hair, only now the tender elixir of your fragrance filling the tiny flickering cups of the sun-dappled canals.

Donna interrupted his reverie. "It's a better heaven, way better than 'God as Bat.' Way better. Just awesome!"

"What are you talking about?"

"Another painting in the Frari. Claudio took me to look at it. At the top of that painting God looked like an old hairy face on bat wings. These angels are such a better heaven. Way better. Look at the angels, all that buff flesh."

"Buff?"

"You know. It's fantastic."

"No. You are fantastic. Thank you for leading me here, showing me here. Illuminating everything. I feel such relief coming here. It's like breathing again. It's like the clot dissolved, the stent slid away, flushed away so I could sweat it out, or pee it out, or shit it out."

"That's gross!"

"So much of life, Donna, is! Enviably gross! Come, give me a kiss."

She pulled away from him in the pew, "Jesus!" she said, "That's so sick."

"Yes! Sick with love. Sick with the possibility we might be pulled together up into that angelic orgy." He motioned to the top of the altar. And he noted that she had not slipped free of his right hand still on her left shoulder. He let his fingers tighten, thumb digging in and finger pressure asking her to turn toward him. Stunningly, she seemed to comply, yielding and easing closer, drawn to him not by words only by furtive finger signals. It was as if the energy poured out of the painting decorating them both in a luminous, white, embracing light. For an instant he imagined they could be gathered up into that whoosh of Tintoretto's genius, shedding garments, afloat in the orange pink light, bathed in swirling blue and flesh tones. Yes, he was wonder-filled as Donna came so much closer—he could feel the softest down of her cheek ooze through the fuscous air suffusing his lips with a galvanizing tenderness–yes, he could partake of the miracle Agnes wrought, renewing his life, his receptivity to all creation.

He closed his eyes, imagined living always in the top of the painting among angel flesh, but rather than kiss Donna as she yielded to him he remembered the responsibilities gently flowing out of the bell tower in Waterbury and finally whispered to her: "When you talk to Claudio, please remind him we've got to make a presentation to Centro Maree."

"You're such a romantic. Vacuum Sewers till you die. . .."

"It's what I do, but who's to say we could ever get free of that painting?"

"Wouldn't you want to find out?"

"Yes, oh yes! I want to find out." And he kissed her with a sloppy ferocity that set them both laughing.

When that ended Donna said, "I'll tell ya something. I knew what a spritz is. I just wanted to let you do your guy thing."

PART IV

A Presentation at Centro Maree

Claudio said, "I was thinking, Hugh, your heart attack turned out to be a sort of *Death in Venice Manque,* or maybe *Death in Venice: A Lame Sequel,* or maybe," his hard-breathing, near- laugh increased "or maybe, *Son of, but not as good as, Death in Venice.*"
"I'm not amused."

"Okay, just *Death in Venice, Part II.*"

"Let's talk about the presentation to Centro Maree, and skip the literary allusions. I didn't come here to die. Neither did I come here to discuss novels."

"It's not really a novel. And it's too sour on Venice."

"Probably nobody at Centro Maree has read it. That's our starting point, don't you think?"

"For someone who can't speak a word at the meeting, you seem pretty involved, pretty worried about something you can't even comment on. I told you the only problem will be Luigino, and I'm working on convincing him—a convincing, incidentally, that will have to go on well before the meeting. If you think a conversion can happen at the meeting, you're wrong. So let me worry about it."

"I can't stay in Venice forever, you know. I have other contracts, and other contacts out of Waterbury. The world wants Vacuum Sewers, and I'm going to deliver."

"I wonder if the world really does want Vacuum Sewers," Claudio said, pouring himself another glass of Schioppettino; the wine that had become the very cement of their almost business relationship. "You and I know it will save Venice, catapult Venice into the position she naturally inherits at the edge of the newest global technologies. But can we convince the bureaucrats that ours is the best path to Elysium?" He took a long swallow, "Can we?"

"If we don't ask, we won't really know, will we?"

"In Italy it never works to ask a question you don't already know the answer to."

"And what is that supposed to mean?"

"Everything is preparation and network; things have to be clicking so smoothly that you don't need to ask. Don't you get that?"

"I get, that for some reason you don't want to make a presentation to Centro Maree soon."

"Exactly. We have to persuade Luigino first. Then when he's on board, we can proceed to Centro Maree."

"But he has nothing to do with Centro Maree."

"That's right. He has nothing to do with Centro Maree. But he has everything to do with solid waste disposal, crap removal, from Venice. IN-SULA controls what comes into or goes out of Venice. At least most of the time. And Luigino is Mister Big in INSULA He has the connections to pry money out of Rome ."

What irritated Hugh most about Claudio was his constant pose as the all-knowing interlocutor, the very key to success in La Serenissima—his steady assumption of superiority, his remorseless automatic soft-spoken insistence on deference. "So we need to find the chink in Luigino's armor–the little crevice by which we can pry open his commitment to vacuum sewerage as the wave, so to speak, of the future."

"Something tells me you've already located a chink."

"Maybe a crevice. Named Antonio, Luigino's son."

"Why not just make the pitch to Centro Maree and be done with it? I've never seen the connection with weather/tide forecasting anyway."

"INSULA has been the strongest supporter of Centro Maree, and that alliance is justification for Maree's really amazing allocations from the government. INSULA is the strongest player in Venice and they're fused with the weather/tides guys. Weather prediction is crucial for them, and if Centro Maree decides now they need a change–your damn pipes to Mestre—and that change is going to cost them livelihoods, then they'll hardly support Centro Maree. And whiff goes the allocations. Centro Maree won't endorse anything without Luigino's permission."

"And we're going to influence Luigino by kidnapping his son? Kidnapping Antonio?"

"No. We're going to get him laid."

"And that's going to facilitate Vacuum Sewers all over Venice?"

"It's going to put Luigino in our debt. And he'll accept that a couple of his subcontractors are going to lose their livelihood, because eventually sewerage won't go into the canals."

"I don't see how getting Antonio laid can be sales leverage?"

"Luigino's convinced the kid is gay."

"And we're going to use that information to hold Luigino hostage?"

"Absolutely the opposite. We're going to disprove it. We're going to set Luigino free from his fears, and he's going to be so thankful he'll do anything we want."

Claudio finished his wine, set the glass down in the narrow parlor of Hugh's apartment and walked toward the sealed glass doors shielding green shutters. He opened the glass doors and swung them back, then lifted the clanking latch of the shutters. He eased them back in their captivating accordion effect, revealing a screenless *altana* that overlooked Campo San Maurizio. Faint Vivaldi music drifted in from the museum at the far side of campo.

"Yeah," Hugh said, "they play that music all day till 9 p.m. Damn sowing machine music."

"Oh no!," Claudio said, "he's a truest genius Venice ever produced. Bach learned everything from Vivaldi. Western music owes its existence to Vivaldi. He created all the forms. Just as Beethoven stole everything from Boccherini."

Hugh joined Claudio on the *altana*. A tourist family took over the east side of the well-head at the center of the campo below; two priests were on the other side of the well-head. The priests were examining a laminated map, presumably of Venice. The family came over to the priests and asked some kind of question.

"That's unusual," Claudio said, "a direct approach to priests—you don't see that often."

"Maybe they're German or American. Probably they're looking for directions."

"I don't think so. Something more urgent."

"Absolution?" Hugh asked, smiling.

"Not likely. I'd bet they're looking for a bathroom."

"And the will have difficulty finding one in Venice," Hugh said.

"Not if we succeed," Claudio laughed. "Little kiosks of vacuum driven relief in every campo. Designed by the finest living architects, each one playing Vivaldi."

"Vivaldi and Boccherini among the sprays," Hugh said.

"I'm thinking we have two allies in the Antonio challenge. Agnes and Donna. Do you agree?"

"I agree with Agnes at least. We know she's a business woman, with a clear price tag."

"Really?"

"I know it for a fact, and I know also that we can meet her price."

"I'm unfamiliar with her mercantile aspects," Claudio said with a certain expression at once quizzical and condescending.

"I guess you need more networking. Or maybe you could be more straightforward. She speaks with remarkable bluntness when it comes to price."

"Really? And what is her price?"

"100 euros for a 'session' I perceive to be less than one hour. Apparently 250 euros for all night, although that was never truly settled."

"Hugh, you have a side I've not seen before. Remarkable! Italy is working its magic on you. Are you sure she wasn't just jesting, or maybe joking with you?"

"About such matters I'm never clear," Hugh answered

2.

In early June the Adriatic had a white choppy surface belying its usual dark blue/green somnolence. And the usual detritus was not so visible: seaweed, sticks, white paper waste, medical shards perhaps, even plastic bottles and furtive, surprising kelp tangles. Claudio's cousin owned a hotel a block off the beach of the Lido, and in this pre high season moment he lent a cellar apartment to Claudio, and that gave him access to the rooftop *altana* and hot tub. During the day, tourists at the hotel always headed off to Venice to visit churches, scuolas, palaces, and so Hugh and Claudio had the roof to themselves.

In a deliberate plan, each of the white plastic sheathed tables held a heavy pair of binoculars, secured by a six and half foot very light-weight chain welded onto the umbrella pole in the middle of each table. If you sat in the best positioned chair you could train the binoculars on the white/tan sheen of the 12 mile long beach. And on the beach some boys were playing an improvised soccer game with a black volley ball. After a minute of careful scanning using the binoculars, Claudio passed them to Hugh.

"Move slowly along the shore toward the fence separating this beach from the condos that used to be the DesBain Hotel. Eventually if you move the binoculars slowly you'll see the soccer game near the fence. Antonio's there. He's the whitest boy on the beach. In pale blue. Some kind of surfing short. Almost alabaster, almost albino."

"I don't see him."

"Start out to sea and come back to beach right near the fence. He's not a goalie, but you'd think he was. He hangs back from the action, near the goal. Reticent. Maybe absent minded."

"Absent minded?"

"Maybe distracted. Not into the game."

"Like us. A loser." Hugh said.

"Yes," Claudio said, "maybe convinced he can't quite compete. Not good enough. Afraid. Reluctant to test himself against the giants of Centro Maree. Content with small contracts in Bridgeport or West New Haven, is that it?"

"Very funny."

"I thought so. But check him out. He almost blends in with the beach. Ivory complexion and a focus a million miles away. Skinny too. Arms like match sticks, legs like a frog, a chrome frog in the sunlight against the green and dirty sea."

"I was thinking the Adriatic looked suspiciously healthy today."

"You're not seeing it. Can you make him out?"

"Yes, I can see him. Now what?"

"Keep watching. See if he notices. See if he looks along the fence back toward the road."

Hugh panned to his right, and there at the edge of the sand on an enormous turquoise towel lay ravishing Agnes in the skimpiest chrome red bikini or perhaps it was just a thong, Hugh couldn't tell as his blinking increased against the stained black eyepiece.

"Does he notice her?"

"No. . . no, he seems lost in some private reverie."

"She'll knock him out of that."

"Yes, now she's waving to him, signaling him over. She's dropped the bikini top. Jesus!"

"She knows her trade. She's the Vacuum Sewers of seduction," Claudio said. "Give me the binoculars."

"Get your own."

But Claudio took them away from Hugh. "Yes, she's holding out some lotion. She pitches forward and now there's not much to be seen. But he's spreading the lotion on her back, her supple soft back, working that delicious liquid into the bread of her being. These are really powerful, you can see the down of her buttocks glistening with the oil."

"Oh to be his fingers now," Hugh said.

"Yes, indeed," Claudio echoed. "She'll lead him to our cellar apartment. I gave her a key and pre-paid for everything. Nature only has to work its will, nature and lotion and the sweet sucking sound of vacuum tubing coiling all around Venice."

"Ah, sweet Agnes of ISMAR, seal the deal," Hugh said.

"She puts on a white jacket to lead him off the beach. He follows like a puppy anticipating a meal."

"A meal indeed."

"And, indeed, I have a meal here in this basket." Claudio put the binoculars down and brought up the large square basket. He took out a bottle of Schioppettino and a roll of goat cheese wrapped in waxed tissue paper, then a baguette and small, serrated knife. Claudio held the Schioppettino between his feet on the deck, worked a corkscrew into the bottle top and slowly withdrew the cork. "We need to let this breathe a while," he said while Hugh took the two stubby wine glasses out of the basket. "Do you suppose someday we'll think back and imagine this moment as the beginning of an unrivaled fortune. The day it all began. Venice returned to her place at the very helm of new technology of waste disposal, returned at last to her leadership position in human health?"

"If not health," Hugh said, "then at least unrivalled removal of our well-formed turds, with a pumping station at the top of the carpark, and probably on the Mestre side of the bridge."

"Yes, pumping stations," Claudio said slowly, savoring the phrase.

Hugh began slicing the baguette. "She'll swallow him whole, like Jonah in the whale."

"And why not, at his age who would not want to be swallowed whole by the immense softness of a woman, the enfolding thighs slightly more spacious than the sky itself."

"The gracious Rubenesque extent of her gigantic ass, the billowy grandiosity of her bottom afloat above and beneath him. " Hugh elaborated as Claudio poured the Schioppettino.

"Let it breathe a while longer. It will pick up the scent of the Adriatic and meld it with that peppery aftertaste into something really amazing. They handle kegs of it from Fruili as if it could explode—ever so gently, so caringly. One thing about Italian craftsmen. The conception may be flawed, but the execution is always and everywhere perfect. They handle the kegs as if they were a woman."

"A woman so undamaged as to be sold to a Saudi Prince." Hugh said. "We have a lot riding on and with Agnes of ISMAR."

Claudio laughed, "But nature is on our side, is it not?"

"Nature and this Schioppettino," Hugh answered, "although I doubt he's a drinker."

"He could be and that's how Italy outshines the U.S. By making nothing of it. Nothing at all."

"There's more to it than that." Hugh took a drink.

"I told you to let it breathe. You're in too much rush."

"It's only twenty five Euros a bottle. Let's not enshrine it. What's muscatel cannot be Chateauneuf du Pape."

"I thought you didn't know much about wine."

"More than you, apparently."

"I know a great deal about Italian wines," Claudio said, smiling and still declining to pick up his glass. "I know that French wine lovers stupidly degrade our Veneto wine."

"So stupidly." Hugh agreed. "They can't recognize how trouble-making our Veneto wines can be. Or how liberating. How empeppering!"

Claudio laughed and at last took a slow swallow.

Hugh said, "I'm not sure Agnes will be gentle or caring. She's all business. Maybe we've sent a tigress to do a kitten's work. I don't know much about Luigino's boy, and I suppose this a lousy time to be catching up."

"Right. He's sixteen–that's the key information," Claudio said. "He's Luigino's son, that's more key information. Agnes is a wonder worker, that's all we need to know." He cut a thick slice of the goat cheese, chopped the end of the baguette off, halved it, and put the cheese in. Then took a healthy bite off the end.

"Do you suppose they're taking a shower?" Hugh asked, fingering his wine glass.

"Let it linger," Claudio answered, "I told you it needed to breathe, needed to right itself after the voyage from Fruili. It needs to be calm, like Antonio. At sixteen you shoot off too quickly, don't you remember?"

"Oh, I remember," Hugh said, "I remember all too well. The instantaneous delivery––would that I could get it back." He swallowed long and hard at the Schippettino.

"Doubtless she'll teach him control. She'll earn her money. I told her to bolster him in every way, build him up, leave him swelling and shuddering."

"Maybe you missed your calling as a hack poet." Hugh said, finishing his wine, and taking a bite of his baguette. "Maybe you should be writing porn in Amsterdam, instead of collecting data here in Venice."

"I do so much more than collect data. Even you must know that."

3.

In another half hour Agnes came out on to the roof. The sun in descent over the Adriatic slipped behind grey clouds and the air seemed momentarily chill and dark. Her words, Hugh thought, matched the suddenly sullen sky.

"You owe me 25 more Euros."

"And why?" Claudio said with mock menace.

"Because I had to be the DM, and I've never been the DM."

"What are you talking about?"Hugh asked.

"It was humiliating. When I took off my clothes, he insisted the DM would never be naked. How could I run a 'one shot game' much less a 'full campaign' if I were naked? How could I? No DM would do so."

"DM?" Claudio asked, "What is that, a kind of Dominatrix?"

"He said it was a 'Dungeon Master,' a kind of narrator for the game." Agnes said.

"Game?" Hugh asked.

"You've never done a D & D before?" Agnes asked with apparent shock.

"He wanted to play a game?"

"That's what he likes to do," Agnes said. "So I put my clothes on and asked him what's next? He said I had to make up the story, tell the story and that would be the game and we'd finish in less than an hour."

"Any story?" Claudio asked.

"Yes, whatever I wanted. Whatever the DM decreed. So I told him about the time I went to Malmo, Sweden when I was eleven. He liked that. He's about eleven too, you know. I went to Malmo and I saw a movie about a beautiful princess who wore twirly dresses and carried a small pink bag full of earrings. He liked it a lot. Afterwards he explained it could never be made into a full campaign. Too few characters. But really a lovely story of the girl in Sweden with the earrings. Then I started laughing. He didn't like that. So I came up here. I never want to be a DM again. It's extra when I'm a DM. 25 Euros extra."

"Nothing happened? No sex at all?" Claudio said.

"A DM is not a sexual being, he said that. D & D can never be a sexual game, he said that. He's quite good at explaining the limits of the game."

"The limits of the game," Hugh repeated, finishing his Schioppettino and refilling his glass.

"I'll have one too," Agnes said, and dutifully Hugh brought another glass up from the basket.

"Nothing else happened? Nothing?" Claudio said.

"How could it? A DM does not permit it."

"This is very bad," Claudio continued. "Very bad."

"How is it bad? I say. Now on to Donna, who can get the job done! She's more his age. It's a better prospect." Hugh said, pouring Agnes's wine.

"There's no time. The meeting with Centro Maree is scheduled this Friday. I don't think I can get it postponed."

"So you actually scheduled it?" Hugh said.

"They scheduled it. The only time they had. I had no choice. And now Luigino's not on board."

"We don't know that. Maybe the kid will brag about his time with the DM." Hugh answered. "Maybe all that Luigino will know is that his boy had a session with the luscious Agnes of ISMAR. He can fill in the details, file down the rough edges, feast on the term DM. Who knows what he might imagine about it. It's better than actuality, just like Venice. Then is always better than now."

Agnes said, "What are you saying? There was no *then* with Antonio."

"We can't say that for sure. Only Antonio can say that." Hugh answered. "Who knows how he might recast the *then*? He might recast himself as the very link between East and West, the imperial power of the world–ala Claudio's constant vision. The Queen of the Adriatic."

"Avoid 'Queen'" Claudio said. "The kid's got to be a king. A king of Luigino's estimation."

"Saying it will make it so," Hugh continued.

"Frankly I don't care, anyway," Agnes said, "I just need 25 Euros to be the degraded DM."

"Done!" Hugh said putting 25 Euros on the table top.

Agnes reeled it in, folding it into her large red handbag. "Sometimes I think you two live in some strange, drifting, imaginative world, and I can't tell whether you're floating on sewerage or something else. But I'm done with it. So's Antonio, who, after all, is just a sweet game player with a sixth grader's sense of reality."

"Unlike his initiating sex goddess." Hugh said.

"I admit I'm not orgasmal Zena of the Jungle. I admit it. What do you admit?"

Claudio answered, "We admit nothing. And Everything. I admit we wanted you to seduce him. But you didn't, and now we have to pick up the pieces and find some alternative. I don't think Donna is it. Certainly not in the time left."

"Maybe Vacuum Sewers will have to limp along on its own," Hugh said, "Sell itself. Be worthy without your machinations. I believe it can. It will prevail. I absolutely believe that. Maybe that's the problem. You'ved never believed it. Maybe you're the worst partner possible. Maybe I would have been better alone, naked, linguistically dumb and blind, with just the product to sell. Where has all your relationship leverage gotten us? Where indeed? A boy twisting toward maturity through a Dungeon and Dragons mist. With his puzzled father on the sidelines. And we're no closer to a contract than any schmuck off the boat from Romania."

"Don't pick on the Romanians," Agnes said, sipping her wine.

"They're not Romanians. They're gypsies," Claudio said. "And they're all thieves. And now we've got to have an alternative plan."

"I don't," Agnes said.

Hugh said, "We could have the Romanians kidnap Antonio and we could rescue him, bring him back to his grateful father, who would, naturally, sponsor Vacuum Sewers all over Venice. I better go back to Bridgeport. Jesus! How bad are things—when I dream of going back to Bridgeport?"

"Things are that bad," Claudio said. "How fast can we get Donna?"

"I don't like it," Hugh said. "She's not a business woman—not a market woman like Agnes here. We'll have to convince her she'd be doing a good deed. And we're not very good at that."

"We'll have to get a whole lot better and fast."

"Wouldn't it be better," Agnes said, "just to give the boy's father some cash directly—*tangente* is very Italian, isn't it?"

"We'll give him so much more than cash—the knowledge his future is safe and sound, his family is whole and healed and functioning in precisely the ways he has always ordered his life. Is there anything more valuable than that?" Claudio said. "The idea is to create a debt he'll be thrilled to payoff, in the way we specify. Support for solid waste and weather prediction–it's a winning combination. The City will have to go along. I'll summon Donna."

Hugh said quietly, "Wrong word."

4.

It was Agnes's suggestion that they plan a casual dinner at Hugh's place and in the course of a wine-filled evening Hugh and Claudio should exit, giving Donna and Antonio the use of the apartment. What could be more streamlined and sensible? Hugh got three rotisseried chickens from a Punto grocery store near Campo Manin. Claudio carried in a large salad and plate of prosciutto and mixed olives. Agnes decided not to join in, opting for her own adventures near the Arsenale boat stop, but only after instructing Claudio to tell Donna that Antonio liked playing D & D, but the night should consist of more engaging, deeper, more fulfilling games. And besides, relations with underage males had never been prosecuted in Italy. Agnes insisted on reassurance for Donna on that point. Hugh thought the directive excessively legalistic, and he found the whole discussion more than depressing, indeed saddening, as if something precious was slowly being dragged away from him in a way that tugged at his insides. Or was it more like a cut over a thumb joint that he needed to keep using for everyday activities? A little stab of pain as quickly forgotten as recognized. Did the whole gambit mean his own affection for Donna was as meaningless at he occasionally imagined? Was laughter toward his feelings as appropriate as inevitable?

When Donna and Antonio arrived, a bit flushed but beaming, from the four quick flights up, Hugh suddenly felt relieved. They seemed so appropriate together–in matching jeans and T shirts, blue and greens–and lithe and supple and awkward before their elder hosts. Hugh recognized the silliness of his infatuation, the embarrassment of it. How she must have mocked him later. Were they already laughing over his imbecilities–a dull and flabby entrepreneur who dreamed of getting lost in a painting? Hugh fought down an urge to apologize to Donna. But instead, he resolved to fix on the notion that she had, in fact, kissed him back.

He imagined discussing it with his daughter. Did she kiss him back, he might have asked her of some romance he briefly observed on some porch-way, in some car—in his memory she tentatively revealed to him as if asking for advice. Had she ever? Of course not, he understood. Only now here they were, the icons of his memory, the little dolls of his manipulations, the great game's recruits. So pristine as if walking on sunlit beach of the Lido with the sullen Adriatic misting, tossing soft white billows from an imagined midpoint. They sat like imploring puppies at his kitchen table and Claudio filled their glasses, but Hugh saw them only as they walked across the Adriatic out of billows coming toward him and mocking his frantic gestures to save them from drowning. Hugh felt cheapened by his plotting, by his subscription to Claudio's vulgar plan. These luscious adolescents needed to grapple on their own, uninstructed, indeed left to improvise their steps into adult ecstasies surely on their own. In a quick surge of self-loathing Hugh turned and went out onto the *altana*, suddenly interiorly instructed to clamp on to Vivaldi's rhythms as if the sewing machine grinding would release through the soft air expiation for his now-soiled longing. What an embarrassment he had been to her, to them both. Acting out his lust now through their wondrously soft, sleek skins. In a long swallow he finished his wine and quickly went back in for more.

"Claudio says the meeting with Centro Maree is all set," Donna said.

"Oh yeah, but that's Claudio's bailiwick. I'm ancillary," Hugh said.

"Bailiwick?" Antonio asked.

Hugh sat down at the table and reached for the plate of split chicken, "You tell him," he said to Donna, "we're paying you to clarify such things to non-native speakers, aren't we?"

"Paying her?" Antonio continued.

Could it be, Hugh thought, that vulgar Agnes had actually asked the kid for the 25 Euros, since an extra role had been required of her?

"As part of her work on the dig," Claudio hastily said, eyeing Hugh skeptically.

'Whatever," Donna said.

"Bailiwick?" Antonio repeated.

"Meaning area of expertise, or special ability. In this case Claudio speaks Italian. Mr. Frendell doesn't." Donna said.

The "Mr. Frendell" annihilated Hugh's heart.

"We're trying to get a contract from the city to clear out all the sewerage," Hugh explained. "The meeting at Centro Maree is critical for our plans, but not for yours. I know it's nothing to you both." Hugh thought, so I concede they are a couple, an item, forever lost in each other's arms. Oh Donna, you've gone into the painting with another. Come out, now, from the painting. Come out and join me on the *altana* as the music churns our mutual energies into something unimaginably wonderful.

"So everyone has a bailiwick?" Antonio said.

"Only a few of us," Hugh answered, "a very, very few. Claudio does with regard to Venice."

"And Mr. Frendell," Claudio delightedly emphasized the formality of the address, "has one with regard to vacuum sewerage. I understand you have one with regard to D & D."

"I used to play that," Donna said.

"Terrific," Antonio answered. "I play it all the time. All the time."

"But not tonight," Claudio said.

"Why not? We've got enough here for a campaign, a small campaign."

"We don't have the time. Mr. Frendell and I have a meeting at nine in San Polo," Claudio said with a sweet finality.

The conversation disappeared into mastications. Claudio produced small bowls of linguine and apologized that the pasta had not been served first. He poured dollops of a pink cream sauce over the pasta. More Schioppettino.

When the chicken consisted only or stripped bones piled in a pasta bowl, in place of dessert Claudio suggested lemoncello or grappa.

"That's a bit much," Hugh said.

"Nonsense–it's just a digestive. Settles the meal."

"I don't think grappa is a digestive," Hugh said. "I wouldn't recommend it."

"You're right," Donna said, "I know what grappa can do. Rolfe gets really stupid on the stuff."

Hugh remembered her mentioning Rolfe once before, but he couldn't summon up her statement about him. Was Rolfe in the painting too? Perhaps it was time for steady Hugh to bow out. "I'm more a watercolor person," Hugh found himself saying, "pale and easily passed over."

"And where did that come from?" Claudio asked.

"From not knowing the language," Hugh said.

"I don't follow it," Donna said.

"Lemoncello has a kind of watercolor lightness to it." Hugh said, "and that's all I meant."

"You're acting a little strange, Hugh," Claudio said. "Have some grappa and let it clear your mind." He poured two short glasses of the clear and potent liquor. "We don't need any more watercolor lightness," Claudio said. "We need tough oil paint, and layered on. I think they sell it in San Polo. Let's go there now." He pulled Hugh through the hallway to the front door, yelled some sort of encouragement to Donna and started down the four flights to the campo.

When they were seated at an outside table in San Polo, Claudio said, "What were you up to with them? What was going on in your mind?"

"I was afraid I was losing her," Hugh said.

"Really? You thought you had her?"

"Of course not. It was a dream, but a lovely dream. I haven't had such a lovely dream in so long."

"You shouldn't drink grappa. You get really slushy."

"I don't think much of us as matchmakers. We shouldn't be playing with them."

"Of course we shouldn't be playing with them. Of course we shouldn't. But if we want to put Venice back in a leadership position, what are our choices? You want to get your contracts, and Venice needs new technology to solve its oldest problem. Their discomfort is — and how can we use the word 'discomfort' in assessing what's going down there, right now as we talk? You can almost see, almost feel the vacuum tubing rushing through Venice as we speak. Snaking its way over the bridge to Mestre and back into every *calli* of Venice. What's their awkwardness in comparison to that? I mean what is it? First love, first sex, first Vacuum Sewers for Venice. Is that really a trade-off? What's wrong with you? We're giving Antonio the time of his life and we're getting contracts for the times of our lives. I say there's nothing wrong with that. Now let's have a digestive here, and imagine how they're getting it on."

"Red fire first, and dead cats afterwards, *Maria Virgine!*" Hugh said.

"Exactly! You got the sound perfectly. Precisely Venetian!"

5.

Centro Maree was on the second floor of a building adjacent to City Hall, across the alley *Calle del Carbon*. The steps up to the *piano nobile* were concaved marble just like those at Hugh's home building and the flight up was twice Hugh's Connecticut-conditioned expectation. A storey in Venice was always two storeys in Hugh's mind. Of course the building was a former palace and the main *sala* housed the 12 workers of Centro Maree four of whom would carry on through the midnight watch. Each one had his own monitor so that in the mid afternoon sunlight coming through the tall windows overlooking the Grand Canal, the room nonetheless had a certain greenish silver sheen to it. On each monitor a series of graphs slowly uncurled with multicolored lines. Apparently the plan was to have Claudio and Hugh sit in two orange canvas chairs in the middle of the room, rimmed by the twelve monitors, so that the workers could swivel around in their leather armchairs and concentrate on the data Claudio would provide.

Hugh knew immediately Claudio would not be happy with the amount of light in the room.

His powerpoint projections of the blessed tubings, the signature lines of vacuum sewerage, since they were pale green on a cream background, would not be very visible. And therefore the very modernity of the presentation, the slick technological appeal, would be lost on the Maree fellows. For a moment Hugh imagined they might end up laughing at the presentation. More than laughter, perhaps tossed candy wrappers or old stained napkins pelting him from the guffawing audience. Only nifty graphics would save them, but the lines wouldn't be smartly visible on the screen attached to the massive drapes blocking the windows facing a small campo near the Rialto bridge. The profusion and precision of Maree's monitor graphics would end up mocking Claudio's pale projections. Hugh moved toward the stairs hoping to meet Claudio and explain the difficulties before he entered the room, but just as he started in that direction, Claudio and evidently the important officials of Centro Maree came into the *sala*, and instantly chairs were offered to them. Claudio proceeded on to the center and stood by the canvas chairs. He did not motion to Hugh to join him and so Hugh backstepped toward the nearest monitor.

Claudio put his faded and bruised backpack on the second orange chair, and took out his small laptop. From a socket between the chairs he pulled up a cable and attached it to the computer. He made some adjustments and suddenly the screen was illuminated. And wonder of wonders, the colors on the graphics had changed, darkened. The tubing lines snaked across the map of Venice in vermillion; Hugh admired Claudio's digital wizardry. But instead of launching into the pitch Claudio mentioned something about Luigino. Hugh imagined Claudio was saying the necessary presence would be a bit late. The Maree watchers swiveled back to their monitors. Nothing would happen, it seemed, without Luigino. So Claudio had been correct, Hugh thought, still wondering what might ensue if Luigino simply didn't turn up. Back to Waterbury, back to modest contracts in Bridgeport and West New Haven. Back to Euro-less Jenean. No diva from ISMAR.

At length Claudio flicked through slides and returned to the first one and began speaking in a soft Venetian dialect. Chairs swiveled back to watch him and the slides. The pitch was largely economic at the outset. Vacuum sewerage would mean less allocations to dredge the canals, and it would be important to see that saved funds were not deflected to the absurd MOSE project (always a favorite target for Venetians) attempting to close off the Adriatic during high waters. Hugh could not follow the language of Claudio's expression but he knew the basic drift of the argument. There were other payoffs, especially environmental ones. Venice's water would clarify, sanitize, glisten again. The lagoon would become again the misty jewel of memory. Fish stock would increase. Barge traffic would lessen and the occasional stench of Venice would disappear. Alfresco dining along the canals would flourish again. Falling in the canal would not require hospitalization. Hugh assumed Claudio was elaborating those points, illustrating and re-illustrating them in a ploy waiting for Luigino to arrive. When that happened, Claudio could move to the next justification–an analogy with the changes Claudio's teams had effected in cargo delivery. He could then mention the new warehouse near the car-park, so that goods could be loaded to a boat going only once to each island, dramatically lessening boat traffic and wave damage to building foundations within the city.

Yes, he could point out the initial opposition but the benefits were now undeniable. Change could be positive, change could magically transform old arguments into sudden joint ventures of new possibility. Hugh knew Claudio could escalate the celebration into revelation of change pervading all of Venice as the new march to recognition, to dominance, to full reassertion of La Serenissima's imperial role in the burgeoning coastlines of the Adriatic, new brilliant linkages to the expanding Muslim world, new entries to central Asia and beyond. The technical genius of the Veneto could blossom into the fertile wastes of new Persia. Yes, Claudio could captivate them with his vision that the tiny snaking red lines on the screen transformed Venice, were Venice clever enough to seize on them. Vacuum sewers to the moon and beyond.

Claudio had only begun to itemize the full spectrum of persuasion when Luigino and son Antonio came into the main *sala*. But something was very wrong. Antonio was looking around, searching out someone, Hugh thought, and Luigino had strode defiantly toward Claudio as if deliberately interrupting his presentation. Indeed, he was now shouting something in Venetian and pushing at Claudio who stumbled backwards against the orange chairs. And suddenly Hugh understood he, himself, was Antonio's searching target. The boy locked eyes with him and came at him running and screaming "Why? Why? Why?"

"What?" Hugh said, but Antonio didn't stop for answer. He swung a wild right fist tagging Hugh's left ear and sending him sagging. Only to be followed by Antonio's swiftly lifting knee into his stomach.

"Pay her to shame on me! Why? Why?" Antonio shouted again, as Hugh doubled over and dumped on the polished marble floor.

"Stop! Help!" Hugh bellowed as Antonio began kicking him. But the kicks were tentative, pulled up at the last minute before impact as if the boy knew he shouldn't be abusing this old, overweight fellow at his mercy now. Quickly enough the Maree personnel seized the boy and hauled him away from any further damage to Hugh, who felt free now to experience his pain fully.

Luigino was still shouting at Claudio who kept edging backwards toward the screen and drapes. He held his hands up as if to stop potential blows, but Luigino speared his fists below them shoving them into Claudio's stomach, always just out of range of Claudio's retreat.

Hugh slowly unfolded to his feet and stared directly at Antonio restrained by two very puzzled Maree analysts. It was the look in the boy's eyes that Hugh fixed on, a gaze at once raging and searching all the while shouting something in Venetian. A look so frightened and frightening as if to frame potential violence with a question, a clubbing that none the less asked of itself why was it necessary, how could it have come to this? Hugh, through blood metallic taste in his mouth and incessant loud ringing in his left ear, came to believe the boy somehow felt humiliated. He had been flailing to recapture a certain dignity and his eyes kept searching, questioning, as if to penetrate outside malevolence, to drive it into a corner and make it own up to its dastardliness. Why were you so hurtful? Why did you manipulate me for your own sorry uses? Why so much evil, such unmonitored evil, such withering slicing of my very person? Why make me a joke, a laughter-inducing cipher in your sick universe? Why was I so vulnerable to your ministrations in the name of what? For whom? On what account? Had he pulled his kicks because he wanted a coherent explanation? For an unbalanced moment Hugh recognized himself in the boy: without proper language or grasp in a city so self-complete historically as to mock all rage, spurn all aspiration, there he was listening fervently to Venice's message, underscored by his own almost gleeful agreement: "Take your vacuum sewerage lines and swim away."

6.

After the disaster at Centro Maree, Hugh and Claudio avoided contact for three days. Then on a grey afternoon Claudio called and suggested they go for a boat ride and yet another rowing lesson. Over the years Claudio had tried to teach Hugh the intricacies of Venetian single oar rowing.

"I don't think so," Hugh said, "I've given up that ghost, as well as much bigger ones."

"Meaning what?"

"Meaning I've decided to go home and give up the dream of dredging Venice of its filth."

There was a pause and finally Claudio concurred, "It will be a long time before I can get Luigino to see the light about Vacuum Sewers. So let's have a drink at Florian's some night before you leave—that's the proper touristy exit, isn't it?"

"Yes, a B & B on the rocks at Florian's. I'll pick the night. It'll be soon. Jenean wants me home."

They settled on a Tuesday evening. They met at Florian's and sat at a table beyond the arcade, on San Marco's plaza well away from the maroon awnings and consequently with a splendid view of the whole square. Near the church, in the smaller square near the water Hugh could see hawkers pushing the latest trinket: a rubber band-driven, ascending propeller that in its spinning cast a brilliant white light into the moist night sky.

"I've come to identify with them," Hugh said, pointing to the fellows selling the propellers. "I found out they're from Bangladesh. I wondered how they got here and whether they really thought they'd make a fortune selling trinkets in the piazzas of Venice."

"It's a front for something else," Claudio said.

"One of them told me they'd tried to sell knock-off handbags, but the North Africans threatened them, so they switched to tchotchkes. Last year it was gel balls that lit up when you threw them onto the stones. This year it's propellers. They came all the way from Bangladesh. I realized I wasn't any different—just a foreigner trying to sell something in Venice."

"We didn't aim at the tourists," Claudio said. "We have something of value, for Venice. Something lasting."

"But it doesn't light up the night sky," Hugh said, "and it didn't mess with a boy and his father."

"Luigino and Antonio will sort that out. The boy got credibility dumping you on the floor."

"I wonder how we get comparable credibility."

"I've been thinking about that, actually," Claudio said. "And I have one idea worth turning over. Yes, one idea worth our time and effort."

Hugh took another sip of the B & B, inhaling the delicious sweetness and fire of the drink as it warmed his throat, and he heard an interior summons cautioning him to think only about the hot, honeyed liquid, not about Claudio's "one idea." But, of course, he could not stop himself.

"What's the idea?"

"It's pretty simple. We need a miniature model of a vacuum sewer line from toilet to processing plant, but done so artistically that we can display it next year at the Bienniale. Not as a country display, of course. Of course not that, but as an appendage away from the display, but distantly linked to the Bienniale Park. Alberto has a cousin who sometimes sets up displays at San Stae church. Maybe in front of San Stae, near the boat dock. I'm not sure about the details. Alberto would have to discuss it with whoever. But a functioning and artistically designed model. Maybe it could generate some real interest. We might not need Luigino."

"It doesn't strike me as proper penance for screwing up Antonio's life."

"Penance? I'm not into penance."

"Well, maybe compensation then. Not adequate compensation."

"You want me to balance it with Luigino? Is that what you want?"

"Well, it's an aspect of the game."

"I don't think so. We both took hits. You actually bled. That should be enough."

"Well, it's a thought."

"It's a stupid thought."

"It's not stupid, when I think about how stunned the kid looked. How assaulted and humiliated. He really was asking why we did it."

"We didn't. Donna and Agnes did."

"No, we did it. I don't like hurting children. I can't insulate from that. It's not what I do. It really isn't."

Claudio took a long sip from his B & B over ice in a tumbler. A diminished chamber orchestra diagonally across the square toward the back of St. Mark's began playing what seemed to be a cello concerto. The initial string sound was raspy but lilting, and, as if on cue, pigeons nearby flocked into the air, circled and resettled closer to the Correr Museum at the other end of the square. Perhaps they moved a chilly breeze across the flagments. Claudio said, "Stop brooding and begin thinking about making the model artistically dramatic, yet illustrating what we could do for Venice."

"I'm not so interested in doing for Venice. Venice has been done enough," Hugh said, apparently resenting the music.

"Think how Tintoretto would have designed our model vacuum sewer system. The energy he would have put into the model. I'm thinking something maybe only ten or twelve feet long, maybe five feet wide, with actual clear pipes so you could watch the flows. We could use colored water——maybe tracking sponges with Led lights embedded, or strobe spots highlighting everything so that it would stop traffic on the canal."

Hugh reached across the table and took hold of Claudio's wrist. "Stop talking about it. It's not going to happen. It was a bad idea, made worse, spoiled by what we tried to do. I'm getting shut of it. Do you see that? It's dead. Dead, just carrion on the piazza. Dead. Even Dr. Risica couldn't resurrect it. Tintoretto and a thousand acolytes couldn't pull it off. Give it up. Understand how, even if you could pull it off—who knows probably Alberto knows some sculptor who could pull it off—even if you could pull it off, it would summon up such pain, such memories of pain and stupidity that it wouldn't be worth it. Not for me anyway. Maybe for you, supreme Venetian, but not for this Waterbury boy. So I'm done with it. I'm tired of looking into the abyss of Venice's sick politics. I've given up on Venice. It's not going to happen. Not with me around, anyway."

Claudio set his glass down. The diminishing ice lightened the brown tint of the B & B. "Have you been rehearsing that speech?"

"I've been thinking about it. That's true. And I'm not going to follow you into the abyss."

"I don't think you follow me much anywhere. You don't even know what I'm saying."

"I sure as hell took your lead on this sorry caper. And what came of it? A wounded kid, a wounded, wondering kid. And not even a pilot contract to cover the embarrassment. Never again."

"That's tonight's message. I get it. But we both know it won't hold." Then, suddenly Claudio switched to Venetian, quietly muttering what Hugh took to be a paean to Venice's immortality. And from his deepest soul-swoon Hugh listened to his own imagined translation: "One night Venice will stand on a distant sandbar in the Adriatic and turn back toward us, beckoning, shedding swirling gossamer blue clothing, to reveal gel, peachy, pliant flesh, and we'll run hysterical into the surf to get at her."

"An intriguing vision. Maybe you could get me buried on San Michele." Hugh said standing, and finishing his B & B.

www.ingramcontent.com/pod-product-compliance
Lightning Source LLC
Chambersburg PA
CBHW072355030726
47505CB00014B/1837